As the train rocked its way south, Emily ate an orange she had no appetite for. It was just something to keep her occupied. She pried off the sections one by one, remembering how she used to save the "babies" for Anna when she was little. They'd had other rituals, most of them made up, like the "Pinkie Club"—a silly game Emily had invented of linking her little finger with Anna's when crossing a busy street. It meant she trusted her young daughter not to pull away suddenly and dart into traffic. Anna would respond by proudly lifting her chin and holding her crooked pinkie aloft as delicately as an English noblewoman at high tea. . . .

—from "The Pinkie Club," by Eileen Goudge and Mary Bailey

"Wonderful! . . . An inspiring anthology guaranteed to touch the heart and lift the spirits of mothers and daughters everywhere."
—*Romantic Times*

Mothers and Daughters

EDITED BY
JILL MORGAN

A SIGNET BOOK

SIGNET
Published by the Penguin Group
Penguin Putnam Inc., 375 Hudson Street,
New York, New York 10014, U.S.A.
Penguin Books Ltd, 27 Wrights Lane,
London W8 5TZ, England
Penguin Books Australia Ltd, Ringwood,
Victoria, Australia
Penguin Books Canada Ltd, 10 Alcorn Avenue,
Toronto, Ontario, Canada M4V 3B2
Penguin Books (N.Z.) Ltd, 182–190 Wairau Road,
Auckland 10, New Zealand

Penguin Books Ltd, Registered Offices:
Harmondsworth, Middlesex, England

First published by Signet, an imprint of Dutton NAL, a member of Penguin
Putnam Inc. Previously published in a Signet hardcover edition.

First Signet Mass Market Printing, May, 1999
10 9 8 7 6 5 4 3 2 1

Jill Morgan wishes to thank editor Jennifer Sawyer Fisher for her enormous help in bringing this "labor of love" to publication.

In addition, I am very grateful to Signet editors Audrey LaFehr and Charlotte Herscher for their dedication and assistance during the development of this book.

Contents

Mothers and Daughters: The Legacies

Jill Morgan

Editing an anthology such as this one is a little like putting together a photo album from family snapshots discovered in a bureau drawer. The stories in this book spoke to me in the same way old family photos do, with poignancy, humor, and in loving recollection of the unique relationships between mothers and daughters. These are stories that touch the heart and draw us closer.

Mothers and daughters will always be reflections of each other. In these twelve stories, the reflections are punctuated by wisdom, wit, and other gifts of understanding. These stories explore the reaches of the heart and find the gifts of legacy waiting there. The stories are fiction, inspired by the real-life relationships of the mothers and daughters who wrote them.

When my newborn daughter, Lisa, was laid in my arms, I felt a kinship with this small, perfect being who linked us both to the long line of strong-willed and independent women in our family. Today I know that twenty-four-year-old Lisa has turned out to be no exception to this genetic attribute. If there is a legacy passed down from mothers to daughters in our family, it is this fierce insistence on self-reliance.

My mother, Juanette, never allowed me to pay the check when we ate at restaurants together. This used to infuriate me, for on many occasions I desperately wanted to treat my mother to a special meal. From babyhood, my daughter observed Mommy and Grandma both lunging for the check as soon as it arrived at the table, and she saw the sly tricks Grandma used to play in managing to capture the prize. Now it is Lisa and I who vie for the check at a restaurant.

"Why do you do that?" I say in exasperation each time she succeeds in being faster or sneakier.

"Because I'm just like you, and you're just like Grandma," Lisa replies, and I am forced to admit she's right.

A thousand other legacies have passed from my mother to me, and from me to my daughter. Daughters have always struggled against acknowledging such similarities in their youth—I *am not* like my mother!—but later in life, in loving recognition, admit to these inheritances of character and personality that link them to their mothers.

We are a reflection of our mothers, and if we are fortunate daughters, our legacies will be many. One treasured legacy I hold from my mother is the courage with which she faced her death from cancer. By her example of calm strength and undaunted spirit, I gained an inheritance of hope and courage to face my own final challenge when that time comes.

In my daughter, I see my mother's honesty, bravery, stubbornness, and devotion to family. In these ways she is a likeness of my mother that also shines in me. Through my daughter's eyes and caring actions, I see my mother once again. And sometimes I see myself. The reflection is startling.

Often I think of my childhood, the long walks my mother and I made carrying groceries from the market and the old songs she taught me along the way. The songs were from her childhood, a memory she shared with her daughter and that I shared later with mine. Those old songs are with me still in sweet recollection. When I think of them, I recall those warm nights and the pretty sound of my mother's voice. Of such memories the best legacies are made.

The stories written for this anthology speak to us of the bonds between mothers and daughters. Within these pages are glimpses of humor, protectiveness, caring, and lessons in courage—all examples of the many types of inheritance that daughters gain from their mothers and that sometimes mothers learn from their daughters. The stories from our assembly of celebrated authors are uniquely enhanced by their daughters' collaboration on these works of fiction.

If mothers are the heart of a family, then daughters are its link with the past and the future. Daughters are a reflection of what came before and a vision of what will be. Like their mothers, they will become the caretakers, the archivists, and the enfolding strength of their own families . . . and the legacy continues.

PART ONE

Mothers
and
Young
Daughters

Try to Survive

Joan Lowery Nixon
and Eileen Nixon McGowan

Photo by Carl Masterson

Katherine Joan McGowan with her mother, Eileen,
and her grandmother Joan.

INTRODUCTION

Maybe I shouldn't have laughed with such wicked delight and said, "What goes around comes around." My daughter Eileen's adorable daughter, Katie J., who was only three, had hidden her shoes because she was not about to put them on, no matter what her mother said. After all, child care books tell us that three-year-olds are noted for their independent spirits and strong single-mindedness and occasional rejection of parental authority.

"This is simply a preview of her adolescent years," I told Eileen. "It gives you a warning of what's in store for you in another ten years."

"Mom," Eileen protested, as she pulled Katie J.'s shoes out from under the sofa, "I was never like that."

"You were worse," I said.

Eileen's loving glance at her daughter was tempered with a sigh. She asked, "With three daughters, Mom, how did you ever survive?"

"The same way you will," I answered. I couldn't help it—I laughed again.

That evening Eileen came by with the idea for our story and six very funny pages of narration and dialogue. From there we went on to coauthor "Try to Survive."

I was living in hell.

Her torments were unintentional—I was fairly sure about that. However, by having to publicly endure them I was completely humiliated. Absolutely mortified. There were times in which I wished I were dead. Like when we went shopping at the mall before Christmas and three of my friends walked over to say hello.

Mom smiled and said, "Hi, girls. Have you been to see Santa?"

I winced with inner pain. *How could my mother say such incredibly goofy things to my friends? Didn't she realize that she sounded on the verge of senile when she spoke?* I mean, I may have been only fourteen, but I was decidedly more socially equipped than my thirty-eight-year-old mother.

"Hi, Mrs. Landon," they answered and laughed politely.

"I realize that you're much too old for Santa," Mom said. "So are we all headed for Victoria's Secret?" Everyone broke into fits of giggles. Everyone but me, that is.

I didn't encourage my friends to hang around, not with Mom standing there foolishly beaming at them like one of the good fairies in *Cinderella*. When they left, Mom actually said, "Happy shopping!"

I groaned, then pulled myself together and asked, "Why, why, *why* must you be so embarrassing?"

Mom took a long, deep breath and answered, "Julie, I merely tried to be polite to your friends."

Although she'd put on that calm-mother voice, I couldn't help noticing an exasperated tone. It occurred to me that the older I got the more exasperated Mom sounded. It was her age, I guessed.

She was probably much closer to menopause than she'd care to admit.

Mom pushed back her curly brown hair. Curly brown hair. Yuck. That was something in the genes department that she passed on to me and that I'd just as soon not have had. I mean, people *do* inherit hair that's sleek and golden—if their mothers have the right genes, of course. Like Vicki Summerbee, my best friend. Vicki's mother's hair practically shone in the dark. So did Vicki's.

When I didn't answer, Mom asked, "What do you expect me to do, Julie? Ignore your friends? Acknowledging their existence is the polite thing to do."

Mom just didn't get it. Whenever we were at the mall—especially when she was in her jogging outfit, and it was painfully obvious that she doesn't jog—and I ran into my friends, whose mothers trusted them enough to go to the mall by themselves, the last thing I needed was to be seen with my mother. I drew myself up to my full five feet, two inches and explained, "My friends probably think I have an overprotective mother who doesn't trust me with my own money."

For a moment Mom looked bewildered. "What does overprotective have to do with . . . ?" Then she stopped speaking, and her eyes took on a kind of twinkly, smiling look. "Honey, maybe I am a tad overprotective," she said, "but let me point out a few things. One, I enjoy your company. I like doing things with you. And two, what do you mean 'your own money'? Did you win the lottery and not tell me?"

Anyone would have agreed with me that comments like that were totally uncalled for. Poor Mom. At times she belonged on another planet. It was a relief to buy a Christmas present for Dad and the jeans and shirts I needed and then leave the mall.

Within less than an hour we climbed into our car. Our car, if you can call it that. "The Spore-mobile," Mom jokingly named it. The car had developed a mildew smell a few months before Dad left us. At the time the mechanics couldn't find the problem, and since then money had been so tight we weren't able to buy another car.

Mom's attitude was, "Well, it runs."

Mom sent in a coupon and two dollars to some company for a box of perfume samples. Each day she sprinkled a few drops of perfume on the upholstery to cover up the mildew smell. I was likely to arrive at school reeking of Shalimar or Chanel Number Whatever. Mom thought the whole thing was funny. You see the problem.

Mom laughed a lot anyway, often at the most inappropriate things, like my friends' jokes. She would hand around soft drinks and brownies while she was loudly ha-ha-ha-ing, and I positively died. Either my friends were extraordinarily sensitive, caring people or incredibly patient people—they acted as though they liked Mom. Our house became a hangout house, even when Mom was there.

I usually tried not to think about Vicki's mother, Lynn Summerbee. Oh, man! Vicki had the coolest mother. Vicki's mother worked out in a gym every day. I even heard her tell someone that she was able to get back into her size six clothes *one week* after Vicki was born. My mom joked about still trying to lose the baby weight fourteen years later.

Vicki's mother always looked fabulous, as though she had just stepped out of a fashion magazine. Once I tried explaining to Mom how important it was to develop a real sense of style like . . . well . . . Mrs. Summerbee, but Mom just laughed and said, "If you put Vicki's mother next to me we'd look like a 'Before and After' picture."

Unfortunately she was right.

When we got home I went up to my room to put away my stuff. I suppose Mom thought I'd be busy for a while, because she got on the phone to call Grandma. The reason I know is that I picked up the phone to call Vicki, and I heard Mom say, "She didn't die on the spot, so the embarrassment couldn't have been too great."

Grandma said, "What goes around comes around," and the two of them began to laugh like maniacs. Totally disgusting behavior for women who are supposed to be grown up and mature. Naturally, I hung up.

Grandma was generally very nice. She didn't fit the white-hair-and-cookies image of a grandmother. For years she'd done a lot of volunteer work for a little-theater group, sometimes even playing a small part herself.

Once a fire started backstage during a performance. The play was a murder mystery, and Grandma was playing a corpse, but she jumped up and told people how to file out of the theater and kept them from panicking, so her picture was on the TV news. Grandma was still wearing a blond-red wig, which was part of her costume.

She studied her picture and said, "My, that hair looks good." Since then she'd kept her hair dyed the same kind of blond-red. Grandma had crinkly little laugh lines around the outside corners of her eyes because she laughed a lot. Like Mom. But not as loudly, thank goodness.

On occasion, when I felt the need to express my totally honest feelings about something Mom had said or done in public, Grandma would put an arm around my shoulders, hugging me, and winking at Mom. "My, my, Diane," she would say, "I seem to have heard that song before." Mom always grinned. I supposed that that was their futile attempt to be funny in the face of an embarrassment crisis.

Normally I'd get on the phone and say hello to Grandma, but at that moment I wasn't in the mood for Grandma's and Mom's silly laughter.

I looked at the box with Dad's Christmas present in it. Mom and I had bought him a good-looking blue sports shirt. I'd have to wrap it and put a card with it and give it to him the next time he came by. Before Christmas, I hoped.

Dad had never given Mom a present since the divorce, but every Father's Day, birthday, and Christmas, Mom took me to the mall to pick out a present for Dad. I gave her full credit for that, because it had to be hard on her. And Mom never said anything mean about Dad. Not even when he "no-showed" for the hours with me that the court gave him. Mom just hugged me and said, "Well, he's doing the best he can, Julie, and he really does love you."

I heard the radio go on in the kitchen, and Mom

began to sing along to this awful, corny song that had to be a selection for the elderly people who listen to golden oldies.

"Wo-oh-oh-oh-oh!" Mom wailed, slightly off-key, and I winced, thankful that none of my friends was present to hear her. How could she behave in such a terribly embarrassing way?

The day after Christmas, Mrs. Summerbee dropped Vicki off at our house so she could stay with us for a week. Their arrival didn't come at the best of times. Our dog, Gloria, had tried to eat a plastic Christmas ornament, and she threw up all over the living room rug just as the doorbell rang. Mom had stopped working on what she calls her Traditional Holiday Chocolate Pie to clean up after Gloria, so there she was, in her "baking outfit"— sweatpants and an extra-large T-shirt with I SHOT J.R. fading on the front.

When I opened the door, Lynn Summerbee stepped gracefully into our living room, looking like a model. She was wearing a black Christian Dior dress I had seen in a magazine, and her golden hair spilled across her shoulders like an ad for shampoo. Vicki stumbled after her, dumping a big suitcase, and leaned against the wall trying to catch her breath.

Vicki had told me that it was hard to live up to her mother's practically perfect appearance, but my thought was, *Hey! At least your mother isn't trying to keep the sweatpants industry in business.*

Anyway, Vicki was going to stay with us because her mother was leaving to go skiing in Aspen with a group from her office, which included her new boyfriend, Charles somebody or other.

"Diane, dear," Lynn Summerbee said, holding out her arms.

Then she saw and smelled the dog mess, so she skipped past Mom and settled on the sofa. We all tried not to look at the smelly spot on the rug as Mrs. Summerbee told us about her vacation plans and the gorgeous red satin gown she was going to wear at the formal dinner party where she and Charles would ring in the new year.

I glanced at Mom, who was smiling politely, even though there was dog vomit on her tennies. Oh, man! Lynn Summerbee's office staff went to terrific places like Aspen, while the people in Mom's office thought they were living it up if they got together for the dinner special at Denny's. Lynn Summerbee had a glamorous boyfriend, and Mom hadn't had a single date since the divorce. Lynn Summerbee was wearing Christian Dior, and Mom was wearing dog vomit!

"I really must run," Mrs. Summerbee said and got to her feet.

"We'll take good care of Vicki," Mom told her, "but you'd better give me your hotel's phone number, just in case of emergency."

"Phone number?" Mrs. Summerbee looked startled, then shrugged. She fished a tiny notepad out of her handbag and wrote on it. "This is the name of the hotel. The operator can always give you the number . . . if you need it."

Mom took the paper and said reassuringly, "Have fun, Lynn, and don't worry about Vicki. She'll be fine."

Later, as Vicki was hanging up her clothes in my closet, I said, "I'd love to have your mother as a mom."

Vicki gave me a really strange look. "You're kidding," she said.

"No, I'm not," I told her. "Your mother's so glamorous and beautiful and so . . . well, perfect."

"It's funny," Vicki said, "but I was thinking that I wouldn't mind having your mom around instead of mine."

"Why? Are you totally nuts?" I asked.

Vicki shrugged. "I just think sometimes I'd like a mom to do parent stuff with. You know, go out shopping together, that kind of thing."

"Shopping?" I thought about our latest experience at the mall and shuddered.

"Your mom talks to you," Vicki said quietly. "And she laughs a lot."

I groaned, thinking about the way Mom always laughed so loudly that sometimes people turned to look, and to keep from dropping dead on the spot I had to pretend I was invisible. As fast as I could, I changed the subject to some good gossip I'd heard about our history teacher. No more talk about mothers. That subject was incredibly boring.

Mom was a little short of cash, so she, Vicki, and I didn't go anywhere for New Year's Eve. Fortunately, Mom is a great cook, and she made a really great dinner for us and used the good china and crystal.

While we were eating, Mom told us some stories about when she was growing up and dating, and they were hysterical. Vicki and I laughed and laughed. Mom told this really funny story about a date in college where she was trying to look sophisticated but had mistakenly worn one black and one navy blue shoe, and we laughed so hard that Mom waved us to stop eating.

"We can't laugh and eat at the same time," she said. "One of us is going to choke."

"Your stories are wonderful, Mrs. Landon," Vicki said. She wiped her eyes on her napkin, and I realized I'd been laughing so hard I was crying too.

Vicki, being my best friend, was more or less bound to say something complimentary to my mom, but I had to admit that Mom *was* a good storyteller . . . in a weird kind of way.

Mom chilled sparkling apple cider and set crystal champagne flutes on a tray so we could toast the new year at midnight.

Unfortunately, Mom was at that age when her body was beginning to break down, and she fell asleep in her chair during the ten o'clock newscast on TV. Vicki and I had to wake her up so she could ring in the new year with us. I thought of Vicki's mother, who right now was probably swirling around the dance floor in her red satin gown, and I sighed. Poor, pitiful Mom.

The day after Valentine's Day Vicki's mother dropped by with a huge heart-shaped box of chocolate truffles. It hadn't even been opened.

"Larry gave them to me," she said. She glanced at the box, shuddered, and thrust it into Mom's hands. "I am not about to allow chocolate truffles to ruin my figure, so I thought about you, Diane, and how you'd probably enjoy them."

Mom just smiled and asked, "Does this mean we're valentines, Lynn?"

Mom and her infantile humor! My face turned hot in utter humiliation.

Mrs. Summerbee didn't get it either. She just muttered something about the beautiful weather, edged toward the door, and disappeared.

"Yum," Mom said around a mouthful of chocolate. She already had the box open and had chosen a second truffle. "Here, Julie, help yourself."

Fleetingly, I thought about Mrs. Summerbee's wonderful figure, then put it out of my mind and reached for a truffle. George . . . um, Larry, had wonderful taste in chocolate.

Mom, who had a smudge of chocolate on her chin, sighed happily and said, "I hope when Easter comes Larry will think in terms of chocolate-cream, pecan-coated Easter eggs. They're my favorite."

But Mrs. Summerbee went to Grand Cayman Island with a group of friends over Easter week, which just happened to be our spring break at school. Mom had arranged to take some of her vacation days to be home with me, so Mrs. Summerbee left Vicki with us.

They arrived just as Mom had finished planting a row of geraniums across the front flower bed. Mrs. Summerbee was dressed in a white silk suit with a blue silk blouse and looked like a model in a fashion show. Mom, on the other hand, was wearing her "gardening outfit"—a ratty straw hat, mud-splattered sweatpants, and an oversized

T-shirt that read, HAND OVER THE CHOCOLATES AND NO ONE WILL GET HURT. I cringed.

Vicki plopped her suitcase down on the front walk as her mother, keeping a safe distance from mine, said, "Diane, dear, I'd love to stay and chat, but I've got to meet Phil at the airport in less than an hour."

Mom smiled and said, "We'll take good care of Vicki. Do you have your hotel's number in case I need to reach you?"

"Oh," Mrs. Summerbee said and began rummaging through her handbag. "I do somewhere. Don't I? Yes, here it is." Making sure that she stayed as far as possible away from Mom's gardening dirt, Mrs. Summerbee handed the slip of paper to Vicki.

"Will there be a dinner dance?" I asked, remembering my dreams of the swirling red satin gown.

"Yes," Mrs. Summerbee said. "I know I'm rushing the season, but I bought this darling sleeveless white chiffon gown with a full, full skirt that swirls beautifully."

I closed my eyes, sighing with pleasure. When I opened them I found myself looking at Mom. Oh, man! I couldn't even imagine Mom in swirling white chiffon.

Maybe if she had a makeover, maybe if she lost twenty pounds, maybe if she bleached her hair blond . . .

"Have fun tripping the light fantastic," Mom said to Mrs. Summerbee.

Maybe if Mom ever learned to stop saying impossible, humiliating, embarrassing things! But she wouldn't. She couldn't.

I helped Vicki carry her suitcase into my room and sat on the bed while she hung her clothes in my closet.

"I love your mother's white suit," I told Vicki. "I love the way she dresses. She doesn't look like . . . well, any old mom. She looks beautiful."

Vicki, her head inside the closet, mumbled something that sounded like, "She'd agree with you."

"She goes to such glamorous places," I said and made a face. "Mom's idea of a big time is to take me to the dollar movie and get us medium popcorns, large Cokes, and boxes of Junior Mints."

Vicki straightened up and looked at me with a kind of strange look on her face. "I'd like that. I hope she'll take us while I'm here."

We started talking about movies, and Mom, who had showered, came in to join us. We started laughing about some of the comedies, and before long we climbed into the Sporemobile and rode to the dollar movie to see *Return of the Killer Tomatoes*.

On Easter Day we all dressed up and went to church. I had saved some of my allowance to get Mom a chocolate-cream pecan-covered Easter egg, and she'd gotten one for Vicki and one for me, so we all pigged out and felt kind of sick and had a lot of fun.

Mrs. Summerbee came back with a fabulous tan, wearing a gorgeous lavender suit and beautiful black coral earrings that Phil had given her. She raved about the clear turquoise water and the marvelous snorkeling, and I loved listening to every word.

Mrs. Summerbee had sipped champagne in a

hot tub and floated over a dance floor in white chiffon. While Mom—oh, man!—laughed while she was drinking a Coke and it came out her nose and spotted her T-shirt that said NOBODY'S PERFECT.

The embarrassing things I had to put up with!

"Diane, dear," Mrs. Summerbee said, "on the next holiday . . ."

Mom broke in. "The next holiday is Mother's Day, Lynn."

Mrs. Summerbee looked blank for a moment, then smiled again. "No, no. I was thinking of the Memorial Day weekend. Arthur has been talking about . . ."

"Sure. Leave Vicki with us," Mom said. "But let's get back to Mother's Day. There's a brunch at the hotel, and maybe you and I and the girls can go together."

I could hear Mrs. Summerbee gulp, and her hands sort of twitched, like she wished she had something to hang on to. Finally she managed to say, "What a charming idea. We'll keep it in mind, Diane."

"Okay," Mom said and smiled as though she were perfectly happy.

"Good," Mrs. Summerbee said, looking relieved. "So if nothing else comes up . . ."

"It will," Vicki muttered under her breath.

I looked at Mom with despair. Maybe if she got her hair styled or bought a beautiful silk suit like Mrs. Summerbee's or . . .

Mrs. Summerbee was about to take Vicki and leave when I suddenly shouted, "Oh, no! We forgot!"

Vicki's eyes grew wide and we said together, "The time-line chart!"

"It's due tomorrow," Vicki said.

"It's for history class, and we were supposed to work on it over our spring break," I said.

"Then get busy," Mom said.

"We can't!" I hurried to explain, "We have to draw the time line on a big sheet of posterboard."

"No problem," Mom said. "Everybody hop in the Sporemobile. We'll all go to the convenience store down on the boulevard and get the poster-board."

The tip of Mrs. Summerbee's nose seemed to turn up. "The Sporemobile?" she repeated in a horrified voice.

"It's what we call our car," Mom explained.

"It's okay," Vicki hurried to add. "This week the mildew's not so bad. The car smells like Ysatis."

Mrs. Summerbee gave a little shiver and said, "There's no need to take your car out of the garage, Diane. Mine's parked on your drive. We'll go to the store in mine."

We did, and it was heavenly. The seats were covered in pale, smooth leather, and it had a won-derful new-car fragrance. I sank back into the soft-ness and sighed with pleasure. What a difference from the old Sporemobile.

Mom had to give Mrs. Summerbee directions. I guessed that she'd never been to a convenience store before. Anyhow, as we pulled into the park-ing lot, an old blue sedan came shooting past us, barely missing the left front fender on Mrs. Sum-merbee's car.

"Oh, my!" Mrs. Summerbee cried.

Mom whirled around to get a good look at the driver of the blue sedan and yelled, "Stupid driver!" even though our windows were up and he couldn't possibly hear her.

I was mortified by Mom's behavior. Mrs. Summerbee's "Oh, my!" seemed a much more dignified response. Besides, the sedan had slammed off the curb into the street and sped away.

Mrs. Summerbee parked her car and we all piled out. With Mom leading the way, we hurried into the store.

"Stop!" Mom yelled, and we did, bumping into her.

It took a moment for everything to make sense: the man lying on the floor in front of the checkout counter, with blood spreading in a puddle under his shoulder; the woman who had fallen nearby, clutching her leg and moaning. Oh, man! My heart began pounding so hard I thought it would jump right out of my body. I pressed my hands against my chest, as if I were trying to hold it in.

"Armed robbery!" Mom said.

Mrs. Summerbee screamed and took a step backward.

"Lynn," Mom said, "call the police. Tell them to send an ambulance."

"I—I can't." Mrs. Summerbee made a retching noise. "I'm going to be sick," she whimpered and ran out of the store.

Mom knelt beside the man and felt for a pulse in his neck. "Julie, call the police," Mom said, but Vicki already had the phone in her hand and was dialing.

My legs wobbled, but I managed to reach the

woman and drop beside her. I took her hand, feeling for a pulse in her wrist. I remembered how to do it from the Red Cross course I took to get my baby-sitting credentials when I was twelve. The woman opened her eyes and looked at me. "She's conscious, Mom," I said, "and her pulse is strong. Her leg is bleeding but not a lot."

Mom glanced over at the woman and said, "She shows the signs of going into shock. Don't let her, Julie. Keep her talking."

"About what?"

"About anything." Mom bent over the man again, tearing his shirt away from his shoulder.

Vicki stood over Mom. She was as white as a sheet of paper, but she said, "What can I do, Mrs. Landon?"

"Find gauze pads and rolls of gauze," Mom told her. "Bring lots. We need to apply a tourniquet here."

"Talk to me," I said to the woman, but she just stared. Her eyes seemed kind of filmy.

"What's your name?"

There was a silence, then she whispered, "Margo Khan."

"Tell me . . . tell me about your children. Do you have children? Who's taking care of them?"

The woman stirred, and she seemed to actually notice that I was there. "Elizabeth," she said. "Elizabeth."

"Where is Elizabeth?"

"Day care."

"How old is she?"

It seemed to take a terrible effort on her part, but Mrs. Khan began to respond and told me about

Elizabeth and when she was supposed to pick her up and all sorts of stuff. Besides being careful to remember how to reach Elizabeth, I didn't pay much attention to what Mrs. Khan said. I just concentrated on doing what Mom had told me— keeping her talking.

For the next few minutes Mom was back and forth between the shooting victims, patching up both of them. Vicki and I did whatever she told us to do.

I was never so glad to hear anything as I was to hear the sirens on the ambulance and police cars that arrived on the scene.

The paramedics quickly took over. "Good job," one of them told Mom. "You did a good job."

Of course the police had lots of questions. Vicki and I hadn't seen anything much except that the car was a blue sedan, but Mom knew the make of the car, and she gave a detailed description of the driver to the police.

Two television crews showed up, and they photographed Mom while she was talking to the police.

Vicki tugged on my arm. "Julie, I can't find my mother," she said, and her eyes suddenly blurred with tears.

We staggered outside, hanging on to each other for support. Even though our job was over, I was still shaky. I'm sure that Vicki felt the same way. I looked around the parking lot. Mrs. Summerbee and her beautiful, good-smelling car had disappeared. "Your mother told us she was going to be sick," I said, and I knew my excuse sounded lame. "Maybe she had to go home."

"Without me," Vicki said. Tears spilled over and ran down her cheeks.

I put my arms around her. "No, it's not like that. It's just . . . I mean, your mother had a good reason." But I had no idea what it could be. I just held Vicki and let her cry it out.

By this time the ambulance had left for the hospital, and the police had nothing more to discuss at the time with Mom, so they drove us to our house.

"All I want is a long hot shower," Mom murmured, "but we'd better get Vicki home and make sure that Lynn is all right."

"The posterboard! We need it," I said.

"Posterboard. Right," Mom said with a sigh.

Exhausted as we all were, we immediately climbed into the Sporemobile. Mom drove us to another store and bought the posterboard, then took Vicki home.

Mrs. Summerbee opened the door just a little more than a crack. She clung to the doorframe and stared at Mom's messy appearance. Her face grew pale and I thought she might barf. "The people who were shot . . . did they . . . ? Are you . . . ?" Her voice cracked.

"Luckily, it looks like they'll make it," Mom said.

Mrs. Summerbee opened the door a few inches more and gushed, "Oh, Diane, you're so clever about things like that. I knew I'd just be in the way . . . it made me so ill . . . you didn't need to deal with my problems, too . . . you understand why I left."

Mom just let Mrs. Summerbee go on and on. Then she said, "We'll get Vicki's things to her tomorrow. She's a wonderful girl, and you can be very proud of her. I hope you'll let her stay with us again."

On the way home Mom said, "I'm very proud of you too, Julie. You kept your head. You did everything just right. Let's hope we saved a couple of lives."

"Mom," I said, "you stayed to help, and Mrs. Summerbee ran away."

"Don't judge her," Mom said. "We don't understand all her problems."

"What I mean is, Grandma kept people from panicking when the theater caught on fire, and now you helped some people who were shot. Is it like heredity or something?"

"Or something," she said. "There's some of Grandma in me and some of both of us in you. You were very brave, too."

"Yes," I admitted with sudden satisfaction. "I was."

The whole scene kept running through my head like instant replays during a televised football game. The car, the people on the floor, the blood, the police, the paramedics, the TV cameras . . .

I sighed, and Mom reached over to pat my knee. "Everything's going to be all right, honey," she said.

"Well, almost everything," I said, "but there is one thing that bothers me. Remember when Grandma was interviewed on television after that fire? She had on makeup and looked good in that red wig. But you . . ."

"But me . . . what?"

"Mom, do you realize that everyone in the city . . .

maybe even the United States . . . or even the world will see you in those awful sweatpants and that terrible T-shirt with the Coke spilled on it and the blood . . . I mean, if *you* had been wearing a glamorous silk lavender suit . . ."

What I'd just said sounded so ridiculous I began to laugh. Mom stopped the Sporemobile in the driveway, and I threw my arms around her neck and laughed until tears ran down my cheeks. Mom laughed and cried with me too.

"Oh, Mom, I love you," I said.

Mom hugged me harder. "Thank God for the legacy," she said.

"What are you talking about?" I asked. "I don't understand."

Mom grinned. "Never mind, honey," she said. "When the right time comes, you will."

I tossed my handbag on the counter and fished two Cokes out of the refrigerator, handing one to my fourteen-year-old daughter, Samantha.

She took the Coke, but she said, "You *have* been paying attention to what I've been saying, haven't you, Mom?"

"Complete attention," I said.

"I was trying to tell you that I just couldn't bear to be publicly humiliated like that again. When we accidentally meet my friends in the mall, why do you have to say such embarrassing, senile things?"

"I didn't say much more than 'hello,' " I answered. "What do you want me to do, Sam? Ignore your friends?"

She leaned against the counter dramatically, an

expression of agony on her face. "That would be a huge improvement over your pitiful attempts at humor. Imagine actually telling them that horrible old joke: 'Where do cows go for entertainment? To the moooovies.' Ick."

"The girls thought it was funny. They laughed."

"Because they're my friends. They had to be polite." Sam swept out of the kitchen with a parting shot. "Worst of all, you not only laugh too much, you even laugh at your own jokes! Why can't you be elegant and sophisticated like Melanie's mother?"

Melanie's mother. I shuddered and made a nasty face. Melanie's mother wore Ferragamo shoes and St. John suits and looked like a fashion model at all times. She was totally cool and sophisticated and was definitely *not* on my list of favorite people.

The phone rang, and I answered.

"What's the matter, Julie?" my mother said. "You sound kind of down."

"I am trying not to be," I told her, "but I just came back from a shopping trip with Sam."

Mom giggled.

"It's not funny," I said. "I was told that I say senile things to her friends, I laugh at my own jokes, and I publicly humiliate her."

"What goes around comes around," Mom said. The giggles turned into gales of laughter.

"Oh, come on," I said. "I was never like that."

"You were even worse," Mom said. She laughed so hard that I had to laugh too. Looked at in a certain light, it *was* kind of funny.

We finally calmed down and Mom said, "She'll

outgrow it. Just keep your sense of humor and remind yourself now and then that she'll go through
the same thing with her own daughter. That way
you'll survive."

"The legacy," I said, suddenly remembering.
"Mom, that's the legacy, isn't it? Keeping a sense
of humor?"

"That's it," she said.

I leaned against the counter and smiled as the
dearest part of my life shouted from upstairs,
"Mom! I forgot to tell you that Melanie's mother is
going to bring her over in a few minutes. Can you
take off that awful old sweater and jeans and put on
something . . . uh . . . well, more sophisticated?"

"My long black dinner dress?" I called back.

"Don't be funny," she said. "And don't tell jokes
to Melanie's mother. They're so pitiful she never
gets them. And don't . . ."

Someday, I thought, *just like Mom before me, and
probably Grandma before that, I'll tell Samantha all about
the legacy. If she has a daughter, she'll need to know.*

Words

Joy Fielding and Shannon Seyffert

Photo by Warren Seyffert

INTRODUCTION

Originally, both my daughters, Shannon, age twenty-one, and Annie, age eighteen, agreed to participate in the writing of this short story. I decided that rather than try to find time when the three of us could work together (not easy with our assorted schedules and personalities) it might be easier, and better for our mental health, if I came up with an idea and we interpreted it from three different points of view. They liked this approach and promised to get busy writing. As the deadline grew near, I kept asking if they'd started writing. The answer was always, "No, but I'm thinking" or "No, but I will soon." This became "No, but I have exams to study for" and "No, but I'm writing it in my head." Followed by "I'm very stressed right now" and "Just when am I supposed to find the time to do this?" Finally, my younger daughter opted out of the project. Shannon, still busy writing the story in her head, showed great reluctance to actually write anything down on paper. It was at this point, a month after our deadline, that I began to wish I had insisted we write the story together. At least that way I could have maintained the illusion of control. I nagged and nagged, although I have to confess I hadn't actually started writing anything myself. Finally, I said the story had to be finished by the end of the week or the deal was off. At that point I went into my office and Shannon went upstairs to her room. "Try to work in a game of Scrabble," she instructed me. The next morning she handed me her finished copy. I read it, shed a few motherly tears, then fitted the two halves together, making a few minor adjustments here and there. She then read the completed story and offered her comments. I made further adjustments. Finally, it was done. It was a frustrating, pressure-filled, but ultimately rewarding experience. The best part was when we actually worked together, so I think if I were to undertake such a project again, I would choose to write the story together, the very approach I had initially dismissed. At any rate, it was fascinating to see what Shannon came up with, and I think she did a terrific job.

O h, God, they're fighting again.
 I can hear them going at it—each word a jagged pebble aimed directly at my heart—despite the fact that we're separated by two floors and the door to my makeshift office is closed. They don't know I'm home. I snuck in a few minutes ago, like a thief in the night, although it is only four in the afternoon, breaking and entering, although only my heart is breaking. I could hear their raised voices even before my key was fully in the front door lock. "Stupid cow!" "Bitch!"—the words spraying from the upstairs windows and onto the street below, like dirty water tossed carelessly out of a bucket. I should have turned around right then and there, run as fast as I could, as far as I could—except where would I go, and what would

be the point? You can't hide from words. They always find you.

And so I silently pushed open the front door and tiptoed down the stairs instead, to the small room beside the garage that Todd was fashioning into an office for me when he suffered a heart attack five years ago and died at the ripe old age of forty-six. Despite no previous symptoms, no family history, there he was dead on the floor at age forty-six, leaving behind his wife of eighteen years and their two daughters, Kelly and Danielle, now screaming at each other two floors above my head. I closed the door behind me, collapsed into the old green-leather sofa that Todd and I bought when we were first married—occasionally I still catch traces of his scent, or think I do—and allowed the sobs that had been steadily building inside my body to break free. I'm not crying for Todd, although I miss him terribly and wish he were here with me now. I'm crying for myself. And for my girls. They've already lost one parent way too early. How will they cope with the loss of another?

"Don't be alarmed," the doctor told me only an hour ago, cradling the results of my recent mammogram under her arm.

But, of course, that's exactly what I was—instantly, totally, unbearably alarmed.

"Your mammogram shows several suspicious areas . . ."

"Suspicious areas?"

"Several areas of calcification . . ."

"Areas of calcification?"

It seemed preferable to keep repeating everything the doctor said rather than asking new questions, rather than flying across the room and wrestling her angrily to the ground, demanding, "What the hell are you talking about? What exactly are you trying to say?"

"We have to do another test," she continued gently.

"Oh, God."

"Please try not to let this upset you. This is not uncommon. There's a good chance it's nothing."

"My mother died of breast cancer," I reminded the doctor, a pretty young woman of Asian descent.

She nodded, well aware of my family history. "I've scheduled the test a week from this Thursday. I'm afraid it'll take most of the morning. Can you arrange for someone to come with you?"

I think I nodded, although there's really no one. My parents and my husband are dead. My friends all work. I haven't spoken to my sister in years, although she used to phone, leave messages on my answering machine. "Hi, it's Jan. Call me." But I haven't. I don't.

Most of what else happened in the doctor's office is pretty much a blank. I think Dr. Lee went on to explain the procedure. I think there were further attempts at reassurance. I think I maintained at least a semblance of composure. I think I even managed a smile at the bespectacled, gum-chewing receptionist on my way out. "Take care, Mrs. Slopen," she called after me cheerfully.

And just how do I do that? I wondered, catching my reflection in the glass of a nearby door, seeing my mother staring back at me. She was fifty-eight when the cancer was first discovered in her left breast. During the course of the next five years, it spread to virtually every part of her body. There was surgery, followed by chemotherapy and radiation, followed by more surgery and more chemo and still more surgery. Her hair fell out; she lost so much weight her muscles atrophied and her bones turned brittle; her skin yellowed like old newspaper, then grayed like dust. She spent most of the last year of her life heavily sedated, drifting in and out of reality. Jan and I took turns at her bedside, although it's doubtful she was aware of anything but her pain, until Jan said that she couldn't come to the hospital anymore, that it was too much for her to bear, that she couldn't stand to see our mother suffer any longer, as if somehow I could, as if it was somehow easier for me, as the firstborn, to stand beside the hospital bed and watch our mother die.

Will it be the same with my girls? I wonder. My beautiful, beautiful babies, who have grown up and away from me with such speed and determination it leaves me breathless. Who will be the one to stand resolutely by my bedside? Kelly, my little social butterfly, whose heart-shaped face and small, upturned nose, gently flecked with freckles, belie the soul of a budding tyrant? Or her older sister, Danielle, possessor of her father's deep-blue eyes and gentle mouth, who has barely said a civil word to me in months, when she bothers speaking to me at all?

It doesn't matter if they stand beside my bedside. The more important question is, Will they stand beside each other?

How quiet the house has suddenly become, I realize, trying to stifle my sobs before they hear me. In the tiny bathroom adjoining my office, I splash cold water on my face, smooth back the straight blond hair that frames it. My hairdresser, Stephan— Ste*phan*, as he pronounces it—has been trying for months to persuade me to cut it into something more modern. "You'd look much younger with short hair," he tells me. "Look at you. You're so slim, you have a great figure. Short hair would take ten years off you. At least ten years."

In the next instant, I am naked from the waist up, my blouse and bra lying on the floor beside my feet, as I study my bare breasts in the mirror above the sink. I have essentially the same breasts I've had since I was thirteen. Small but perfect, Todd used to say. Maybe once. Now they're just small. Age, pregnancies, and nursing two babies have definitely taken their toll.

I've always been fascinated by breasts. Maybe because I was a child in the fifties, in the era of Jane Russell and Marilyn Monroe, when a picture of Jayne Mansfield falling out of her dress under the disdainful glance of an equally well-endowed Sophia Loren made the front pages of newspapers across the country. At least the breasts were their own, I think, mindful of today's surgically enhanced celebrities, nostalgic for the days when nature was the only option. "When are my breasts going to get bigger?" I remember demanding of my mother when I was fourteen, as if my lack of development in this area was her fault, something she had wished on me to keep the boys away, keep me from the popularity I craved. My mother certainly possessed an ample enough bosom, not large, perhaps, but quite respectable. Wasn't I my mother's daughter? I'd inherited her fair hair and pale-green eyes, even the curve of her calves, why not her breasts? Furtively, I monitored my sister's progress in this department, grateful beyond words when she too progressed no further than an A cup. "Don't worry, they'll grow," my mother promised. I'm still waiting.

At first my mother tried to hide her cancer from Jan and me. Even after it was decided that a mastectomy was the only alternative, she tried to minimize the seriousness of her condition, refusing to be anything but cheerful around us until it was too late for pretense. "I didn't want to worry you," she said when I asked her why she hadn't confided in us earlier.

"We might have been able to help," I told her.

"Jan wouldn't have been able to deal with it. You know how sensitive she is," was her reply.

"Jan is a lot stronger than you think," I argued.

"She's always had such a hard time of things," she continued, as if she hadn't heard me, although I knew she had. We'd had this discussion many times before. It was always the same: Jan was sensitive; she was unlucky; she wasn't focused. Not the way I was. I had so much; she had so little. My husband was a successful dentist who not only adored me but made enough money so that I could afford to stay home and try to get my writing career off the ground; I had two beautiful daughters. Jan had two ex-husbands, a job she hated, and a dog who hated her. She was always struggling to make ends meet. "She's never had any luck," our mother concluded.

Sometimes we make our luck, I thought then.

Sometimes we don't, I think now, reaching down to pick up my clothes, slipping directly into my pink blouse, forgoing the unnecessary bra. Too small for a B cup. "Not small enough for the big C," I say, and almost laugh. One of life's many ironies. I have inherited, not my mother's breasts, but in all likelihood the disease they harbored and sheltered and fed.

Have I passed this legacy on to my own daughters?

Why is it so quiet? Has Danielle finally made good on her threats to kill her younger sister? Oh, God, what will happen to them if something happens to me? Will they be able to put aside their petty differences, draw closer, realize that they're all they've got? Or will their silly squabbles escalate until normal conversation becomes impossible, until there is nothing left to remind them of their sisterly bond but a few rarely glanced at old photographs.

Almost unwittingly, I feel my hand reach for the stack of photo albums on the bottom shelf of the cabinets Todd designed. I quickly locate the one I'm looking for, the oldest one, a dark leather-bound book of heavy black pages onto which the pictures have been pasted. And suddenly there we are, Jan and I, in our matching blue-and-white gingham dresses, sisters separated by only three years and three months, arms swung protectively across one another's shoulders, mouths open in wide smiles of varying degrees of toothlessness. And here again, the following year, cavorting with one another at the beach, and here, at ages ten and seven, playing Old Maid, and here, now into our teens, hunched over a serious game of Scrabble. "Can't you ever let her win?" I hear our mother ask. "Just once." And so I tried to let her win, but even when I handed Jan spaces that would have afforded her triple word points, she was unable to squeak out the necessary points to beat me. "I'm trying," I insisted to my mother as once again, Jan retreated to her room in tears. "Try harder," our mother said. "You know how sensitive your sister is."

Could I have tried harder? Maybe. But even as a child, I was becoming impatient with Jan's so-called sensitivity, which she wielded with the force and subtlety of a baseball bat. And I was resentful of the way in which she was able to manipulate our mother.

"It's not my fault she left most of her money to me," Jan insisted after our mother's death. "I never asked her to do that."

"I know."

"You know that she loved you every bit as much as she loved me."

I know that too. And I know that the reason she left most of her money to my sister had nothing to do with loving her more or me less. She did it because she worried about her more, about me less. She told me of the extra provisions she'd made for Jan in her will before she died, and I lied and said it was okay, it didn't matter. I had Todd and the girls. I didn't need her money. But it wasn't okay, it *did* matter, for reasons that had nothing to do with money and everything to do with fairness. She was my mother and I adored her, and after she died, I felt doubly abandoned. I felt *left out*. And I blamed Jan. And as a result, I lost a sister as well as a mother.

I must be very careful not to do the same thing where my daughters are concerned. I must do everything in my power to preserve the fragile balance that is their relationship. I will take care to ensure that everything I have is divided equally between them, regardless of perceived need. I must not follow my mother's example, however well-intentioned it might have been.

And yet, what kind of example am I setting for Kelly and Danielle? What have I taught them about love and forgiveness, about tolerance and the bond between sisters? How can I tell them to watch out for each other, to take care of each other, to be kind to one another, you're sisters, you're all you've got—words on a Scrabble board, lacking context, just words—when the example they've grown up with says sisters are unnecessary, irrelevant, expendable.

There are other words as well, words that need to be said. I do my daughters no favors by protecting them from the truth. "Why didn't you confide in us earlier?" I hear them ask, their words echoing my own. How can I expect them to function as adults if I continue to treat them as children? They must know how much I love them. And isn't trust a large part of love? There are things they need to know, words that must be voiced out loud.

I take a deep breath and reach for the phone.

Danielle

The truth is, I can't even remember what started the argument. A few misplaced words. Next thing I know, my sister and I are verbally assaulting one another, and the door is slammed in my face before I can wrap my hands around her throat. The worst thing about fights such as this one is not how hurt you feel, but how much you hate yourself for saying the hurtful things you said. I'm used to that feeling. It comes with having a hot temper and little self-control. I know that the ones I've hurt the most are the ones who would sacrifice their lives to save mine. I can only hope that my relationship with Kelly won't mirror that of my mom and Aunt Jan. They haven't spoken in years. Not that my aunt hasn't made countless attempts, however futile. But my mother refuses to take her calls and has never returned a single message. I don't want that to be our story. Part of me wants to enter Kelly's room, unarmed and apologetic; another part of me is much too proud. So instead I decide to head down to the kitchen for a snack. That's when I hear it. Ever so softly, as I stand at the top of the landing, one foot poised to take a step.

My mother is crying.

I didn't even realize she was home. My instinct tells me that something is terribly wrong, for it's not anger I hear but a quiet sadness. I am frozen, my hand gripping the banister. I don't have to ask what's wrong. I already know.

I know because when she went for her mammogram last week, she was desperately trying to mask the nervousness that she so obviously felt. I wanted to ask her about it, but I didn't want to upset her. Or maybe it was me that I didn't want to upset. I'm not sure.

I turn and head back to my room. I don't know what to think. I feel numb and removed from the situation. Kind of the same feeling I had when we lost my father to an unexpected heart attack. He was forty-six. I remember thinking, "No, this isn't happening to me, it couldn't possibly be happening to me." I, like every other young adult, was gifted with an immortality complex that I thought extended to all my other family members as well. Only when I was forced to face the harsh reality of my father's death did that particular complex also die.

Sometimes I think I'm much too young to have such a deep understanding of mortality. That's why I'm so frightened. The numbness I feel has nothing to do with thinking that what's happening isn't possible, but that it *is* possible. The worst *is* conceivable.

I love my mother. I do. Although I don't always show it. Perhaps I never show it. Perhaps hoping she knows it isn't enough anymore. I know that she often thinks of her mother. They shared a closeness she always hoped to duplicate with Kelly and me. I know she tries to be the strong and gentle woman her mother was. I know she desperately wants to create the same bond with us that they once shared. That's why she wanted daughters. To pass that on.

What I've never told my mother is that I think of her the same way she thinks of her mother, that I see her as a wise, gentle soul with an inner strength matched by few. And I know that if ever I were to have a daughter, I would want to be just like her. But I wouldn't want a daughter like me. A daughter who feels so much love for her mother but is unable to express it.

I'm tired, overwhelmed by the need to lie down. I return to my room and climb into bed. Immediate solace. I wander off to dream.

I am sitting on the floor. A hardwood floor in a room that is neither kitchen nor den but a peculiar hybrid of both—bookshelves mixed with appliances, a desk where the kitchen table should be. None of the lights are on. The room is in semidarkness. My mother sits on the floor across from me, eyes focused on something in front of her, concentrating deeply. We're playing some sort of game. My mother is busy arranging a bunch of little wooden squares on a board.

"Pick your letters," she says. "We don't have very long."

Suddenly I recognize the game. Scrabble, I realize, until then oblivious to the board and the small bag of letters lying on the floor in front of me. Scrabble is my mother's favorite game.

"My turn first," she informs me, proudly proceeding to display her word on the board, one letter at a time. B R E A S T S. She giggles, like a little girl. "I got Scrabble!"

I stare at my letters, suddenly aware of the fact that I only have three. "I only have three letters," I whine. "I can't play with only three letters." My mother doesn't respond. I persist. "Aren't I supposed to have seven?"

"I was given seven," she tells me. "You were given three."

"But that isn't fair," I protest.

"Hurry," she warns me. "We don't have too long."

"Okay." I stare hopelessly at my letters: M, E, I. "I can't. I don't know what to do."

"Concentrate."

"Mommy, I'm scared."

"You have thirty seconds." She turns over a miniature hourglass. As the sand seeps through its tiny center, my mother begins to fade.

"No, you can't leave me. You have to help me— like you used to, when I was little. Remember, you used to let me win."

"I can't do that anymore."

"Please."

"I can't help you now."

"Danielle . . ." The voice is low, soothing, achingly familiar.

"Daddy?" I cry, as his shadow floats in and out of view. My wonderful, adoring father. How much I miss him. How much I wish he were here.

"All you have to do is concentrate. Relax. Let the letters find their place," he tells me.

"Daddy, I'm scared. I don't know what to do."

"Hurry," my mother whispers desperately.

And suddenly my father is beside me, his arms around me, guiding me, comforting me. "You can do it," he says.

"Okay," I say softly. "Okay, Daddy, I'll try."

I shift my letters around, studying those already on the board.

"It's right in front of you," my father says as the word begins to take shape. "It's always been right in front of you."

And then I see it. Under the T in BREAST, I place my I, followed by the M and the E.

TIME.

I smile and turn to my father, only to find that he is no longer there.

"Isn't it funny," my mother says sadly, "how we never seem to have enough."

I am suddenly awake. I sit upright and turn toward the window. It's dark outside. The clock beside my bed says eight o'clock. I've slept for almost four hours. I feel out of breath, though I'm not sure why. Already I'm losing the details of my dream, though I still feel my father's presence. It's been a long time since he visited my dreams. I feel a strange sense of urgency, perhaps because I'm supposed to meet my boyfriend in half an hour and I'm nowhere near ready.

I get out of bed. The events of the day immediately surround me. My sister and I were fighting. My mother was crying. There is something very wrong. I know my mother won't tell us about her situation, and I'm not sure whether or not to broach the subject. I think maybe I should let her handle it the way she believes best. At least for the time being. I know that right now she is missing my father. I wish I could provide the sense of support I know he would have provided. Maybe I'll tell her my dream before I leave.

I quickly apply my makeup and search for something to wear. After selecting a black catsuit and small black silk scarf, I gather my belongings, take one final glance in the mirror, and head downstairs.

My mother is seated by herself in the kitchen, seemingly engrossed in a book she's been reading forever. "Hi," I say from the doorway.

She looks up and smiles. Such a wondrous smile for such a simple word.

"Where's Kelly?" I ask.

"She went out with some friends."

"Listen, could you tell her that I'm really sorry about the fight we had earlier?"

"Why don't you tell her yourself?"

I sigh. "Yeah, maybe."

"You slept through dinner. Are you hungry?"

I shake my head. "I had a dream about Daddy," I venture.

Her smile becomes peaceful. "What was the dream about?"

"I can't really remember. I just know he was here."

And suddenly I can feel him, I can feel his presence in the room, and it's as thick and strong as if he'd never left. I believe my mother feels it too. I'm beginning to think she always has. I try desperately to remember what my dream was about. I feel it was important. But all I can do is stare at my mother. My beautiful mother. And I have to hold back the tears.

"So, where are you off to tonight?" she asks.

I want to run to her, to hold her, to comfort her. "Nowhere," I say, dropping my purse to the floor, walking toward her, sitting down beside her.

"Good," she says. "I need to talk to you."

I say nothing, wait for her to speak.

"I was at the doctor's today," she begins, as the breath stops in my lungs. "Apparently my mammogram was a bit suspicious."

"You have cancer?" I hear myself ask, nails digging into the bottom of my chair.

"Hopefully not," she says quickly. "But I need to have another test. Next Thursday."

"Will it hurt?"

She smiles. "I don't know. I didn't think to ask."

"Are you scared?"

"Yes."

"Have you told Kelly?"

"Not yet."

"Are you going to? I mean, maybe you shouldn't. Maybe she's too young. . . ."

"I think she should know."

I nod agreement. "Do you want me to come with you—next Thursday?"

Tears fill her eyes. "Thank you, sweetheart. I can't tell you how much that means to me." She takes a deep breath. "But I've already asked Jan to take me."

"Jan? Your sister?"

"Jan," she repeats. "My sister."

I love you, a voice inside me screams. *I have always loved you. But I have never loved you more than I do right at this moment.*

I want so desperately to say the words.

I want to tell my mother how much I love her.

"Do you want to play Scrabble?" I ask instead, my voice on the verge of breaking. Her face lights up. Once again, I've made my mother smile. She runs to get the Scrabble set.

It is Friday night, I'm supposed to be at a party with my boyfriend, and instead I'm sitting in the kitchen playing Scrabble with my mother. And I've never been happier.

Letters

Debbie Macomber and Syrena Gaffney

Photo courtesy of Macomber Family

INTRODUCTION

When Syrena and I were asked to participate in this project, we were excited. Syrena had been working with me, honing her writing skills for several months, and this was an opportunity of a lifetime for her . . . and me. We talked extensively about how to go about writing a short story together, tossing ideas back and forth. We made a couple of attempts, but soon discovered that our writing styles are very different. How to blend a story with two very different authors posed something of a problem.

"Letters" was Syrena's idea. An exchange of letters between a mother and a daughter, both with attitudes, both with lessons to learn. I started the first letter and Syrena answered. Soon our computers were humming. We took two months to finish the project, exchanging letters every few days, learning, laughing, and growing. By the time we finished, we had discovered that our styles, outlooks, and approaches weren't so very different after all.

Mother and Child Reunion

June 7

Dear Janey,
    You've been at camp a couple of days now

and I'm hoping that you've had time enough to cool down. I feel bad that we were forced to spend our last hours together arguing over something stupid. I won't use this letter to lecture you. I made my views on the matter of body piercing plain before you left. From the way you were shouting on your way out the door, I'm in no doubt of your feelings either. Perhaps the best thing for us to do is agree to disagree and leave it at that. As far as I can see we're too far apart to meet in the middle on this issue. In fact, let's drop the subject entirely. Entirely!

Everything at home is great. Actually it's a lot more peaceful around here without your music blaring at all hours of the day and night. This job at camp will do you a world of good, teach you the meaning of a dollar and appreciation of family.

I need to put the clothes in the dryer and get this in the mailbox before the mailman arrives. It would help if you wrote once in a while, you know. I'm your mother, and no matter how you feel about me just now, the fact that you're my daughter will never change. With that in mind, I'm hoping that we can both look past our differences and make an effort to get along. Could we try to do that?

Write soon.

Love,
Mom

P.S. If you're in contact with Darrin, would you kindly let him know you're at camp.

We've been getting phone calls past ten p.m. and when we answer, whoever's on the other line hangs up. It's got to be Darrin. One more time and your father's going to get caller ID.

June 14th

Mother,

I just love the way you decide to "end" a subject, especially when it's in your best interest to not talk about something. Well, not this time. I'm seventeen years old and don't deserve to be treated like a child any longer. Besides, you're too late! My new friend and co-counselor Autumn and I talked it over and agree that I'm old enough to decide what I want to do with my own body. As of Thursday I now have a pierced belly! How's that for a "subject ending"?!!

By the way, camp's great! Especially since I don't have you nagging at me left and right, criticizing everything I do. The first group of kids arrived yesterday and already three have left sick, or should I say homesick. That's the last thing you'll ever need to worry about with me!

I talked to Darrin and told him that our relationship is over. I met a great guy here, and he's twenty. So, if that was Darrin calling past ten, it should stop.

Bye,
Jane

P.S. Dad, please tell mom to stop calling me Janey. I hate that, it's sooo immature! Thanks dad, love ya!

June 18th

Dear Janey,

Your letter arrived this morning. I cannot believe that after everything your father and I've said about you piercing your body that you would go ahead and do it anyway. I can't help feeling you did this simply to defy everything we say and believe. Well, the deed is done, and all I can say is that I hope you don't live to regret it. I can only imagine the condition of the needle your friend used. Promise me this one thing, if it isn't too much to ask—please keep the area clean and as free from germs as possible. The belly button is a direct line to your bloodstream.

It's sometimes difficult to remember that you're my daughter, seeing how hardheaded you are and how stubborn you can be. I don't know what I did to deserve this rebellious nature of yours. I will tell you this, though, and believe it if you want: The only one you're hurting is yourself. If your belly button becomes infected you're the one who'll suffer. Just as you'll be the one who will have to stare at the unsightly image of it ten or fifteen years down the road. My guess is that then you'll lament you didn't listen to your parents and wish you had!

I hate to bring up another unpleasant

subject, but both your father and I consider a seventeen-year-old girl much too young to be dating a boy of twenty. I understand about summer romances and won't make an issue of this one, but I am relieved to know the dorms aren't coed. I'm sure, now that the newness of camp has worn off, that you'll appreciate the burden of responsibility for the ten-year-old girls in your charge.

I know you'll do your best to be a good camp leader.

Love,
Mom

P.S. Darrin didn't get the message; he phoned again last night and I was forced to tell him that you have a new boyfriend now and don't wish to hear from him any further. Are you sure he knew this? Because he sounded surprised.

June 24th

Mother,

Don't bring daddy into this. He didn't say a word when I mentioned body piercing. He at least listened to what I had to say. You weren't even willing to hear me out. Anyway, you didn't say anything about me not getting my belly button pierced, you were too "concerned" about me piercing my tongue! I'm smart enough to be sure Autumn used clean instruments—after all, I do have my ears pierced.

This group of girls is great and we get along fine. They don't think I'm stubborn or hard-headed! Sometimes Chad comes over late at night to sing and play his guitar for us. He's really nice, Mom. He wants to backpack through Europe with his guitar, and he invited me to go along! I told him that I'd have to think about it and that my parents are extremely conservative, especially my mother. Sometimes I wonder if you and dad remember what it was like to be young. I think dad does because he never gets into these "discussions" with us, even though he backs you up when you do drag him in. (I feel that it's just a marriage thing, though.)

I can't believe you told Darrin that I have a boyfriend!!! He wasn't supposed to know yet. You just don't understand anything, do you? Well, it's lights out, and I gotta go.

Bye,
Jane

P.S. Stop calling me Janey!!!

June 27th

Dear Jane,

Your father was kind enough to remind me that there are many things to be grateful for in this body piercing phase you're going through. First off, you're right, you didn't have your tongue pierced and if you had to pierce anything I guess the belly button wasn't the worst place. If you can live with that, then so can I.

Tell me more about Chad. You say he's nice, but that doesn't really tell me anything about him. Sweetheart, I do remember what it's like to be young. It seems like only a few years ago I was arguing with my own mother. She didn't like my music or the way I did my hair, and she refused to let me phone boys. Can you imagine? Yet I appreciated the fact that she cared enough about the way I looked and behaved to show some interest. I didn't appreciate it at the time, mind you, but later. I hope you'll be able to look back at these years someday and feel the same way.

I can't get over how quiet the house is with you gone. I miss your help. Your brother does what I ask him to do, but nothing more. Remember what you were like at age thirteen? I had him put the dirty dishes in the dishwasher and he did, but he left all the leftovers out on the countertop. When I told him he needed to put the food away he stuck the bowls in the refrigerator without lids. I need to be more patient with him, I guess. And more patient with you, too. Who says I never admit I make an occasional mistake? I'll say one thing—when you cleaned the kitchen, it was spotless, unlike Billy. (I can still call him Billy—when he turns seventeen I guess I'll have to change his name to Bill.)

Okay, about telling Darrin he has a little competition. You didn't tell me not to say anything. I'm not a mind reader, Jane. If I said something I shouldn't have, then you should have made the point clearer. Okay?

Love,
Mom

P.S. Are any adults around when Chad comes over to the dorm to play his guitar and sing? A boy who would bum his way around Europe sounds shiftless and irresponsible to me.

July 3, 1997

Mother,

I don't know why you assume everything in my life that you disagree with is a phase. Not to worry, Autumn's boyfriend, the one who actually pierced me, gave me some cleaning solution for free. I think he's great. You wouldn't like him, though, he's got too many tattoos and too many pierced body parts, especially in places I shouldn't mention to my parents. Also you should know: I'm living with my decision just fine!

Chad is really a great guy and he treats me fine, a lot better than Darrin, anyway. He's more mature and he listens to what I have to say. I wish you'd listen as well, but as you said, I guess that's just how mothers are. You said you didn't get along with your mother either. Well, I bet all your arguments were about your hair—I saw those pictures of you in your high school annuals! I'm just having a little fun with you, Mom, so don't

have a tizzy. When I'm a mom I hope I won't
be uptight about things like you and grandma
are; after all, I'm being raised in the information age. There aren't as many taboos in this
day and age as when you were growing up,
so we can express ourselves and learn more
about each other.

I feel more independent out here. I'm not
constantly being told how to do the dishes.
As long as I complete my assignments with
the girls, I can do as I please (well, to a certain extent, anyway) and listen to whatever type of music I want. We get a free time
every afternoon and almost everyone listens
to my music—well, there's a few hicks and
G-wanna-bes. I have my own private area in
the woods where I go to read or dream. It's a
nice little area without a younger brother
bringing his lovestruck friends to stare at
me. But sometimes I miss my Nutella and peanut butter sandwiches. I don't, however, miss
them enough to want to come home. By the
way, what's going on with you guys over the
4th of July? Let me know how it goes. Since I
won't be there.

Even though I don't care what Darrin
knows, it was still rude of you to say anything about my personal life to him, or to
anyone for that matter. I don't go running
around saying when you and Dad argue and
who you talk to afterwards, do I? No. Well, I
expect the same courtesy from you. My life
is my business, and I should be the one to

share it with whomever *I* desire to share it with. Hopefully you won't make this mistake again!

Well, I gotta go! Give my love to Dad. Bye!

Jane

P.S. Thanks for not calling me Janey, even though I know it's probably Dad's doing. See, I appreciate things!

July 7, 1997

Dear Jane,

We had a great 4th of July—thanks for asking about our plans. We joined your grandparents at the lake and had a barbecue. You know how your father loves to barbecue—he did a great job. Naturally your grandmother asked about you and you don't need to worry about hiding your pierced belly button from her because I told her myself what you'd done. She was shocked, but like me she recovered quickly. Your grandfather made a great joke out of it and will probably ask you to show it to him the next time you're home.

You asked why I called this body piercing thing a phase. Well, Jane, because that's exactly what it is. You make "phase" sound like it's something bad, and that isn't necessarily so. We all go through periods when something of one nature or another interests us. Remember how I started knitting last winter and once I'd finished that scarf for your father, I moved on to needlepoint? Knitting was just a phase, so to speak. You go through them. I go through them. Everyone does. What I'm saying is that there's no need to be so quick to take offense.

As for what you said about feeling more independent, that's great. You're seventeen and at the age where you're making your own decisions. I'd like to think that those decisions would be made with a mature outlook. In other words, you need to consider the consequences of your actions. Actually, I couldn't be more pleased that you're growing up. In another year you'll be off to college. An adult.

You seem to think it was rude of me to tell Darrin you're seeing someone else now. What I consider rude is leaving and not so much as letting him know. Apparently you hadn't bothered to tell him you'd gotten the job at camp. Darrin deserved to be treated better than that.

I've got to get dinner going. Your father will be home soon.

Love,
Mom

P.S. What makes you assume that me calling you Jane is your father's doing? By the way, who's Ben? He phoned and left a message on the answering machine the other day. I don't remember any friends of yours named Ben.

July 10, 1997

Mother,

I'm glad that you had fun at the lake. Don't be mad, but it sounds like I would have been bored. We didn't have any kids during the fourth so we had a major kegger . . . just kidding. We did have a little Bar-B-Q of our own, though—no kegs were allowed—we did have apple cider (yippie skippie). After the Bar-B-Q picnic we watched the big fireworks from across the water. It wasn't that spectacular since we were a long way off. Then we had a bonfire on the beach, sang songs, and just had a cozy time telling stories and jokes. Nothing big. Some of us did go to the carnival in town and were disappointed. It just wasn't like the one at home. They didn't even have the Zipper or the Octopus, can you believe that!

Yesterday, one of the girls from my cabin broke out with the chicken pox. We had to notify all the parents. Over half the kids had to go home today. I've had chicken pox before, right? Well, I'll probably talk to you on the phone before I receive another letter from you anyway. Would the chicken pox be considered as a "phase"? Nah, I guess not. One thing I'm glad of, though, is that your knitting was a short phase before you decided to make a matching scarf for me. Don't take offense, but your scarf looked just awful!!!

Mom, I want you to know I did think long and hard about piercing my belly and I know

I won't have any regrets. And I can't believe you actually told Grandma and Grandpa about my belly ring. Okay, maybe I can believe it. He'll start lecturing me on "how awful it'll look when I decide to have children someday," and I'll say, "I just won't have any" or "I'll adopt!" But nothing will satisfy Grandpa.

Who cares about Darrin, but, please, tell me what Ben said. Did he really call or did Billy make it up and tell you that he left a message for me and that he "accidentally" erased it. Please, I gotta know!

Oh, someone just puked, so I should jet now. Bye!

Jane

P.S. Just in case you wanted to know, family day is Saturday, August 16, and I *suppose* everyone is invited. Oh, yeah, who says that I'm going to college? Becoming an adult doesn't mean college. That's just another excuse to stay young and play-act that you're an adult!

July 14, 1997

Dear Jane,

It was good to chat with you yesterday, however briefly. I was glad to be able to reassure you that you've got nothing to fear from the chicken pox. I will say that I got a good laugh about you thinking you could see the bumps rising up on your arms and legs. The imagination is a powerful thing.

I promised I'd review the tape from the answering machine to be certain exactly what it was Ben said. I hope you appreciate the time and effort it took to find it. The message was actually very short. He said, "I'm calling for Jane, give me a call when you can." He didn't leave a phone number. Who is this Ben? What about Chad? You haven't mentioned him in the last couple of letters.

Your father and I checked the calendar and I'm sorry, Janey, but we can't make it to camp on August 16th. Your father and I made plans with some friends to take a wine tour. We would like to visit the camp, however. Is there another weekend where we could stop off and have you give us a mini-tour?

Gotta scoot.

Love,
Mom

P.S. I found a bunch of your old jeans and decided to do you a favor and mend the knees. I don't know why you want to wear those pants with giant holes in them, anyway.

July 19, 1997

Mother,

This is the last Saturday I'll have completely to myself this month. I went for a swim this morning in the outdoor pool. And to think I used to be scared of the water. It was cool and refreshing, especially after this heat wave we've been having. It's been up in the '90s all week. How's the weather been at home? Oh, next time I call, don't talk so long, there are other people waiting to use the phone. It may be hard for you, considering the way you love to chat. Just remember to try to keep it under ten minutes. Thanks.

I can't believe Ben didn't leave his number! Can you do me a huge favor and call 'Cinda for me and ask her if she has Ben's phone number? I met him at the mall with 'Cinda. Don't worry, Mom, he's not as old as Chad! Why should you care about Chad? You've done nothing to encourage my relationship with him, so what's the big concern now?

Don't worry about not being able to make it to family day. I didn't really want you to come anyway. I hope you and Dad have fun toasting it up on your "whine tour." Not many of my friends' parents are coming either. No biggie.

Bye,
Jane

P.S. I can't believe you *fixed* my jeans! They were *meant* to be that way. That was the *whole* point!

July 25, 1997

Dear Jane,

I knew you were going to be upset about your father and I not making it to camp for "parents' day." I do feel bad about that, but try to understand, we've had these plans with the McMahons for months. We're driving to the Yakima Valley where there's a number of wineries. We've been looking forward to it all summer, so please don't be upset. I guess I must be feeling guilty about it.

Believe this or not, Jane, I do care about your friends and was interested in hearing more about Chad. You seemed quite taken with him at the beginning of the summer. What concerned me was all that talk about not going on to college after you graduate and touring Europe instead. First of all, your father and I would never allow that and secondly, you could never afford it. You have all your life to visit Europe. College is the most important thing you need to think about. That's your future.

I'm sorry this is so short, but I've got a pounding headache. Your brother has been playing Grunge music all morning. I don't think those are your CDs? He knows better than to go into your bedroom after what happened last week. I'll feel better once I've had a couple of aspirin.

Love,
Mom

P.S. You asked me to contact 'Cinda for Ben's phone number, but there won't be any need to do that. He stopped by the other day. How old is this young man, anyway? He looks like he might be college age, in which case I think he might be too old for you. Before you call and demand to know, his number is 345-9087. He was rather polite though, and good manners say a lot. Oh, not to worry, I was teasing about mending your jeans.

July 29, 1997

Mother,

Honest, I'm not upset about you and Dad not coming for Parents' Day. It's actually for the kids at camp, not the counselors. You're always assuming things! So have a great time drinking it up with the McMahons in Yakima. Have a glass of wine on me, okay?

You won't be hearing about Chad anymore, I decided to end it with him. Don't get all cocky, it had nothing to do with you. I had my reasons, that's all. Besides, Ben's a lot cuter! Thanks for giving me Ben's phone number. You don't know how much this means to me. Oh, sorry I didn't call you. I used my phone time to call Ben. He's totally awesome!!!! I still can't believe he stopped by to see me. I wish I were home *just* to have seen him.

Now what's this about Billy, my room, and what did he do with my CDs? If he ruined anything he's dead! He hasn't been feeding my fish too much, has he? What about my iguana—how's he doing? Don't tell me he put all my fish in one bowl to clean out my aquariums—even I don't think he's stupid enough to put all my betas together and with the other fish.

'Til Next Time,
Jane

P.S. About Europe and college, maybe I could go to a college *in* Europe.

August 6, 1997

Dear Janey . . . sorry—Jane,

Thanks for being so understanding about your father's and my weekend away with the McMahons. I did phone and try to re-arrange the time, but they're busy people and the 16th is the only weekend they have open. If it were possible for us to be two places at the same time, then you know your father and I would be with you too.

You'll never guess who I ran into. 'Cinda! I was in Albertson's, minding my own busi-ness in the produce section, when she came up and asked about you. I'm telling you, Jane, I didn't recognize her and I doubt you will either. She had her tongue pierced and was all excited and told me in far more detail than I wanted to hear about how it was done. I hope to high heaven that whoever pierced your belly button used sterile instruments. I've mentioned this before and don't mean to harp on it, but infections happen. By the way 'Cinda's hair is now pink, but I don't think the color was intentional. The only reason I'm telling you is so you won't be shocked later.

Don't worry about Billy, he's taking good care of all your creatures. As to what happened in your room with Billy. Your father and I talked it over and decided we should tell you. I caught Billy reading your journal. I wouldn't mention it except he was silly enough to write comments in the margins. Your father and I highly disapprove of him invading your or anyone's privacy. I refused to listen to anything he tried to tell me, although I was tempted. He's lost all phone privileges for an entire month. Enclosed is his letter of apology.

I'm pleased you were able to connect with Ben. What did he have to say? As for attending college in Europe, it doesn't do any harm to dream, but that's far beyond what your father and I can afford for you. What about a scholarship? You could do it if you'd apply yourself!

Write soon.

Love,
Mom

P.S. 'Cinda said she was thinking of having her nose pierced next. Thank heavens you chose your belly button instead of that or your tongue.

August 6th

Dear Jane,
Sorry I read your journal.

Billy

August 17, 1997

Mother,

Sorry I haven't written sooner. I've been so busy coordinating the events for Parents' Day. Most of the time we had fun, but some parents were really annoying, especially to their kid. You'll probably receive this letter after you get back from your trip. You would have enjoyed it here. There were a lot of other conservative parents you would have enjoyed meeting. There was one little girl who decided to show off to her little brother and see how far out in the lake she could swim. She was doing really well until she started getting tired coming back. I had to jump in and bring her back to shore. Swimmer's itch really sucks!

I talked to LaCinda ('Cinda) last week and she mentioned that she was thinking of getting her eyebrow pierced, also. Now, I think that's going a little too far. I'd never do anything like that. My belly button is good enough . . . for now anyway!

Billy does know that when I get back that he better be on his best behavior or I will kill him. Well, I just might decide to do that anyhow. He has never met with the wrath of a woman, or at least this one, to this degree! What he did was unacceptable and no amount of apologizing will make up for it. He will be my personal slave until I see fit for his release! Do you think that's too harsh, Mom, or should I be harsher? Oh, well. What's done is done. At least I didn't have anything too personal in there.

I don't feel like talking about Ben with you right now, okay? Just know that he's a really great guy who's trying to find what he wants to do in life. Good head on his shoulders, don't you think? Time will tell.

I'm bushed, so I'll end it here. Love ya.

Jane

P.S. Give my love to Dad!

August 24th

Dear Jane,

Your father and I are pleased with how well Parents' Day went, and from the sounds of it you were a real hero, swimming out to rescue that youngster. We're proud of you! We had a great time with the McMahons in the wine country. Cindy and I have been friends from the time we were teenagers. A lot like you and 'Cinda. Cindy reminded me of how much my mother and I used to fight and how stubborn I used to be. Me? Imagine that! When I told her that you'd pierced your belly button, she laughed and asked me if I remembered the time the two of us bleached my hair and did such a horrible job that chunks of it fell out and I was almost bald on one side. Oh, Jane, you can't imagine how awful that was. I looked like a freak. Cindy and I laughed until we cried. What I'm saying is that despite our difference of opinion on certain matters you and I are actually quite a bit alike. That's a scary thought, isn't it?

Billy misses the phone, and although I don't think a thirteen-year-old boy would openly admit it, he misses you too. He asked when you'd be home again and it's hard to believe that it's only a couple of weeks more. We'll have a lot to do when you get back, shopping for school clothes . . . are you going to want a perm because I'll make the appointment now if you do. I've already got you scheduled for a physical with Dr. Frank for the first Monday you're back. It wouldn't hurt if he looked at your belly button either. That would put my mind to rest.

Gotta scoot. Write soon.

Love,
Mom

P.S. What's up with you and Ben? Hey, you can tell me anything, really, Jane, I mean that. I might yell and get upset but you're my daughter and we should be able to talk. I'm on your side. Darrin stopped by the other day. He's looking like a lost puppy these days. I think he misses you, but I agree with you, he's immature and needs to grow up. Actually your choices in friends have always been good. Your father and I trust you when it comes to choosing the boys in your life.

August 30, 1997

Mom,

I'm glad that your trip was a great success. It's nice to know that you too have some good friends. I miss my friends, and I guess I miss you guys too; well, just a little! I can't believe that you tried to bleach your hair back-in-the-old-days. No wonder you almost went bald, nothing was perfected then. I could just imagine grandma's reaction!

This has been a dull week around here. Chad and Autumn (my old good friends) are always all over each other. I'm so glad that I got rid of that loser! My new kids find him arrogant and annoying and so do I. The administration is beginning to get more and more strict. I guess they've about had enough of this camp thing, too. I can't believe that I can't wait to leave, but, yet, I can't. Whatever.

I guess I can forgive Billy, after all he probably read my journal just to remember me. A friend of mine and I talked about that and what she said actually made sense—about how going through my personals was his way of showing how much he really misses me. It's hard to comprehend Billy missing me, but I guess I miss him too.

I keep saving my letters for bedtime, then I get too tired. So, I'll let you go now.

Love,
Jane

P.S. Nothing's up with me and Ben. He's a great guy and we share a lot of common interests. But, some of his friends are stupid and think he should go for someone else that has more free time, that doesn't have a curfew. But, we talk all the time and he says he really likes me, so someday something may happen. I can't wait 'til it does!

September 3rd

Welcome Home, Jane,

I'm sticking this letter on your bed because I wanted you to know that I enjoyed exchanging letters with my daughter this summer. When you first left for camp I was as glad to see you go as you were to leave. We could barely speak a civil word to one another. Having you gone has opened my eyes. It helped me appreciate the woman you're becoming, one with a decent head on her shoulders. You're growing up and it shows in the decisions you're making and the friends you're choosing, especially in how you're handling relationships.

All this is leading up to an idea. How about if you and I continue with the letters? I think it might be easier for us than sitting down and talking since we both seem to let our emotions run amuck. I get loud, you get mad . . . or is it the other way around?

I'm glad you're home, and more importantly I'm glad you're my daughter.

Love,
Mom

September 4th

Mom,

I almost didn't see your note on my bed when I pulled down the covers last night. Thank you. I'm glad to be home, too. Being away made me appreciate things. I know I'm not the easiest person to get along with at times, but then who is? I ended up looking forward to your letters. But, don't tell anyone! Just kidding.

I'm glad you're my mom, even though I sometimes wish that I had more freedom (hint, hint). But I know you want what's best for me and I've noticed, from our time apart and from listening to other kids, I've actually got it pretty good. Even though I don't want to realize it at times. I love you, too, Mom.

Love,
Janey

No Place for Children

J. A. Jance and Jeanne Teale Jance

Photo by Glamour Shots

INTRODUCTION

We are survivors. We are also a mother and daughter who have been through a lifetime's worth of emotional battlefields, including the loss of a husband and father to the ravages of alcoholism. Sometimes we've emerged from the fray a little the worse for wear, but we've made it.

Teachers of fiction writing often admonish students to write what they know. If the writer sticks strictly to the facts, though, the art of fiction is lost. In No Place for Children *we took liberties with one of the most hurtful aspects of divorce—separate holidays. We gave ourselves permission to add something to the story that wasn't part of the reality for our newly divorced family—a hopeful if not necessarily happy ending.*

The process of writing the piece helped ease some of the lingering hurts from those tough times and heartbreaking events. We wrote No Place for Children *in hopes that it might offer comfort and encouragement to other despairing mothers and children faced with similarly painful holiday separations.*

Ultimately, after a number of bleak, lean years, our fortunes took a turn for the better, one that gave us a real-life happy ending with a newly reconstituted and thoroughly blended family. It seems likely that our ability to live in and enjoy the present comes as a natural out-growth of our having both experienced and conquered the past.

Dragging a child by each hand and juggling her purse as well as two shoulder-held carry-ons, Leah Mason fought her way upstream through the long and crowded concourse. Holiday traffic in and out of Sea-Tac Airport had been a nightmare. Now after spending forty-five minutes waiting in the check-in line and another ten getting through security, there was barely time to make it to the gate before the preboarding announcement. For families with young children. Or for children traveling alone.

This was the first time Leah would be separated from either one of her two children. Danielle and Richy were flying off to Las Vegas without her. There they would spend Christmas with their grandmother Maggie Mason and with Richard, the children's father and Leah's ex-husband. Glancing down, she caught Danielle peering up at her—for reassurance, perhaps. Knowing the chaos Richard's erratic behavior had sprinkled through holidays past made that reassurance hard to find. Leah tried her best.

"It'll be great," she managed hollowly, hoping her voice conveyed more confidence than she felt. Danielle, two years older than six-year-old Richy, didn't seem fooled. "Are you sure Daddy'll be at the airport to pick us up?" she asked.

Disturbed to think that her mask could be that

transparent, Leah swallowed hard before she answered. Danielle was old enough that she had personally witnessed some of her father's bizarre behavior, had suffered the heartbreak of his often broken promises. Her question, wise beyond her years, went right to the heart of Leah's major concerns—to one of them, anyway. What if the plane landed in Vegas and Richard wasn't there? If he stopped off in a bar along the way, there was a good chance he'd show up late or not at all. The travel agent and the ticket agent both had been very specific about airline procedure: If the person designated to pick the children up wasn't waiting at the arrival gate at McCarran Field, most likely the kids would be shipped right back to Seattle on the next available flight.

"Mom," Richy whined, "let go. You're hurting my hand."

Until Richy complained, Leah had no idea how tightly she was holding her son's pudgy little hand. As soon as she loosened her grip, he slipped out of her grasp and darted away from her through the people and carry-on luggage jammed into the waiting area. Dropping to his knees, he skidded up to the window and blew a cloud of steamy breath onto the chilly glass.

"Is that our plane out there?" he called back to her, pointing out the window through the unending gray of a drenching December rainstorm. "Is that the one?"

Leah's instinct was to race after him, grab him by the hand, and corral him once more, but Danielle, still attached to Leah's other hand, had stopped cold, pulling Leah to a jarring stop as well. "Why couldn't Grandma come get us?" Danielle asked.

"Because Grandma doesn't drive," Leah answered. While he was alive, Maggie Mason's husband, Richard Senior, had done all the driving. But Grandpa Mason was gone now—dead of a heart attack fifteen months earlier.

"You mean Grandma doesn't know how?" Danielle persisted. "Couldn't she go to school or something and learn?"

"Is that the pilot out there under the plane?" Richy continued. "And why's he wearing those funny things on his ears?"

Before Leah could wedge through the press of people, a young uniformed woman stepped up to the door and began punching a keypad to unlock the door to the jetway. Her appearance was the signal for one whole section of people to rise and edge toward the doorway, trapping Leah and Danielle in their midst.

"That's not the pilot, Richy," Leah replied. "He's probably already on the plane."

"Who is it, then?"

"I don't know. Probably a mechanic. Come on now," she urged. "Get back over here. It's almost time to go."

To Leah's surprise, Richy did exactly as he was told. The first time. He came back and squeezed himself into a nonexistent spot between Leah and Danielle. For weeks he had talked of nothing else—of getting to go on the plane, of getting to see his daddy again. Now, suddenly, he seemed to lose heart.

"Do we have to go?" he asked wistfully, clinging to Leah's skirt. "Couldn't we just stay here with you?"

Dreading saying good-bye, Leah Mason had spent days preparing herself for this moment. She had tried to imagine every possible scenario—including this one of Richy suddenly refusing to go. But in all her preparations, she had failed to realize there would be an audience all around them—that the leave-taking would take place squashed in among crowds of people with heavily laden suitcases and bags full of gaily wrapped presents. She hadn't anticipated that a herd of interested bystanders would be there, gawking and absorbing every nuance of their unfolding family drama.

Now, though, feeling her personal life on display in front of strangers, she thought she sensed them hearing and weighing each word. She was sure that from the smug comfort of their special holiday outfits, they looked down on Leah's children and realized they came from a single-parent home. The onlookers either knew or guessed that Richy and Danielle were being shipped off to spend time with an absent father. In front of her, an elegantly dressed blue-haired lady with a first-class sticker prominently displayed on her ticket packet looked back at them and shook her head in silent disapproval. Leah's whole being shriveled under the weight of that gaze. It was as though the woman had instantly divined every sordid detail of Leah's marriage and divorce.

"Poor little children," the woman's accusing

eyes said. "How sad to be the product of a broken home!"

"Shattered" would have been closer to the truth, Leah thought. Everything was gone now—Richard, the house, the cars and stereos. Other than the few things she had managed to pack into the car when she left town, there was nothing left.

"You have to go," Leah said stiffly to Richy. "It's not a choice."

"But why?" he pleaded, his voice verging on tears.

"Because that's what your father and I agreed on," Leah said, keeping her tone as steady as possible. "Because we said you were coming and you are."

Not that she wanted the kids to go. Every cell in her being screamed its objection, but that was what the divorce decree ordered. Richard was to have the children for two weeks at Christmas and for two months in the summer. For the time being, having lost the house and both of his leased cars, Richard had moved back in with his mother. That meant that for this trip at least, Maggie would be there to run interference. Even though Maggie had always turned a blind eye to her son's problems, the fact that she would be in the same household with them was some consolation. As for next summer's visit? That yawning chasm in Leah's heart was still months away. She would cross that dreaded bridge when she came to it.

Ever since the plane tickets had come in the mail, Leah had agonized about letting the children go. How could she have agreed to something so dumb? How could she have accepted a custody agreement that required her sending Richy and Danielle off to stay with someone who didn't have brains enough to take care of himself, much less two small children? The truth was, the divorce had been Leah's doing—one of those quicky, do-it-yourself, no-fault deals, done in the interest of saving face and money both.

Leah could hardly blame the judge for the outcome. She had kept her mouth shut then, just as she had for years before that. She had kept hidden the history of steadily escalating drug and alcohol abuse and of escalating violence as well. Consequently, the custody agreement had been made in a vacuum, with the judge knowing nothing about what was really going on in the household. Other than the nominal child support the judge had insisted upon, Leah had asked for nothing—not out of guilt or pride or altruism but because she knew that there was nothing left to take. Struggling month after month to pay the bills with less and less money, she had known full well that the affluent lifestyle she and Richard had enjoyed for so many years was a house of cards within minutes of falling. By the time the divorce was final, it was gone.

Much to her surprise, the child support payments came anyway. She wasn't sure how Richard was doing it, but as long as he was keeping that much of his bargain, Leah had to do the same. Christmas vacation was his.

"Couldn't you come, too?" Richy was asking. "Please."

The gate agent was speaking into her mike. "At this time we are pleased to announce preboarding for Flight 1624 from Seattle to Las Vegas. This is a preboarding announcement only . . ."

"Because I can't," Leah whispered. "I don't have a ticket."

"We could buy one."

"No, we can't. Come on now. It's time."

"Tickets, please."

Leah fumbled the boarding passes out of her purse and handed them over.

"Two traveling alone?"

Not trusting her ability to speak, Leah simply nodded. Then she pulled off the two separate shoulder bags. She had packed them both with goodies—books and Crayolas and coloring books—to see the kids through the long plane ride. "Now, remember," she said, finally finding her voice. "Put these under your seats and don't open them until the flight attendant says it's okay."

"But I don't want to go," Richy said.

Behind them a man cleared his throat. Armed with a briefcase and the studied boredom that comes with thousands of frequent-flyer miles, he was impatient to board.

"You've got to, Richy," Leah insisted. "Now mind your sister." She kissed the top of his head. Then she turned to Danielle, handing her the rest of the tickets. "Whatever you do, don't lose these. Be good, okay?"

Danielle nodded numbly while a trail of tears dribbled down her pale cheek and dripped onto the collar of her coat. Her daughter's forlorn but stiff-backed stoicism as she disappeared down the jetway was enough to break Leah's heart. She reeled backward, away from the gate agent, unaware of the people she jarred and the luggage she stumbled over in her wild flight from the gate. The tears she had held in check for weeks now, all through the holiday preparations, surged to the surface in a flood. Blindly she fought her way into the nearest rest room. Once there, she locked herself in a stall, then stood, leaning against the door, sobbing her heartbreak for all to hear while Richy's plaintive question played again and again in her head. "Couldn't you come, too?"

Leah knew that if she hadn't been so stubborn, she could have. Maggie, Richard's mother, had invited her—had even agreed to pay her fare and put her up in a hotel if Leah didn't think Richard would behave. The offer had been both kind and generous, but Leah had declined, and not because she didn't trust Richard. It was more because she didn't trust herself. She feared that seeing him again, even after all these months, she might still be susceptible. Might once again fall victim to his charms, which, when Richard Mason wasn't drinking or drugging or beating her up, could be considerable.

She had tried leaving three times before she finally made it stick. Nine months after the divorce was final, Leah still wasn't confident of her immunity. Going to Al-Anon had helped her come to terms with the fact that she couldn't fix Richard, she could only fix herself. But she understood that it was far easier to keep all that in perspective with him a thousand miles or so away. She was afraid she might waver if he was right there in the same room with her, pleading with her and swearing that whatever had happened before would never ever happen again. It would. Bitter experience had taught her that Richard's promises were like that—easily made and just as easily broken.

By the time Leah had herself back under control enough to leave the rest room, the plane had pulled away from the gate. It was probably just as well that she hadn't been at the window to watch them take off. Making her way back down the concourse, she headed for the garage. When they had arrived at the airport over an hour earlier, the short-term-parking level had been totally jammed. She had finally located a spot for her ten-year-old Pontiac on the top floor of the garage. Now it took half an hour to make it down the winding ramps and out to the payment booths.

She drove back to the freeways through drizzling rain. Not wanting to be exposed to any more Christmas cheer, Leah left the radio off. Consequently, she had no notice of the jackknifed semi on I-5 near the brewery until she was already trapped in the three-mile backup. Adding that to everything else that had happened that day, she might well have dissolved into tears right then, but she had no tears left. She had wrung herself dry, standing in that rest-room stall sobbing her heart out. There was nothing to do but sit and wait until traffic once again started moving.

Her pager went off three times while she waited. She had asked the property manager to get her a cell phone. Each of the three pages came from Andy White's office—maybe now he would finally get off the dime and do it. She'd have to call him once she made it back home. Leah had worried about how long the airport trip would keep her away from her job. She had asked Dora Hagendorn, one of the complex's elderly tenants, to stay in the manager's apartment and let people in or out as needed while she was gone.

Leah hoped nothing serious had happened in her absence. She didn't want anything to jeopardize her position as manager of the Regency Apartments. The building was no longer nearly as nice as the name implied and as it once had been, but the two-bedroom manager's unit provided a roof over their heads. And it beat living in a shelter.

That had been her lowest point. She had used up all the cash she'd received from pawning her wedding and engagement rings. Out of money, out of a job, and without a place to stay, Leah had gone to a Factoria-area shopping center hoping to land a job as a clerk. Not only had she not been given the job, the Pontiac's ailing transmission had given up the ghost right there in the parking lot. With nowhere to go and no way to get there, she and the kids had bedded down in the car, expecting to spend the night. Sometime late that night, a Bellevue cop had awakened them and given them a voucher for a one-night stay in a hotel room. The officer had also given Leah a list of agencies that might help. From the motel they had gone to a temporary shelter and from there to emergency housing.

Even now, Leah burned with shame to think that she had fallen so far and so hard. She had always thought of herself as a resilient person, but it had all been too much. The car had quit at a point when she couldn't handle one more thing. And, humiliating as it might have seemed, she knew now that it was also the best thing that had happened to them since leaving Vegas. It was through help from their caseworker at the YWCA that Leah's car had been repaired and she had been steered into the apartment manager job—one that gave her a place to live and a small salary to supplement her monthly child support checks. She and the kids might not be well off, but at least they were getting along.

Coming from Vegas, Leah still couldn't get used to wintertime Seattle's early nightfall. By four, when the snarled traffic finally started moving again, it was almost dark. Leah came up over the rise on the freeway and saw the Christmas tree lights on top of the Space Needle and on the Queen Anne radio tower behind it. As soon as she saw the lights, she looked away. Seeing the Space Needle tree reminded her of the ugly little Charlie Brown tree the kids had insisted she put up.

Scrawny and crooked, the tree didn't have much to recommend it. There were no lights on it because Leah couldn't afford to buy any. The decorations were all handmade. She and the children had baked flour-and-salt cookie-cutter ornaments and painted them with some tempera paints Leah had found for a dollar at the Goodwill store over on Dearborn. Danielle had scavenged several boxes of Styrofoam popcorn from down in the trash room. She and Richy had patiently strung the clam-shaped pieces on dental floss, making garlands that, from a distance, might have been mistaken for real popcorn. There were hand-cut paper snow-flakes and Crayola-colored paper balls, along with a floppy tinfoil star pinned to the tree's topmost branches.

The tree may not have been a thing of beauty, but it was precious nonetheless. Leah realized that it was only while they had worked on it that she had found herself touched by the Christmas spirit. Now, though, with the kids gone, Leah dreaded walking into the apartment and seeing the de-jected little tree. It would look bare because the few inexpensive gifts she had managed to squeeze out of the grocery money had disappeared from underneath it. Those were what she had packed up and sent along in the shoulder bags.

No, the calendar may have said December 23, but as far as Leah Mason was concerned, Christ-mas was over. "The minute I get home, I'm taking down that damned tree," she told herself aloud. That way she wouldn't have to look at it.

Except, by the time she opened the door to her apartment, taking down the tree was not an op-tion. It was lit up with so many lights that the spindly branches could barely support them all. The tinfoil star had been moved down a limb or two. In the star's place stood a magnificent angel, dressed in an elegant velvet gown and armed with a lighted wand. When the door opened, Dora Ha-gendorn guiltily limped away from the tree.

"There you are," she said. "I hope you don't mind. With Henry gone, I don't put up a tree any-more. These decorations were down in my storage unit just gathering dust. As a matter of fact, I was about to go back downstairs and bring up some boxes of balls."

Leah didn't know whether to laugh or cry. She couldn't tell Dora that the last thing she wanted in her house right then was a decorated Christmas tree. "Thank you," she said graciously. "That's very thoughtful of you."

When she stepped closer to examine Dora's handiwork, she noticed with some surprise, that there were a few gifts under the tree as well—one each for the children and two for her.

"Where did those come from?" Leah asked.

Dora shrugged. "Santa, I guess," she said. "I'm just sorry I wasn't able to have them wrapped properly before the children left. Speaking of which, Danielle called a few minutes ago—from the airport."

Leah's heart lurched. "The airport?" she echoed. "You mean the plane came back?"

"Oh, no. From the airport in Las Vegas. She wanted you to know that they were there safe and sound and their father had come to get them."

Relieved, Leah glanced at her watch. Impossible as it seemed, in the time it had taken her to get back home from the airport, the kids had already arrived in Vegas. "Good," she said. "Thanks for letting me know."

As soon as Dora went upstairs, Leah called Andy at Puget Sound Property Management. "Is there something wrong?" she asked.

"Wrong?" Andy returned, sounding puzzled. "Not that I can think of. Why?"

"Because you called three times while I was

stuck in that traffic tie-up on I-5. Maybe it's time to do something about that cell phone?"

"Maybe so," he agreed. "But no, all I wanted to do today was find out when I could come by and drop off your Christmas bonus. Are you going to be home for a while?"

"Sure," she said. "I'll be here from now on."

"Good," he said. "Depending on traffic, I should be there within the next half hour."

Before Leah had time to hang up, Dora Hagendorn was back, tapping on the door. When Leah opened it, the white-haired woman stood smiling in the hallway, her bony arms laden with half a dozen boxes of Christmas tree balls. "I haven't had so much fun in years," she said. "I'm just sorry I didn't think of doing this before the children left."

Leah nodded. "If you don't mind, I'll try giving them a call."

"Sure," Dora said. "Go right ahead."

In Las Vegas, Leah's former mother-in-law answered her phone on the third ring. "Hello, Maggie. Could I speak to either Danielle or Richy?"

"They're not here right now," Maggie replied. "They left a few minutes ago. Richard took them to the mall to do some last-minute shopping."

Leah's heart fell. She knew from personal experience what that might mean. Richard's Christmas shopping trips usually began and ended with a trip to a bar and or a casino along the way. Gambling, drinking, and drugging were necessary ingredients for his version of holiday spirit. In the old days, Leah had always tried to be there to drive him home afterward.

Why did you let the children go with him? Leah wanted to scream at her former mother-in-law. Richard was living with Maggie, for God's sake. Surely by now she knew what he was like. With Dora Hagendorn right there in the room busily hanging elegantly glittering balls on the almost overloaded tree, Leah forced herself to say none of those things aloud.

"Oh, well, then," she said as nonchalantly as possible. "Have them call me as soon as they get home. I'll be home all night."

While Dora finished fussing with the tree, Leah brewed a pot of tea. They were drinking hot tea and admiring the tree when Andy White buzzed from downstairs. He arrived with an armload of poinsettias and a handful of envelopes. He set the flowers on the floor near the door and gave Leah one of the envelopes. Inside was a gift certificate good for a completely prepared Christmas dinner for four reserved in her name and ready to be picked up from a store on Lower Queen Anne sometime before closing time on Christmas Eve. The description on the certificate made it sound like a real feast—turkey, potatoes, gravy, dressing, cranberry sauce, pumpkin pie. Leah's only regret was that Danielle and Richy wouldn't be here to share the bounty. Turkey and dressing was a big step up from macaroni and cheese.

"Thank you," she told Andy huskily, blinking back tears.

He looked around. "Where are the kids?" he asked. "Aren't they here? I have something for each of them, too."

"That's very kind of you," Leah said. "But you

missed them. They're in Vegas spending Christmas with their father and grandmother."

Andy shrugged and placed the two envelopes under the tree. "No problem," he said. "Fortunately, gift certificates to the movies aren't perishable. They'll keep until the kids come home. I have to get going. Merry Christmas." At the door he paused and looked back into the room. "Nice tree, by the way," he added. Then he was gone.

Glancing up from the gift certificate, Leah realized that here was a chance to repay Dora Hagendorn for her many small kindnesses. "Dora, how would you like to come down for Christmas dinner? It says here that it's dinner for four. It would be a shame to have that much food go to waste."

Dora's wrinkled face glowed with pleasure. "Really? When?" she asked.

"Christmas Day, I suppose," Leah replied. "Around four or so."

The older woman smiled. "Thank you. Christmas Day can be pretty lonely sometimes. I'd love to. What can I bring?"

Until Dora said that, it hadn't occurred to Leah that someone else might be dreading the holiday almost as much as she was. This way they could muddle through it together.

"You can't bring anything at all," she told Dora. "Everything's included. Besides, you've already provided most of the decorations on the tree."

"It was nothing," Dora replied modestly. "This was a perfectly good little tree. I just added a few little trinkets here and there."

After Dora went back upstairs to her own apartment, Leah busied herself around the apartment to take her mind off the fact that she was waiting for the phone to ring. She cleaned up the dishes in the kitchen, washed, dried, and folded two loads of clothes, and tried reading the evening newspaper. By nine o'clock she was more than a little uneasy. Between nine and ten the minute hand on the clock barely seemed to move. By ten she was angry. Vegas was Vegas and the malls stayed open until all hours, but still, the kids had had a big day. By now they ought to be safely back home, in bed, and sound asleep. The problem was, Richard had never been a great believer in sticking to a set schedule.

At ten-fifteen Leah gave up and started calling. For the next hour and a half, she dialed Maggie Mason's number every fifteen minutes, letting the phone ring ten or twelve times before she hung up. No one ever answered. Between calls Leah berated herself for letting the children go by themselves. What if Richard had gotten drunk and driven the car into a telephone pole? What if the kids were hurt—or worse? What if . . . ?

By midnight she was frantic. Finally, fearing the worst, she located a telephone operator who put her through first to the Las Vegas Police Department and then to every Las Vegas–area hospital. No one had any information about a possible accident with a driver named Mason—no Richard and no Maggie either. Leah didn't know who to be more angry with—her ex-husband or her ex-mother-in-law. If something terrible had happened, one or the other of them should have called.

Finally about one-thirty, exhausted by worry,

Leah fell asleep on the couch. She awakened hours later with the overhead light still shining in her eyes, the silent telephone still on the coffee table beside her, and daylight just beginning to creep over the top of Capitol Hill. She grabbed up the phone and punched redial. The phone rang and rang. She was about to put it down when Richard answered, his voice hoarse and blurred, as it always was after a night on the town.

"Where are the kids?" Leah demanded without preamble.

"What do you mean? They're asleep. Where do you think they are?"

"Of course they're asleep, damn it. Why wouldn't they be? They must have been out until the wee hours. Wake Danielle up and put her on the phone. I need to talk to her."

"Go to hell!" Richard replied. There was a small click and then the phone went dead. Leah dialed again immediately, only this time the phone didn't ring. Instead, she heard the steady pulse of a busy signal. He had left the phone off the hook.

"Damn you, Richard," she screamed into the mouthpiece. "Damn you, anyway!"

Shaking with impotent fury, Leah wanted to throw the phone out the nearest window. If Richard had disabled the phone in his room, it might be hours before Maggie and the children discovered the problem. They'd be expecting Leah to call, when all the while she wouldn't be able to get through.

One way or another, Richard Mason had always found a way to screw up the holidays for everyone. This was more of the same. The powerlessness, the fury, the emptiness were all achingly familiar. In the old days, Leah would have been overwhelmed. She would simply have sunk helplessly into the misery and let herself drown in it. This time, though, recognizing that she was in danger of losing it, she took action. Grabbing the telephone again, she dialed a familiar number. Within minutes, she was dressed and headed to a morning Al-Anon group that met at nine o'clock in the senior center on top of Queen Anne Hill.

The meeting lasted for an hour. In talking to a roomful of other people who had lived as Leah Mason had lived, she found a measure of comfort. Some of the attendees were divorced or widowed from their particular alcoholic. Some had now sober spouses, while others had spouses who were still enmeshed in drinking. Either way, these people who had themselves lived through hundreds of mangled holidays somehow found the courage and generosity to turn to Leah Mason on that Christmas Eve morning and to give her the solace others had kindly given them at some earlier time. They reassured Leah that they had once been where she was now, and they gave her the blessing of hope that somehow, someday, things would get better for her as well. As usual, and for no reason Leah could ever quite explain, their commonsense counsel made her feel better—gave her the strength to get up and go on.

At ten o'clock, when she stepped outside the building, she was startled to realize that the clouds had rolled away. The sky was clear and bright. Days of drizzling rain had suddenly ended, leaving behind a city dressed in clean, cold air.

"Merry Christmas," people from inside murmured as they made their way past her. "Merry Christmas" and "Keep coming back."

Driving back down the hill and away from that community of goodwill, Leah once again felt herself threatened by shadows of old familiar dread. Rather than giving in and letting it take over, she swung into the crowded parking lot of the grocery store, the one listed on Andy White's coupon.

Inside, the place was a madhouse. She, along with several other customers, had to wait for two or three minutes before a carry-out boy returned from outside with a set of empty grocery carts. At the deli she collected her dinner. The food came packed in a large box that filled most of the shopping cart. After that, she strolled through the store, picking out fresh vegetables for a salad and a half pint of whipping cream to dress up the pumpkin pie. Other than those few items, she really didn't need anything, but she was reluctant to leave the place. It was crowded, but the people jamming the aisles were in a surprisingly festive and unhurried mood. Being with them made her feel better, helped hold off for that much longer the next time she would dial Maggie's phone in Las Vegas only to hear that infernal busy signal.

Once she reached the checkout stand, she fumbled the gift certificate out of her purse. The clerk smiled when she took it. "Christmas present?" she asked.

Leah nodded.

"Nice. I wish someone had given me one of those," the clerk continued. "In our family, I have to do all the Christmas cooking."

Just then the pager in Leah's purse went off. Glancing down at the number, she was relieved to see her mother-in-law's number in Las Vegas flash across the display. She heaved a sigh of relief.

"Good news?" the clerk asked. Leah nodded. "That'll be $7.58," the clerk added with a chuckle. "When it comes to the smallest order for the day, I think you win the prize."

Smiling stupidly, Leah dug the correct change out of her purse and handed it over to the clerk. "Merry Christmas," she said.

"Merry Christmas to you."

Elated, Leah raced home. In the underground garage, the elevator seemed to take forever. Once in the apartment she set the dinner box on the kitchen table and raced for the phone. Richard answered.

"Danielle, please," Leah said.

"What do you mean 'Danielle, please'?" Richard replied. "Where is she?"

"Where is she?" Leah repeated. "Isn't she there with you?"

"No, she isn't here with me." Even over the phone, Leah could hear how angry he was. "What have you done with her? Where is she? And where is Richy, too? I just got up and went looking for them. Nobody's here. Their beds haven't been slept in. Their luggage is gone and so are their Christmas presents."

Leah was dumbstruck. "They're not there?"

"I already said that, didn't I?" Richard repeated. "Are you stupid or what?"

In the old days, that kind of remark from Richard would have wounded Leah and sent her into a tailspin. He had said it often enough that for years she had believed she really was stupid. Fortunately, in the months since her divorce she had developed a certain amount of self-respect.

"Where's your mother?" she asked.

"She's not here either. How the hell am I supposed to know where she is? It's the kids I'm interested in. If you've done something with them, I swear, I'm calling the cops. Do you hear me?"

Leah's call-waiting signal buzzed. "I've got another call, Richard. I have to hang up now."

"Oh, no, you don't. I'm warning you. If you've got the kids somewhere, if you've sent someone down here to get them, I swear I'll . . ."

"You'll what, Richard?" she asked, fighting back. In the old days she would have caved right then, but she was on her own now—surviving and taking care of herself and the children. She wasn't the same person anymore.

"What'll you do to me, Richard? Take me to court? Try it. This time I'll tell it all exactly like it was. I won't hold anything back. Not the drinking. Not the drugs. And not the beatings, either."

There was a pause. "You wouldn't do that," Richard said, sounding aghast.

"Wouldn't I? Try me," Leah said. "I'm hanging up now, Richard. I have another call."

By then, though, whoever had been calling on the other line had hung up without leaving a message.

It took time to move things around in the refrigerator enough to be able to put away all the packages of microwavable and reheatable goodies from the cardboard box. Once those and the salad makings were refrigerated, Leah started a pot of coffee and sat down to think. There had been times during her marriage when Richard had turned violent—times when Leah had considered putting the kids in the car and escaping to a motel. Maybe that's what had happened to Maggie. Maybe she had taken the kids and run away from home overnight. She could well afford it. If that was the case, there was nothing Leah could do but wait for some word.

Throughout the remainder of the morning and afternoon, Leah resisted the temptation to call Richard back to see if he had heard anything. It was almost four when there was a small tap on the door. Ever since coming back from the store, Leah had buzzed in a series of delivery people bringing last-minute Christmas packages to residents. Since there had been no buzz, Leah assumed her caller had to be someone from the building—most likely Dora Hagendorn dropping by in hopes of a cup of tea and a few minutes of friendly chat.

"Surprise!" Laden with shopping bags and surrounded by mounds of luggage, Danielle and Richy stood in the doorway, both of them grinning up impishly at their mother. Behind them, her arms filled with gaily wrapped packages, stood Maggie Mason. "May we come in?" she asked.

Stunned, Leah could barely believe her eyes. "What in the world . . ." she began.

Just then, Richy dropped his shopping bags and launched himself tearfully at his mother's hip. "Daddy didn't really want us there. He took us to a smoky casino and just left us. We waited and waited for him to come out, but he never did."

After hugging Richy so hard she cut off his ability to speak, Leah reached for Danielle. "So I called Grandma," Danielle said, taking up the story where Richy had left off. "She caught a cab and came to get us. And she told us that, if we could catch a plane, she'd bring us back home for Christmas."

Leah turned to Maggie, who was still out in the hall. The older woman's eyes brimmed with tears. "We had to fly standby," she said. "They said if I came straight to the airport right then, they might possibly be able to get us on the early-morning flight. I didn't know until the last minute that we'd all get on. That's why I didn't call. I didn't want to disappoint you. Then, when we got to town and you didn't answer the phone when we called, I decided to do some last-minute shopping before we came here. I hope you don't mind me showing up unannounced like this. If you want me to, I can get a hotel . . ."

"Come in, come in," Leah said, laughing and crying both as she grabbed Maggie by the arm and pulled her into the small apartment. "Don't be silly. Of course you won't stay in a hotel."

"Where'd all the lights come from?" Richy asked, staring at the tree.

"And the beautiful angel!" Danielle added wonderingly. "Where'd you get her?"

Out in the hallway, Leah was shoving the collection of suitcases into the apartment. "Kids," she said. "Help me with these. Take your suitcases back to your room and take Grandma's into mine."

"But . . ." Maggie objected.

"No buts," Leah told her firmly. "You can sleep in my room. I'll sleep on the couch."

Leah waited until the children were out of earshot. "What happened?" she asked.

Maggie Mason shrugged. "I've learned more about my son in the last few months of living with him than I knew in all the previous thirty-four years. A lot of it I could have done without knowing. He promised me before the children ever arrived that there wouldn't be any drinking. I told him if there was, it would be the last time he'd see them. Casinos are no place for children, you know. He must have left them in the lobby of that place for hours before Danielle called me to come get them."

Amazed, Leah dropped onto the couch. She waited while the children returned to collect Maggie's suitcases and drag them away.

"I had been thinking about this for months," Maggie continued, once they were out of earshot. "Talking to Danielle on the plane, I've made up my mind. I'm going to sell out in Vegas. I never liked it all that much anyway. I believe I'll see about moving into a retirement home up here. That way I'll be able to see you and the children whenever I like. Besides, it's probably the only way I'll be able to get Richard out of the house—to sell it out from under him. Let him try being homeless for a while and see how he likes it. Maybe he'll finally come to his senses."

Leah felt herself blushing. "You know about that, too—about the shelter?"

Maggie nodded. "Danielle told me. You could have called me for help, you know, Leah. I would have been happy to give it, but no doubt you needed to learn to manage on your own. I've been going to a few meetings myself," she added. "I'm not nearly as blind about some things as I used to be."

Richy bounded back into the room. "Is it time to open the presents yet?"

Maggie shook her head. "Not yet. I believe your mother likes to open them on Christmas morning. Isn't that right, Leah?"

"Yes."

"So we'll just have to arrange them around the tree as best we can. You and Danielle can do that. Then we should see about getting ready for dinner. I'll bet you haven't gone out to dinner for a very long time, have you?"

Leah shook her head. "We go to McDonald's sometimes," Richy told her.

Maggie smiled. "For tonight I have something in mind that's a little nicer than that. As soon as you finish arranging those gifts, you and Danielle should change into one of the new outfits we bought downtown. Hurry now. I'm starving."

With her children safely back home and bustling happily around a gaily lit Christmas tree, it seemed as though Leah Mason had stepped into a scene from some impossibly lovely dream. But then reality cut in. The phone rang.

"So where are they?" Richard demanded. His voice was heavy, his tongue thick. Leah knew at once he was drinking again—drinking and already drunk.

"The children are here," Leah said. "And so's your mother, Richard. You don't have to worry."

"My mother's there, too?" Richard roared. "By God, you're both in it together. I'm calling the cops. I'll have the two of you arrested for custodial interference. And you can believe this is the last time I'm paying one thin dime of child support..."

Reaching down, Leah depressed the receiver to disconnect the call. She knew her phone package came with an option called call-blocking. She had never used it before, but if it became necessary, she would find out how to enable it. She waited for more than a minute. To her surprise, the phone didn't ring again.

Danielle popped her head out of the bedroom. "Was that Daddy?" Leah nodded. "What did he want?"

"He wanted to know if you were safe, that's all."

"No, he didn't," Danielle replied bitterly. "If he cared about us, he wouldn't have left us alone." She disappeared from view, slamming the door behind her.

Leah turned back to Maggie. "He threatened to put us in jail for custodial interference," she said. "And he's going to stop paying child support."

The money Richard paid wasn't much, but without it Leah knew she wouldn't be able to make ends meet. She wouldn't be able to survive on her modest salary from the property management company alone.

Much to her surprise Maggie greeted that awful news by breaking into gales of laughter. "Richard said that, did he? Since when has he been paying child support?"

"Hasn't he?" Leah asked. "The checks come into the bank right on time each and every month."

"They do that because I send them," Maggie Mason said. "And I'll continue to do so regardless of what Richard says."

Leah was dumbfounded. "You mean you've been paying the child support all this time?"

"Richard hasn't worked in months," Maggie replied. "You didn't think I'd let the three of you starve, did you? You go change now too. On the way home, I had the taxi drive us by a nice restaurant just up the street. I made reservations. They're booked solid for this evening, so the only time they could squeeze us in was right at five o'clock. Afterward, maybe we can go to a Christmas Eve service somewhere. Do you know where we can find one?"

"I don't know of one right now," Leah told her. "But after all, this is downtown Seattle. I'm sure there are several. We should be able to find one that will work."

She started for the bedroom to change. After a step or two, she stopped, went back to Maggie, and hugged her close. "Thank you," Leah whispered. "Thank you so much for everything."

"You're welcome," Maggie Mason murmured, hugging her back. "And Merry Christmas."

Through tear-dimmed eyes Leah saw Dora Hagendorn's Christmas lights blur into shimmering globes of light. In that teary haze Leah Mason realized that the crooked little tree perched on top of an aging television set was by far the most beautiful one she had ever seen.

And this Christmas—the one she had given up on—was her very best Christmas ever. "Thanks for coming, Maggie," she whispered. "And Merry Christmas."

The Luck of the Draw

Faye Kellerman, Rachel Kellerman, and Ilana Kellerman

Photo by Jonathan Kellerman

INTRODUCTION

Writing in collaboration is always a daunting project. Scribing a short story with two partners—who also happen to be my daughters—seemed to me to be a recipe for disaster. We are three females with seven opinions. Yet, I knew they'd be wonderful because our family dinner table conversations are always filled with hilarious narratives and poignant anecdotes. The format of our story worked well for us because each was allowed her own voice. It was my eleven-year-old daughter, Ilana, who came up with the idea of winning the lottery. A mall was the chosen setting because shopping is one of our most frequent shared activities.

My daughters were wonderful work companions. They were cooperative, timely, gracious, and just plain funny. Their characters were strictly their own, their story reflected their own distinct personalities and style.

To tell you the truth, penning this short story was remarkably easy—much easier than our actual shopping excursions. Thank you, girls. You are my treasures.

Amanda's Turn

I thought Jack was kidding when he told me the news. But when he pulled the kids out of school,

I knew he was serious. He sat them both down to tell them the same thing he had told me. That he had won the lottery.

"Not the big, big money," he explained. "Five out of six on the Scratchers."

I was stunned. Jack hadn't gone into the specifics. Our younger daughter, Beth, clapped her hands and paraded around the room. Our elder daughter, Toni, asked the obvious question.

"How much?"

Jack answered, "The amount isn't important."

We looked at him, dumbfounded.

"Well, put it this way. Not enough for me to quit the firm." He added this with a wink. "But guess who's going to get her own car on her sixteenth birthday?"

Toni leaped up and hugged him with all her strength. I was happy for her but angry with Jack. Money did not give him the right to make unilateral decisions.

"What about me?" Beth asked.

Jack broke from Toni's grip. Again, out came the wink. "Well, we might splurge on something special for you."

"Like?"

I said, "No need to go into details right now." I realized my voice was harsh and softened my tone. "I need to talk to your father, girls. Right now and alone."

After they had left, he was peeved. "Look, I realize I should have discussed it with you first. But did you have to cut me off in my moment of glory?"

I said, "How much?"

He was clearly irritated. "Two mil."

I gasped. Then I did the mental math. Two million amortized over twenty years came out to about one hundred thousand a year. After deducting for taxes, we now had an additional seventy thousand dollars of disposable income.

Yes, we could easily afford a car for Toni. And a new stereo for Beth. And that small speedboat that Jack had been eyeing. And what about redoing the kitchen?

I broke out into laughter. I gave my husband a bear hug.

On weekends the mall was always crowded. But ritual was ritual, and every Saturday, my mother, my daughters, and I trekked through the ganglia of stores and tried to bond. Sometimes these excursions were pleasant. Sometimes they were exhausting. Since winning the lottery, those days had become tedious.

Beth was nagging me. "Why can't I have the dress? We can afford it."

I counted to ten so I wouldn't lose my temper.

That seemingly innocuous phrase.

We can afford it.

And then I launched into my standard explanation. "Just because we can afford something doesn't mean I'm obligated to *buy* it."

Beth was now sulking. My mother tried to comfort her, which made me angrier. I tried to contain my ire and be rational. "I bought you clothes a few weeks ago, Beth."

"But they didn't have the white dress in my size, Mom. You said you'd buy it for me."

"I said you could wait and I'd buy it when it arrived in your size. *Or*, I said, you could have the plaid dress. You chose the plaid dress. End of story!"

Beth muttered to herself.

I tried to be motherly. "Honey, yesterday I saw a gorgeous suit. It was beautiful and it fit me perfectly. But I didn't buy it. You know why?"

"Here comes the lecture," Beth said. "Because it's not healthy to have everything you want."

Of course that shut me up.

"Where's Toni?" my mother asked.

"She went into her store. She's looking at some pants."

"You bought Toni pants last week," Beth said. "Why does she get pants this week and last week?"

"I bought her a pair of jeans. Today she's looking at dress pants. Beth, it doesn't matter what Toni has or what Toni does. We're not dealing with Toni now, we're dealing with you. And you made your choice and that's it!"

"You're not being—"

"I don't want to hear this!"

With that, Beth stomped away.

"Where are you going?" I shouted at her.

"I'll be at Body Beautiful . . . *looking* at stuff I can't buy!"

At least she hadn't added "because my mom isn't fair."

My mother tried to be helpful. "They'll get over it. Things'll be back to normal. Once they've . . . adjusted."

I turned to my mother, smiling sadly. "Know

what, Ma? Every day I thank God that we didn't hit the big one."

She laughed, then frowned. Instantly, I spotted the reason behind her wariness. Toni had returned, carrying three separate parcels. She gave me a cat-in-the-canary-cage smile.

Wryly, I said, "That must be one large pair of pants."

She showed me what she had bought. I told her she'd have to return everything but the pants. She told me I didn't understand. I said that might be, but she'd still have to take back her purchases.

And then the famous retort.

"We have the *money*, don't we?"

At that point I gave my mother the car keys and elected to walk home.

Toni's Turn

When I was called out of class that Thursday, I thought maybe someone had died. Why else would Mom let me miss school? She was up-tight about those types of things. But nothing could have prepared me for the news to come.

"We won *what*?" shrieked Beth, my younger sister.

"Whoa," I muttered under my breath.

The *lottery*.

Of course, my parents wouldn't tell us the specifics, like how much we had actually won. But I was promised a car, so I wasn't about to stage a protest.

So we had finally come into some money. Not

like we were hurting financially, but I knew the money would help us out. Mom was always nervous when it came to money, and I thought the extra cash might put her more at ease. And if she was more relaxed, she'd be more inclined to buy her lovely elder daughter more wonderful tokens of affection.

Yes, this new lifestyle was fine by me.

Later that day I overheard Mom talking to Grandma about the whole thing on the phone.

"Yes, Ma, the lottery. One of those Scratcher tickets. . . . No, not all six numbers. . . . I know—amazing, isn't it? Jack has always had good luck, but still the odds of winning are so low. But you know what's strange? I have mixed feelings about this. On one hand, I'm thrilled. Who wouldn't be thrilled about winning two million dollars . . ."

So *that's* how much we had won!

Mom continued, "But I'm kind of worried this will go to everyone's head. Jack has already promised Toni a car and Beth thinks we're millionaires now. . . . I know, I know. I just don't want to spoil them."

She didn't want to spoil us? Didn't want the money to go to our heads? Who cares if it does when it means we can live more comfortably?

But I knew how to plan my course of action. Not to complain, not to ask for a lot. I'd have to work my way up slowly and be excessively grateful. I would show Mom that I was not taking the money for granted. And then she'd realize that the money wasn't spoiling us. And she could buy us what we wanted with a clear conscience.

* * *

I started my plan Saturday at the mall. At first everything went as planned. With much restraint, I picked out only one pair of pants. One. And they weren't even expensive. Mom seemed pleased.

Good.

A couple of weeks after we had won the money, I was still sticking to my plan.

Beth was a different story. She went psycho when Mom told her no, she couldn't have another pair of shoes and two dresses.

"But, Mom," she complained, "it's not fair. I've wanted these dresses for such a long time. Lisa's mother bought her four outfits last week, and her father didn't even win the lottery."

Grandma tried to cover a smile. I knew my actions would look even better next to Beth's greedy fits.

I separated from everyone to go into one of my favorite stores.

Big mistake number one. Mom had given me her credit card to buy some dress pants.

Big mistake number two. As I looked around, I knew I was losing my self-control.

"Restraint," I muttered to myself. But everything was so cute—and not *that* expensive. Besides, we could afford it.

After a while, eight articles of clothing now officially belonged to me.

I smiled.

Mom did not when she saw what I had bought.

"Toni, I really expected more from you. You're fifteen. How could you do this?"

She wouldn't even look at me.

I said, "But you just don't understand—"

"I do understand," Mom interrupted. "But maybe you don't understand the concept of self-discipline. You girls are unappreciative. I would have never acted like this. You're going to have to go back and return the items."

Return them? I just couldn't understand why Mom was being so uptight. I know she didn't want us to get into the habit of buying everything we wanted, but I thought she could be a little more understanding. I had to say it.

"Mom, I really don't see why you should care so much. We have the money, don't we?"

Mom looked exasperated. When she stomped off, I didn't know what to think.

Beth's Turn

I guess when I found out we had won the lottery, it made my day. I'm in sixth grade, and that day I had just taken a social studies quiz and a big English grammar test.

I'm the worst at grammar.

Mr. Furling had called me out of class and I saw Dad. He took me home and told me the big news. We had won the lottery. I didn't care how much. I paraded around the room. When my dad told Toni, standing for Tonia, that she could buy a car, I thought about my own list of things that I wanted: a pair of Steve Madden shoes, a couple of new dresses, and a CD player with a Spice Girls CD to go along with it.

Even though we had won the lottery, I was still frustrated about the tests I had taken. So when we went shopping and the store didn't have the beautiful long, slinky white dress in my size, I almost cried. Mom gave me the choice of waiting for the dress in my size or getting a blue-and-white-plaid dress that was half-price. I'm not very good at waiting, so I grumpily told my mom that I would take the plaid dress. My sister, Toni, bought a pair of jeans.

A few weeks later, we took another trip to the mall and I saw the white dress in size ten—my size! It was just my fit and I could get great use out of it. So I ran over to ask Mom if we could buy it. She said no. At first, I kept saying please, please, please.

Then I got so upset that I yelled, "It's not like we can't afford it."

Mom started giving me this whole lecture about how she didn't buy a suit because she used common sense. Being argumentative, I told her there was no such thing as common sense because everyone had different genes in their bodies. I also reminded her that she said she would buy the dress when it came to the store in my size. Mom seemed very agitated, explaining that I had made a choice.

Grandma tried to comfort me, but that didn't help. Then I started to compare Toni to me. I said that Toni got to buy two pairs of pants, why couldn't I have two dresses? Mom told me Toni was not my concern.

Tears streamed down my eyes, but I didn't want Mom to see them. When she asked what was wrong, I told her I was sweating from frustration. I remembered I had five dollars in my pocket and I started to walk away. When Mom asked me where I was going, I screamed that I was going to Body Beautiful to *look* because I didn't want to steal any of her *precious* money.

While I was walking away, I saw Toni coming out of her store carrying three bags.

"You're crazy," I said. "Mom won't allow it."

Toni just glared at me like all snobby older sisters do and walked away. When I got to Body Beautiful, I bought mango-flavored bubble bath. I had earned my five dollars washing the neighbor's car.

Then the strangest thing happened. I looked out the mall window and saw Mom stomping down the sidewalk. I felt bad for what I had done and decided to give her the bubble bath.

The Solution

I said, "I called this family meeting because something has to be done!"

My daughters stared at their laps with sullen expressions.

I continued, "Winning the lottery doesn't give you two license to start making demands!"

"So you can continue to be arbitrary," snapped Toni.

"That's uncalled for," Jack leaped to my defense. "Apologize."

"She is being arbitrary," Toni insisted. "You both are. One minute you're both expansive, saying we can afford this and that and taking us out to fancy restaurants. The next minute, I find a blouse—*on sale, nonetheless*—and you won't buy it for me. Oh, you have enough to afford a hundred-dollar bottle of wine, but I can't buy a fifteen-dollar blouse."

Jack said, "What *we* do with *our* money is our concern, not yours."

"Obviously," Beth retorted.

"You know what I think?" I said. "I think we were doing just great before this lottery business came up. I think we should . . . give it all to charity!"

Jack smiled, "I'll tell you girls right here and now, if things don't work out soon, we're going to give Mom's idea some real thought."

I looked at my husband. "Jack, I'm serious. Let's give it away—"

"Amanda—"

"Okay. We'll keep enough for the girls' education. Give them some motivation for doing well in school. But beyond that, I think I've hit upon a perfect solution. We weren't hurting before. Why shouldn't we share our good fortune?"

My family was stunned. No one spoke.

Finally, Beth said, "Dad, *say* something."

Jack faltered. "Honey, I admire your nobility. But there's no reason to be hasty. Besides, we've made plans for that money."

"I know we've made plans," I ventured on. "And Toni has made plans. And Beth has made plans as well. So whose plans do we listen to? And you know as well as I do that someone is always going to feel shortchanged. All the money has done is build resentment!"

Again the room fell silent. I could see desperation on my daughters' faces.

Toni said, "Look, I know I've been selfish." Tears were in her eyes. "I'll do better, Mom. I really can do better."

Beth started crying as well. "So can I. I'm sorry I've been so selfish."

Jack winked and said, "I think you got the point across."

But they didn't understand. I wasn't trying to get a point across. "Then you spend the money, Jack. Put it in your wine collection, give it to the girls, I don't care. I don't want any part of it—"

"Amanda, you're being . . ." He looked at the girls, keeping his accusations in check. "As I stated before, I think your idealism is commendable. Giving money to charity is a fine idea. But that's *your* idea. There are other people in this house. As you always said, we don't make unilateral decisions."

Beth said, "How about this?"

All eyes went to her.

"We give away some money . . . even most of the money. But let's keep a *little* for fun." She paused, then her eyes lit up. "I know who we can give the money to. The homeless guy we always see in the park. He could use some money, I bet."

Jack stifled a laugh. "Yes, maybe we could give him a handout." He turned to me. "If you're serious about this giveaway program, what about the National Endowment for the Arts? With all the budget cuts, I'm sure we could fund something."

"Art doesn't feed people, Dad," Toni said. "How about LIFE—Love Is Feeding Everyone? They feed poor people, Dad, including children. Best of all, it doesn't cost them anything. They use expired but good food from supermarkets. All they need is people to collect it and distribute it. We could give them something."

"You want to really feed people, just go downtown to Mission Street," Jack said. "I'm sure we could supply some meals there."

I put in my own two cents. "I like Children's Hospital. So many sick kids. And even the healthy ones. They're very poor. Their parents have to wait hours just to get seen."

Toni said, "I hope we have enough money for all these good causes—and a *little* left over for fun."

No one spoke.

Beth said, "Not that I mean to be selfish. But . . . does this mean I'm not going to get any new stuff? And what about Toni's car?"

Toni sighed, "You know, I really don't go many places without friends. I suppose I could . . ." Another sigh. "*Save* up for a car . . . like we originally planned."

I said, "A car was promised to you. But it doesn't have to be a new one."

Toni nodded. "I agree. Anything that gets me to school and back is okay. Who needs a Jeep, anyway?"

She was disappointed but trying to hide it.

I said, "In answer to your question, Beth. Yes, you will still get new stuff. You always did get new stuff. But we don't have to spend as if we own the store."

"About that fun money, Amanda?" Jack said. "There was this bottle of Cabernet . . ."

"Oh, let him buy the wine, Mom," Toni broke in.

"I'm not his mother. He can do what he wants."

Toni said, "He wants your approval. Stop being so withholding and enjoy life!"

She was right. I said, "I love Cabernet."

"A bottle a year," Jack announced. "I propose we put twenty percent of the newfound money into our savings, twenty percent in a fund for the kids' education, ten percent for fun stuff, and the rest goes for those who truly need it. A great idea, Amanda."

Toni said, "But Beth came up with the idea of keeping a *little* for fun. And a great idea it was."

Beth beamed golden rays at her older sister's approval. I smiled too.

There were still things that money couldn't buy.

The Pinkie Club

Eileen Goudge and Mary Bailey

Photo courtesy of Goudge Family

INTRODUCTION

When I first sat down to write a story on the theme of a legacy between a mother and a daughter, my thoughts ran toward the obvious: a diary, a family heirloom, a favorite recipe that had been handed down from one generation to the next. But somehow the story I envisioned, wrapped around such a keepsake like layers of deliciously crinkly tissue paper, never materialized. Instead, I turned the pages of my own mental diary, back to a time when my daughter, Mary, and I had not been quite so close . . . when the idea of us collaborating on a short story, or even a shopping list, would have been as unlikely as a trip to the moon.

Four years ago, when she was sixteen, I made the difficult decision to send Mary to a therapeutic school in the Berkshires, a two-hour drive from New York City. She was severely depressed and unhappy, and we all hoped this would be the magical "cure" that would turn her around. What I discovered instead was that when a family member has emotional problems, it affects everyone, and that sometimes the "sickness" is merely a perfectly understandable reaction to an unhealthy situation. Over the course of two years, Mary and I went from barely speaking to one another to finding new ways of communicating. And as I learned more *about the roots of her unhappiness, I saw how inter-wined they were with certain unresolved issues of my own.*

She got better. I got divorced.

"The Pinkie Club" is based on a true incident that occurred shortly before Mary graduated into the "real world." I had just separated from my husband (her stepfather) and was feeling particularly vulnerable. For once, I stopped treating Mary like a "fragile, broken reed" and allowed her the opportunity to show her true inner strength. Through this reversal of our roles, I discovered the greatest legacy of all: trust. The trust I had placed in Mary as a child was brought full circle, and I was seeing how, though clouded by the years of adversity, that early gift had not been lost on her. For a brief moment in time she became the guardian of my emotional well-being, and I depended on her as she had once depended on me.

When I showed Mary the first draft of this story and invited her comments, it was her initial reaction that spoke the loudest. Rather than feeling embarrassed, as she once would have, or angry at me for having revealed something so personal, she was pleased. With tears in her eyes, she hugged me and told me how touched she was by what I had written. Then, like any good editor, she sat down and red-penciled the manuscript, advising me on which sentences to cut and which paragraphs needed tightening.

The following is the result not only of our literary collaboration but of our mutual joy in sharing with others one of those rare moments in life when a mother and daughter travel from their two separate and some-times distant points of view to meet happily in the middle.

So this is what it feels like, Emily thought.

Funny. She'd always thought of a nervous breakdown as something that involved a fair bit of screaming and carrying on, a certain amount of wreckage even. But this . . . she felt like a piece of paper being slowly crumpled by a giant fist. A letter, or a statement of an overdue account, that its recipient had scanned quickly before relegating it to the wastebasket. Even if she could summon the strength to pick herself up after this, what would be the point? Her life was more than just a mess; it had been folded, stapled, and mutilated.

She'd meant her marriage vows. Every last word. But over the past ten years things had changed. She couldn't quite put her finger on exactly how, or what. All she knew was that it was over. And now here she was, taking a train to Philly—where she would meet her daughter and the two of them would head off to visit campuses—acting as if everything was perfectly normal, as if choosing the right college for her daughter was the biggest worry in her life at this moment. As if she weren't leaving Daniel and moving into her own apartment as soon as she got back. As if she weren't, at this very moment, in her hard plastic seat in the ticketed-passenger waiting area at Penn Station, having a nervous breakdown of some kind.

"The four-fifty to Thirtieth Street station is leaving from Track 22." A nasal voice blared from the loudspeaker, causing Emily to jump.

She darted quick glances to either side of her, arming herself against the inevitable stares. Who wouldn't gawk? A middle-aged woman with the hollow eyes and hyperanxious look of a patient on a day pass from a psychiatric facility. But even if she'd had the benefit of the Klingon Cloaking Device, she couldn't have been more invisible. The waiting area was packed, but everyone seemed wrapped in his or her own little self-contained cocoon—the old man beside her working his way through an apple with the utmost delicacy, as if the fate of his bridgework depended on it; the harried young mother struggling to calm her restless toddler; the slouchy teenage boy zoned out on his Walkman. *New Yorkers,* she thought. Emily smiled to herself—a thin slice of bemusement that did nothing to ease her misery.

What would Anna think? Seeing her mother this way would be a shock, no doubt. Her capable, clear-eyed, for-every-problem-there's-a-solution mom, who, just minutes ago at the ticket booth, had burst into tears after spilling her change on the floor. She hadn't picked it up; she'd been too humiliated. Anyway, why bother? What was a handful of quarters and dimes compared to turning her back on the home she'd shared with her husband for nearly ten years? And Anna, of course. Until last year, her daughter had lived with them too.

It seemed to Emily that Anna's departure was when it had all started to unravel. Whenever she tried tracing the problem back to its source, it always seemed to land there, freshly throbbing, like a pulse point signaling some hidden pain: the day they'd packed her daughter's belongings in the trunk of their Datsun and driven her up to Silver

Lake—a facility delicately described as a "therapeutic community." Or maybe the seeds of discon-
tent had been there all along, lying dormant in the
dark, and the problem with Anna had merely
caused them to take root and flourish. All Emily
knew was that after her daughter went away,
when it became clear that Anna wouldn't be home
for Christmas, or anytime in the near future, the
house had seemed as achingly empty as the socket
of an infected tooth that's been pulled.

In some ways it had been a relief. God strike her
dead for saying so, but it was true. Had it gone on
a minute longer, the three of them would surely
have killed one another. Then there had been the
weeks of negotiating the minefield of psychia-
trists, school officials, educational consultants, not
to mention the well-intentioned meddling of her
own family. When the final trauma of actually *de-
livering* Anna to that place was behind them, Emily,
her senses blunted, had waited for her home to be
magically restored to what it had been—a sanc-
tuary of companionable chaos and contentment.
It never happened. Instead, she and Daniel had
drifted off into separate corners, where, little by
little, they withered like geraniums deprived of
direct sunlight. While Anna, after a rough patch in
the beginning, thrived at Silver Lake . . . back home
Emily began to slowly break apart.

Now she sat staring at the bundles on the floor
at her feet before starting to pick them up, one by
one. Her canvas carryall, for the two nights they
would spend in and around Philly. A shopping
bag containing bottled water, a plastic sack of or-

anges, and today's *Times*, unread. An old back-pack of her daughter's stuffed to bursting with all the items Anna had asked her to bring—shampoo, toothpaste, Tampax, her moth-eaten old teddy bear for good luck, a pair of high heels she'd left behind on her last visit. If Emily balanced them just so, she could carry them all without dropping anything or tipping over onto the train tracks. Everything in life, she thought, was simply a matter of balance.

The question was this: How would she manage Anna on top of it all? Her fragile child, glued together like a broken vase that would never be as strong as one completely whole. Emily wouldn't even have to tell her. Anna would know the instant she laid eyes on her that something was wrong. She would recognize the face of her mother's despair as one she'd glimpsed too often in her own mirror. And when Emily told her why she was so unhappy, Anna would be devastated. Not that she and Daniel were so close, mind you, but over the past year their family *had* achieved a sort of balance . . . one so precarious that the tiniest feather stroke could bring the whole teetering structure down with a crash.

Emily took the first empty seat on the train, but instead of stowing all her stuff on the overhead rack, she piled her shopping bag and heavy sheepskin coat on the vacant seat beside her, to make it look as if she were saving it. She felt a little guilty, as if she were cheating somehow. She'd been taught as a child to follow the rules, color within the lines, be courteous at all times—habits so deeply ingrained that they were as automatic as breathing.

But the car was only half full; she wouldn't be robbing anyone of more than her company. Really, whoever might have wanted to sit next to her, Emily told herself, she'd be doing them a favor. She was too unstable right now. Anything might set her off. A thoughtless comment, an accidental bumping of elbows. All week she'd been bursting into tears at the drop of a hat. Everywhere she went was like walking up a down escalator. But when she stopped moving, it was worse. Like being in an elevator slowly going down.

Daniel didn't understand, of course. He'd wanted to know why they couldn't see a counselor, why it had to be like this—more like an amputation than a divorce. But they *had* been through all that, she'd impatiently pointed out. Apparently he just hadn't realized it. All those sessions in Dr. Morely's office, the family groups, the Sunday parent meetings— Daniel had believed they were only about Anna. It hadn't occurred to him that a seventeen-year-old trying to kill herself wasn't something isolated, that it might be connected to them in some way, however remote.

Emily saw her daughter more as one of those canaries miners used to lower down into the coal mine in the old days to test for poison gas. Anna, fragile to begin with, had been helpless against the atmosphere she'd been placed in at the age of seven. There had been nothing obvious, of course. They'd all behaved politely to one another, and taken the requisite family trips—skiing in Vail during winter break, spring and summer holidays in Europe. Daniel never made Anna feel less than welcome, and there had been none of the stereo-typical stepchild resentment on her part. Maybe things would have turned out differently had Anna's real father been more than a granite head-stone she visited once a year in a cemetery. Or if Daniel hadn't had kids of his own—two grown sons and a daughter near Anna's age, on whom he lavished affection. To a little girl as fiercely bright and hungry as Anna, the disparity must have been like getting hit over the head, again and again.

As the train rocked its way south, Emily ate an orange she had no appetite for. It was just some-thing to keep her occupied. She pried off the sec-tions one by one, remembering how she used to save the "babies" for Anna when she was little. They'd had other rituals, most of them made up, like the "Pinkie Club"—a silly game Emily had in-vented of linking her little finger with Anna's when crossing a busy street. It meant she trusted her young daughter not to pull away suddenly and dart into traffic. Anna would respond by proudly lifting her chin and holding her crooked pinkie aloft as delicately as an English noblewoman at high tea. Emily had never once had to resort to tugging on a wrist or even taking firm hold of her daughter's hand.

In her mind, Emily could see Anna as she'd looked then, a stick-thin seven-year-old in a flow-ered dress with a smocked bib. Her fair hair had been long and straight, clipped back at the sides with plastic barrettes in the shapes of butter-flies. In the morning, when Emily brushed her daughter's hair, Anna cried, because of the tangles

that invariably developed overnight in a little
bird's nest at the base of her neck. In frustration,
she would sometimes strike out at the hairbrush
with a small, tightly balled fist . . . but never at
Emily. No. Even when Anna was truly mad, she
kept it inside. She'd swallowed her anger like a
fat, chalky tablet that never dissolved, that instead
of making her better had only made her sicker.

How would she react to the news that her mother
and stepfather were getting divorced? That the
home from which she'd been abruptly removed
last year wasn't going to be there when she returned this summer, her last before college? A ca-
nary who'd just learned to fly on her own—how
would she survive the sea change?

Emily had to hold the newspaper open in front
of her face to hide her tears. Even so, she could see
herself reflected in the window, a milky shimmer
against the bulleting blackness, like something
needing to be skimmed off the top of a bubbling
pot. She was shivering, despite the Saharan heat
pumping through the car. Yesterday she'd begun
circling likely apartments in the *Times* Real Estate
section—Daniel's moving out wasn't an option;
the house had belonged to him since long before
they had ever met. She had become so overwhelmed that she'd had to lie down on her bed for
half an hour, until her breathing slowed and she
could face even the simple task of reserving a hotel room for tonight and tomorrow.

At least money wouldn't be a problem, she reminded herself. Her first husband, Anna's father,
had died five years before she married Daniel,
leaving her fairly well off. And she had her own

business, small but growing by leaps and bounds—
gift baskets were quite the thing nowadays, she'd
discovered. It was something she enjoyed too, because the baskets she created for Just Because
weren't only unique, they made people smile. Like
the "happy divorce" special order that had proved
so popular she'd had a number of requests for it
since—it featured a bottle of champagne nestled
inside a boxing glove, chocolate truffles (to be eaten
alone in bed, naturally), an embroidered handkerchief, a copy of *Singles Survival Guide to Manhattan*,
a black lace teddy, and Extra-Strength Tylenol.

How could she have known that one day she
wouldn't find the idea of divorce quite so amus-
ing? Their marriage had survived the ordeal with
Anna. Who could have imagined anything worse?

No, Emily thought, it was the other way around—
Anna had survived *them*. At Silver Lake she'd
learned first to crawl, then walk, then run . . . then
smile. She'd gone from seeing herself as a patient
to a fully realized person deserving of the happiness that had eluded her for most of her seventeen
years. She'd even made new friends and had gotten in touch with a few of her old friends from
Brearley. And next year she would be starting college, the same as every other kid her age.

She'll survive this, too, Emily told herself. *She still
has me. No matter what, I won't let her down.*

Anna's own train from Boston had gotten her to
Philly a full hour ahead of Emily, so Anna was on
hand to meet her when she arrived. Seeing her
daughter rush toward her, canvas duffel hoisted
under one long arm, a shopping bag flopping at

her hip, Emily felt her heart take flight. Anna's fair hair was still long, but gone was the grave, unsmiling little girl who might have been the model for Tenniel's "Alice of Wonderland." In her place was a young woman in torn jeans and an outrageous fifties Hawaiian shirt, flying across the crowded terminal like a glorious silk banner.

"Mom! I thought you'd never get here!" They collided bumpily, and Anna dropped her bags to hug Emily, who couldn't seem to let go of hers. "Was it horrible? Me, too. I was pestered the whole way by a guy old enough to be my father. Are you hungry? Do you want to eat first? Have you seen the food stalls here—they're awesome. One even has broccoli rabe." Somewhere along the line, Anna had decided she was a vegetarian.

"I remember when all they sold in train stations was soft drinks and pretzels." Emily mustered a smile. "Actually, I thought we'd go out for dinner, a nice restaurant. We haven't done that in a while."

She was thinking about the cafeteria at Silver Lake, with its plastic turquoise trays and flimsy utensils that always seemed bent out of shape—like a bad metaphor pertaining to its community in general. The food was serviceable but institutional nonetheless. And Anna still had three more weeks of it after this before she could come home.

Whatever *that* would be.

"Mom, are you okay?" Anna was peering at her with concern. "You look like you've lost weight. Those jeans are practically falling off you. Here, let me help you with some of this stuff." She pried the carryall out of Emily's arms, juggling it easily with her own retrieved luggage while making one of her famous free-associative conversational leaps. "I hope you brought something to wear for tomorrow's interview. A dress?" she added hopefully.

"I didn't know *I* was the one being interviewed." Emily jogged to keep up with her daughter's long-legged stride.

"We both have to look nice," Anna said somewhat primly. "So they can see what kind of family I'm from. Isn't it bad enough I spent my senior year in the booby hatch?"

"How about if I drool and cross my eyes? Then they'll think it's inherited."

Anna shook her head, holding her lips pressed together to keep from smiling. "Just promise me one thing. Tomorrow, when we get to Bryn Mawr? No jokes, please. Don't get me started. I'll pee my pants."

"Your dress, you mean. You *did* bring one?" Emily countered drily.

Joking their way through a crisis—it was the meat and potatoes by which their family had survived through the generations. Emily imagined her great-grandparents, crammed into steerage on the ship that had carried them from Dublin to America, cracking inane jokes about the lousy weather and the lack of amenities. But what did it accomplish really, except to postpone the inevitable? Laughing through your tears was like taking aspirin for a cold, she thought; it relieved the symptoms but did nothing to cure what ailed.

Emily had reserved a rental car, but the thought of navigating her way through a strange city at night was suddenly terrifying. Just short of the Avis desk, she stopped dead in her tracks, pretending to search for the fax confirming her reservation, but really it was because her legs were trembling so badly she could barely walk.

"I know it's here. I'm sure I brought it," she muttered into the jumbled contents of her shoulder bag.

A boneless hand fluttered onto Emily's shoulder, and a tentative voice—the fearful Anna of another era—asked, "Mom? Is it something I did? Are you mad at me?"

Emily blinked hard and steeled herself. For her daughter's sake, she had to be strong. A year ago, if she'd allowed herself to weaken, where would Anna be now? No. This had to be dealt with. Here. Now. While Anna stood watching her with open, anxious eyes. Not in some quiet restaurant the way she'd planned.

Slowly Emily straightened. "No, honey, I'm not mad at you. This has nothing to do with you, believe me. It's Daniel." She pulled in a deep breath. "We've been having some problems lately. We've talked about it . . . and we decided . . . *I* decided . . . it would be better if I moved out."

Anna stared back at her. She was frowning, a look of intense concentration that might have been mistaken for a scowl by someone who didn't know her. With the canvas straps of her own bag and Emily's dragging at her lanky shoulders, she might have been a discouraged traveler looking up the face of a steep mountainside, calculating how long it would take to climb to the top.

"I don't get it," she said at last, her face slack,

her speech faintly slurred by incomprehension, as if she'd just eaten something cold. "I just don't get it."

In the rented car, as she nosed her way out of the underground garage, Emily attempted to explain. It wasn't that she didn't love Daniel or that either of them was involved with someone else. They hadn't been fighting, not really. They still ate dinner together and slept in the same bed. It was just . . .

"Remember the time we were all in Aspen, that awful condo with animal hides and trophy heads everywhere you looked?" Emily recalled. Out of the corner of her eye she saw Anna make a face. "Remember how you had nightmares, and I wanted to pack up and leave, and Daniel said who cared if the decor sucked, it was only for a week? It feels like that now. Dead. Like I'm in a place that's not about living, where *I'm* only half alive."

She drove carefully, peering nearsightedly at street signs. It was cold, even for January, and each time she strained forward, mist bloomed on the windshield in front of her. They were staying at a Marriott forty minutes or so out of town, halfway between Bryn Mawr and Haverford—the second of the three colleges they were visiting—but whoever had given her directions must have been reading them off a mirror. On the turnpike it felt as if they were going the wrong way, in the direction of New Jersey.

Emily began to panic. Headlights slashed by. Tires hissed on pavement still puddled from this morning's thunderstorm. Strange signs leaped out at her. Why hadn't she thought to bring a map?

What could she have been thinking, relying on some idiot hotel desk clerk for directions? It wasn't like she could depend on her daughter either. Poor Anna. She had to be just as disoriented. Who would have thought to teach Anna how to read a map when she hadn't yet learned to drive? A girl as troubled as she had been, for whom it was challenge enough just to navigate her way through adolescence.

Tears leaked from the corners of Emily's eyes. She scrubbed at them angrily with her knuckles. What was she even doing here? Endangering both their lives with her recklessness in this cold and alien place. She imagined herself stretched out on a bed someplace quiet. A bed with crisp white sheets and pillows that smelled faintly of chlorine. A *hospital* bed. *Yes. Isn't that where they take you,* she asked herself, *when you feel as if your blood is sizzling in your veins and your head is about to explode?*

"Mom, pull over."

Anna's sharp command had the effect on Emily of a red bubble light flashing in her rearview mirror. She half turned to find her daughter bent over, fiddling with the latch on the glove compartment, her long hair draped over her knees. Anna didn't look scared . . . only concerned.

"They usually give you some kind of . . . yeah, here it is." She fished out a flimsy Xeroxed map, courtesy of Avis, spreading it open in the pale light washing her kneecaps. Emily stared at her daughter in surprise.

She flicked on her turn signal and guided the rented Corsica onto the next ramp, regardless of where it might lead. She was crying hard now, and all she wanted was to go somewhere dry and safe and light, where she could curl up in a corner with her forehead on her knees.

Luckily the exit led to a rest area, which was little more than a huge parking lot, at the edge of which stood a McDonald's, all lit up with floodlights like the Taj Mahal. Emily switched off the engine, and sat shivering in the stale leftover warmth of the car heater. Her teeth were actually chattering, she realized dimly. Something she'd thought happened only in cartoons.

Then Anna's arms were around her, pulling her into an awkward embrace. "Mom? It's okay," she soothed. "We're not lost. Not really. We'll find our way back. Why don't we get something to eat? You'll feel better."

Over burgers and french fries and milkshakes—food that Emily would normally have turned her nose up at—she began slowly to regain her equilibrium. She even managed a shaky laugh when Anna joked that her salad tasted like wet cardboard. Anna reached across the table and pressed a hand over Emily's.

"What you said before, about Daniel?" she said softly, her blue eyes that had always seemed so achingly vulnerable narrowed slightly in shared recognition. "I know what you mean. I felt it too. Like that time in Aspen. Like nobody but us got what it was all about, that place. Lizzy and Jeff, they thought it was funny even. All those dead, staring eyes."

"What can I say? They're Daniel's kids. They think like him."

"Yeah, but that's not the point." Emily's beautiful daughter leaned forward slightly, faint shadows cast by her extraordinarily long lashes brushing the smooth skin under her eyes. When Anna was born, just minutes old, one of the nurses had remarked on how unusually alert she was—until someone else noticed it was because Anna's eyes were *glued* wide open by her sticky lashes. "We didn't have to stay. You and me . . . we could have gone home. They would have had more fun without us anyway."

Emily thought for a moment, then said, "I wasn't ready, I guess." She cast a stricken look at Anna. "Should I have been? Would it have made a difference?"

Anna shrugged. "In terms of me? Probably not. I was pretty wrapped up in my own thing by then. Anyhow, you shouldn't think that way. Looking back over your shoulder will only get you in trouble."

Her daughter's sensible words were like a cool hand pressed to Emily's fevered brow. At the same time, below the surface of her pain, a pocket of wonder was forming. A deep, almost mystical awareness that some sort of transformation had taken place without her fully realizing it until now. At what point had her fragile, broken child become this capable, clear-eyed young woman holding a map spread open on the Formica table in front of her? It couldn't have happened overnight. Why hadn't Emily seen it?

Maybe you were too busy thinking she had to be rescued, a voice whispered in Emily's head. *Maybe you had to be rescued a little yourself.*

All she knew was that it felt surprisingly good. Like when she'd been a kid herself, assuming that her parents would simply take care of whatever was wrong, or missing, or turned around backwards. How long since she'd felt this way? Emily wondered. When was the last time she'd been content just to sit back and let someone else decide what to do? The amazement of it being her own daughter taking charge, her far-from-worldly seventeen-year-old who'd spent the past year more or less sequestered, had left Emily more than just speechless. She was absolutely spellbound.

"You seem to have it all figured out." Emily managed a weak smile.

"Only how to get us as far as Bryn Mawr."

Anna lifted her head, keeping a finger pressed to the map so as not to lose her place. Emily noticed its nail was bitten to the quick and felt a flicker of something close to relief. She wasn't ready to turn her back on the past without pocketing at least a few souvenirs. She didn't want to ever forget what it had been like to hold Anna to her breast, to absorb like a porous rock all that wet, clinging misery. *For if you lose sight of where you started from*, she thought, *how can you ever be completely sure of where you're going?*

It wasn't all that complicated, as it turned out. Emily drove while Anna directed. Once they got to Route 30, it was a piece of cake. The Marriott was just off to the left, about a mile outside of town. Emily, a sucker for quaint bed-and-breakfasts, had never been so happy to see a neon sign promising nothing more than a hot shower and a night's sleep. Installed in their generic but functional room upstairs, she collapsed onto the double bed nearest the door.

It was Anna who switched on lights, arranged their luggage, and turned on the TV to see what tomorrow's weather would be like. By the time Emily managed to get undressed, her daughter was already tucked in, with what looked like the world's oldest teddy bear propped on the pillow beside her.

Emily was exhausted, too exhausted even to sleep. After several minutes of staring at the drapes, glowing faintly in the darkness from the arc lights in the parking lot below, she whispered, "Anna? You awake?"

"Mmmm," her daughter mumbled thickly.

Emily remembered when Anna was little and used to crawl into bed with her. Daniel had put a stop to it at a certain point, saying she was too old. And anyway, he'd reasoned, Anna couldn't expect to have Emily all to herself anymore. That might have been fine for a while after losing Robert, when Anna was four and had reverted to sucking her thumb and talking baby talk. But big girls needed to learn how to sleep on their own.

Emily had bought her a night-light shaped like a fat piglet, but still Anna had cried when she was told to go back to bed. Emily, listening to the sound of her daughter's small bare feet padding down the hall at night, thought her heart would break.

Now, years later, in the foreign darkness of the anonymous hotel room, it was Emily who asked softly, "Would it be okay if I get in with you? Just for a little while?"

She could feel Anna smiling at the irony of it as she threw back the covers to let Emily in. The warm bed made Emily think of a fox's den, all furry and close. As she sank into it, she understood at last how profoundly comforting it must have been to her small, frightened daughter all those years ago. And how bewildered Anna had to have been by the concept of it being better somehow to be a "big girl," when what could be more perfect than this?

Now Anna was the big girl and Emily the one in need of comforting. If Emily had long ago been shown a snapshot of this, she would have laughed at the idea. But curled up next to her daughter, Anna's long, athletic arm—the arm of a swimmer or a javelin thrower—flung over her, Emily had no trouble believing it. None whatsoever.

"I hung up your dress," Anna, half asleep, murmured in her ear. "The one you're wearing tomorrow. So it wouldn't be wrinkled." A beat of silence, then, "Don't worry about Daniel. You'll get through it. Trust me."

"I know," Emily whispered, wishing she could be as sure.

In the darkness she felt Anna's pinkie curl loosely about her own little finger, and as her eyes drifted shut she saw them standing on a street corner, two women—one beginning to grow a little fuzzy around the edges, the other as crisp and resilient as a new blade of grass—waiting for the light to turn green.

PART TWO

*Mothers
and
Grown
Daughters*

Crayons and
Pink Giraffes

Eileen Dreyer and Kate Dreyer

Photo by Jessie Wiese

INTRODUCTION

My mother's mother died when my mother was born. My own mother died six weeks before my daughter, Kate, was born. So when Kate and I were invited to join in an anthology about the gifts mothers hand down to daughters, I was a little reticent. It seemed we had a bit of an interrupted line of inheritance. But then, when Kate and I talked about the concept, she told me some of the gifts my mother had handed down: a love of family, a love of laughter, a wonderful sense of the absurd, a sense of fair play, and a rare common sense. Kate, who had never met my mother, knew about these gifts, because I'd taught them to her as Grandma's lessons.

My mother had another gift. She could write. Unfortunately she was born in an era when writing was considered frivolous. She became a nurse and then the neighborhood mom, and she nurtured us all. She knew I enjoyed writing, but she didn't live long enough to see me try and publish. I've been blessed in that I've seen my daughter, Kate, fall in love with the written word. I've seen her dabble with it and then court it. And I've now had the chance to see her publish. It is a gift I will always cherish.

Of course, there is a downside to this. Not that we had any problems. It was a thrill (at least for me—you can ask her when you see her). The problem is knowing once and for all that this child of mine is a far better talent than her mother is. So do I encourage her or lock her in the attic to protect my fragile ego? I'll let you know. In the meantime, we write notes to each other, which my mother would have loved.

"Okay, Dad, I understand. Maybe next week . . . Okay, Dad . . . I love you, too. 'Bye." Hannah hung up the phone and turned to her husband, Jim. "My dad will be over soon," she said, then shrugged, her father's tight voice still echoing in her ear. "Uh, tomorrow maybe."

Jim smiled as if it didn't mean anything. "Don't worry," he assured her in his soft, supportive voice. "He'll love his new granddaughter."

Hannah smiled for him. "I know. I know."

They had been home a total of two hours. They had been parents a total of twenty-four. Hannah should have been exhausted. She should have been sore and anxious and exhilarated. She wasn't. She was just . . . weary. Afraid that the constriction in her chest would cut her breathing off completely.

A small mewling sound from the vicinity of Hannah's lap caught the attention of both parents. Hannah looked down to the shock of bright coppery hair, the guileless dark blue eyes, the scrunched fists of her brand-new daughter. She waited for the thrill of discovery that simply didn't materialize. Or maybe it just couldn't work its way through everything else that was crowded around it in her throat.

"Well, hey, little Rose," Jim crooned, suddenly on his knees beside the couch where Hannah was holding her baby. "Hey, little girl."

Rose couldn't be more disinterested. Hands waving aimlessly, she preferred to watch the ceiling, where sunlight sparked against the white paint. Alongside her, Jim laughed and settled one of his huge fingers into a tiny fist. Jim was so big. A vast man of wide shoulders and great voice and wide brown eyes. And yet he seemed to fold within himself before his daughter.

Hannah watched as Jim followed Rose's movements with his eyes. She knew that Rose would be spoiled beyond belief by the age of four. There would be a pony in the backyard. A Barbie dream vacation house in her room and daily trips to get ice cream.

God, how she wanted to cherish this moment. She'd been waiting for it since she'd seen Jim's eyes light with the news that he was going to be a father. Holding the anticipation to her like a precious secret, because she'd known all along Jim would be this mesmerized. This smitten.

And now she sat here tasting ashes where joy should have bubbled. Anger instead of exultation. And she was so afraid.

"Judy and Stan are supposed to be here any minute now," he said in a singsong voice, as if addressing the baby. "That ought to liven things up."

Hannah was glad. Anything rather than being left alone in this suddenly too empty house that she'd inherited from her parents, where she'd planned all along to raise her own passel of noisy, rambunctious children who would look just like Jim and discover the joys of their noisy, rambunctious aunts and uncles and cousins. And grandparents. Especially grandparents.

Almost on cue, the doorbell rang and a blond elf with bright blue eyes poked her head into the house, "Hey, kids, can I come in?"

Jim turned around, still on one knee. "Well, you're already halfway in. Why not pull the rest of yourself in?"

Jim got to his feet just as his sister threw open the door the rest of the way and walked in. Half of Jim's height and a third of his weight, Judy was the one the family always said had to be adopted, as bright as a penny and Hannah's favorite in-law. And behind her waited the big, square, shy brunette husband she'd just acquired. Not paying attention to formalities, Judy headed straight for the baby, the casserole in her hands somehow ending up in Jim's hands on her way past him.

"I figured with the new baby and all, you wouldn't have time to cook," she said with a bright smile, "so I made a couple of things you can just freeze. Oh, and I meant to say before, Rose is just such a pretty name for the baby. I just love it. To reheat the casseroles, just put them in the oven at 375 Fahrenheit and leave it for fifteen minutes—" Never taking a breath, she plopped down next to Hannah, one hand on her sister-in-law's shoulder, the other reaching for the baby "—and Hannah, I just hope you're doin' okay. I figured I would help out where I could."

Hannah really smiled for the first time, grateful for her sister-in-law's rapid-fire exuberance. "Thank you, Judy. I appreciate it. Stan, come on in the door, honey. Judy's sure not going to wait for you to follow."

His shy smile the perfect antithesis of his wife's, Stan sidled in the door and let it close behind him. Jim just laughed at them both and ruffled his kid sister's hair.

"Thanks, Jude, it's just what we need to save time."

Walking on into the kitchen, he fought his way through the frost to find room in the freezer for the casseroles.

Judy never noticed he was gone. Her eyes and mouth almost comically wide, she was visiting with her new niece. "Oh, aren't you just the cutest thing?" she asked, taking hold of one of those miniature hands. "Yes, you are, just the cutest little thing. Oh, woojee woojee woojee, just the cutest thing . . . I know your mommy must be thrilled that you got here safely after all she's been through, isn't she?"

Hannah smiled at Judy and fought the urge to press a hand against her burning chest. She took a deep breath instead to release the tension inside of her.

Hands shoved in his pockets, Stan edged over so that he stood next to Judy, his attention on the rug on the floor. "So, uh, Jim, are you still coming over next weekend for poker? It's your week to bring the beer and all."

"Yeah, buddy. Don't worry, I'll be there. Have a seat. You don't have to stand all night."

Stan sat down next to Judy and tried his best to get comfortable. He crossed his right leg over his left, then his left over his right. He shifted his weight and put his left ankle on his right knee, then settled in and put an arm around Judy.

Hannah took her eyes away from the baby and looked back and forth from Judy to Stan. "So, Stan, how's law school coming?"

"It's going okay, I guess. Just one more year."

"And then we'll be able to start our own family," Judy enthused, her focus still completely on Rose. "Just like Rose here. Although we won't be able to give her quite as big a family as Rose has, will we? Do you think we could borrow some of your family, Rose? Just a few aunts and uncles. Of course, I wouldn't mind borrowing that red hair, too, can you believe it? It's such a waste that your mom didn't . . ." She stumbled, flushed. "I mean that she . . ."

"Rose would be happy to share," Hannah assured her with as easy a smile as she could offer. "Everything but the hair, anyway."

She didn't realize she'd pulled Rose just a little closer. She could feel her chest ache and swell again, though. Her throat tightened, making it hard to breathe.

The good thing about Judy was her quicksilver mood. Grabbing an apple from the fruit basket in front of her as if she hadn't just been embarrassed, she took a bite. "So, Hannah, are you going to stay home with the baby for a while?"

"Yeah, I think so. I don't think I'm ready to go back to work. I figure in a year I'll be dying to get back into the office." Hannah shook her head and brushed a stray curl from her eye. Red hair. Coppery and bright like her daughter's. Like her mother's. A whimsical color her mother had always told her was fairy-kissed.

"No kidding! I don't know how your mom did it. To stay home for more than half of her life to raise children and take care of the house." Judy laughed around her next bite of apple. "What patience she must have had."

Hannah smiled, glad Judy wasn't stuttering with discomfort anymore. "Yeah, that's my mom. She always said, 'Don't have children until you're ready to be embarrassed.' I must say there's a lot of truth in that."

"Well ya know, I think your mom is absolutely right. We are either incredibly dumb or ready to be embarrassed. But Rose just looks too sweet to do anything like that to us. Such a tiny little thing."

Hannah wished she could be happier about holding a miracle in her arms, but an immense emptiness filled her. She didn't know where to go. Didn't know who to talk to about the doubts she was having. Didn't know whose shoulder she could cry on like a child once again.

"Oh, we're having a picnic next month on the eighteenth," she said. "Just wondering if you could come." Hannah waited for Judy and Stan to nod, then continued. "We can decide later what you want to bring."

Judy waved the apple like punctuation. "Yeah, that would be great. I could make my world-famous strawberry pie. That's how I impressed my Stan, ya know. Took one bite of that pie and fell in love. I think that's the real reason why he married me. Oh, hey, sorry if you guys haven't gotten your thank-you note for the wedding gift yet. You know how the post office can be. You mail something one day, it gets there the next month. I wouldn't forget to send thank-you notes. Some time this decade you'll get them."

"No problem. I understand how that goes."

Judy patted Hannah's shoulder a couple of times. "You're really okay, honey? I mean it's only been a month since your mom . . . since she . . . well . . ."

Hannah smiled. "It's okay, Judy, you can say it. Since she died. Yeah, I'm okay. Having Rose has made all the difference. And, Mom never would have gotten better, you know. She just didn't deserve to go through any more."

Judy watched her for a second like a lab experiment, then smiled. "I'm so glad, honey. I mean, that you can be so positive and all. My God, you've been a rock through this whole thing. I just don't know that I could do it."

"I hope you don't have to."

Hannah stopped her sentence short, afraid her chest would burst. It wasn't as easy as she'd thought. She wanted them to go. But if they did, she'd be alone. Alone with Jim, who knew her too well to be fooled, and that wouldn't be good, either.

But Judy sprang to her feet anyway, startling Rose. "Well, hey, it's been fun, but we shouldn't stay." Judy smiled, flashing twin dimples. "It's your first day home. We'll come and visit more later."

"No, it's okay," Hannah protested, instinctively rocking Rose back to sleep. "I'm really feeling okay."

Judy just shook her head and grabbed her husband's hand. "Come on, Stan, we have dishes to do at home."

Stan obediently got to his feet. "Well, Jim, I'll see you next week. Congratulations, you two."

Hannah knew she should get up and see her in-laws out. She left it to Jim, though. While he walked Judy and Stan to the car, she sat on the couch and watched her daughter. And wondered why she couldn't enjoy her. Why she couldn't at least cry.

Closing the door, Jim turned and looked at his wife. He stood silent for a second, mesmerized by her beauty. Her soft, freckled face. Her piercing green eyes. The glow in her face that made her more beautiful than ever. He just wished . . .

Hannah lifted her eyes to meet his and smiled, and Jim fell in love all over again with the mother of his child.

"She's so beautiful," he whispered as he eased down onto the couch next to them.

Hannah nodded vaguely. "Yes, she is. She really is."

Jim saw her smile and knew she was trying hard not to ruin his first night as a daddy. They'd both planned and worried and waited so anxiously for this moment. He'd sat right alongside Hannah holding her hand when she'd had that first ultrasound. He could still remember the doctor's laugh at his reaction. "Baby? What baby?"

He'd seen the baby the next time, though. And the next. He'd seen fingers and toes and a tiny, fluttering heart the size of a sparrow's, and he'd fallen as helplessly in love as he had with his wife.

It should have been so wonderful. But Hannah shouldn't still be trying to pretend that nothing had changed since the moment she'd held her own mother's hand as she fluttered into stillness in that sterile, echoing hospital room.

He didn't know how to give her that joy back. That stability. That certainty that had been the gift of her mother. He didn't know how to make her feel less cast adrift in a foreign place.

"I think our star attraction is finally asleep," he ventured.

Hannah nodded and stood up, leaning heavily on the hand Jim offered. "I think I'm going to let her try out her new crib."

"Why don't we just go to bed, honey?" Jim asked, indulging himself with the downy feel of his daughter's head. "You need to sleep."

"In time."

Hannah led the way into the room she and her mother had prepared for Rose. Stars dangled from a ceiling painted like a summer sky. Animals cavorted across the walls. Cows, sheep, a giraffe. Hannah's mom had painted the giraffe, its head too big for its neck, and they'd laughed as she'd painted its coat pink and orange. Rose's crib had been Hannah's. Handmade and old, with bright hand-crocheted afghans and plump stuffed bunnies.

Pushing a couple of them to the side, Hannah laid Rose in her crib and gently pulled a blanket over her. Rose clenched one of her tiny fists and breathed out. Hannah watched her for a second, and Jim watched them both. Jim saw the love, the wonder, the pain chase each other across Hannah's bright, mobile features as she looked down on her infant daughter.

"How about some tea?" he asked, his arm around her as they stood over Rose's crib. "It's been a long day."

Hannah nodded. Taking hold of her hand, Jim led her into the kitchen. He began to heat the water on the stove, pull out mugs, and find the tea.

"You realize, of course, Rose is not leaving the house until she's twenty," Jim said brightly. "And when she does leave the house, she's going into a convent."

Turning around, Jim watched Hannah's reaction.

Hannah took a stool from under the counter, her features carefully composed again. "My parents said that about me. Ya know, you and I would have never met if they had followed through."

Jim aimed a coffee mug at her. "We'll see about Rose. I'm a stubborn man."

"Oh, really! I guess my mom was right about you."

"What did your mom say about me?"

Hannah's smile was sweet. "Just that you'd be a good daddy."

Glancing up from filling the bright-blue mugs, Jim brightened. "A woman of extraordinary good sense." He finished, then handed Hannah's mug to her. "How're you doing, sweetheart?"

Hannah never looked at him as she stirred her

obligatory three teaspoons of sugar into the liquid. "Oh, okay, I guess. I'm a little sore and pretty tired, but that's nothing aspirin and sleep can't handle. I'm also hungry. The hospital food was awful. While I was there I liked to play the thirty-second game."

Perfectly happy to play the straight man, Jim frowned in confusion. "The thirty-second game?"

He won a quick grin. "If you can't identify the food within thirty seconds, don't eat it. That left out most of the food, so I was left with Jell-O and white bread."

"We can't have that now, can we? So what do you want? We have soup, white bread, and . . . uh, Jell-O."

"Really?" she asked, then considered. Jim recognized the game, but went along, just happy to see her smiling. "Well, I think I'll have soup. Just make sure it passes the thirty-second test."

Sipping at his tea, Jim began bustling around the kitchen in search of food. One soup can, an opener, and a saucepan later, he was on his way to a late-night snack.

"I remember when I'd walk in on you and your mom having those late-night girl talk sessions over tea," he ventured. "It used to embarrass me silly."

Hannah chuckled. "And you never heard the really good stuff. Those were the times I learned everything I know. Important stuff like how to keep a hotel mirror from fogging, how to keep hose run-free, and how to make you fall in love with me. My mom really liked you. You were the only guy I brought home that she liked."

Hannah stopped, focused on the tea in front of her, stirred it with her finger. Jim saw her fight for control. He stood there a minute, struggling to know what to do. So many of their conversations had become minefields. So many familiar references deadly traps. And he didn't know how to defuse them. He knew Hannah missed her mother. He knew she hadn't allowed herself to grieve. But there was something more. Something she hadn't shared with him, and he didn't know how to force it free.

All he knew how to do was hold her, so he did. "Hannah, I love you."

Hannah sat up straighter and rubbed at her chest. She wiped her wet eyes and made an effort to smile. "I love you too, honey. It's okay."

"It's okay to be mad at her," he ventured, just like the hospital chaplain had told him to.

Hannah blinked at him as if he'd offered to barbecue the baby on the Weber kettle. "What?"

He straightened, unsure of himself again. "Your mom. She should have been here. She should have helped you learn how to be a new mom." Jim shrugged before the sudden stiffening in his wife's posture. "She should have been here to share Rose with us."

Hannah hadn't cried since the night she'd walked out of that hospital carrying her mother's jewelry. She didn't cry now. She just sat there staring at him as if he'd betrayed her.

"I'm not mad at her," Hannah said coldly. "How could I be mad at her? It's not like she chose this moment to have cancer. It's not like she said one day, 'Ya know, Hannah, things aren't stressful enough for you, being eight months pregnant, so I think I'll be rushed to the hospital with chest pain. Better yet, I will have been so afraid of what the doctors told me six months ago that I'll make sure I don't share it with you until it's too late, because I don't want you to worry, even though I know perfectly well it'll only make it even harder for you . . ."

She tightened, impossibly, even more. Chin up. Eyes bright and dry and brittle as old glass. And Jim, hurting and frustrated, didn't know what to do.

"I'm sorry," Hannah relented with a half smile. "It's not fair to take it out on you. I guess I'm just tired."

"You have a right, honey."

Her smile this time was less assured. More honest. "Maybe. But it's still not fair. Now, how 'bout that soup of yours O master chef?"

Jim knew not to push her, "Comin' right up, Mom."

Hannah didn't know what to do. Her heart was in her throat and her patience was at an end. She lay in the dark next to Jim and tried so very hard not to scream.

They'd put Rose down four hours ago. Four hours during which Hannah had been up seven times, and Jim another three. Four hours in which her baby, her sweet, redheaded image of her mother, had fretted and sobbed and shrieked in the echoing hours of the early morning.

And Hannah had run out of ideas.

The clock read four, and Rose was screaming again. Hannah rolled over, exhausted, frantic, frightened, and nudged Jim in the back.

"Jim . . . Jim."

Nothing. Somehow he was sound asleep, and Hannah resented it. She resented him. She wanted to kick him, when his only crime was that he couldn't tell Hannah how to make her baby stop crying.

"Jerk," she said anyway as she crawled out of bed.

It was better than giving way to the tears that were crowding her throat. She'd put off going to bed so she didn't have to face the dark. Sat in that kitchen for an hour after she should have fallen asleep because she didn't want to be alone with her last memories of her mother. Silly her. She hadn't been alone at all. She'd been up with Rose.

Bathrobe, slippers. Long march along the hall to the bedroom next door where beneath the dancing stars and smiling giraffe, Rose was frantic.

"What?" Hannah demanded, her voice shrill and high. "What do you want? I've fed you, I've changed you, I've rocked you. I can't do any more, Rose. I just can't."

Rose's cries were impatient. Her back protesting, Hannah bent over the crib and checked her daughter out. Dry sleeper. No obvious injuries. No signs anywhere of what was wrong. Hannah picked the baby up and eased herself down onto the rocking chair, too sore to rock, and she hummed. Rose wasn't buying it. She arched her back, flailed her fists. Cried harder and higher, until Hannah wanted to cry back. Until she wanted to run. Until she just wanted to shake this baby who wouldn't tell her what was wrong.

Mom, help me. Tell me what to do.

Hannah squeezed her eyes shut, stunned by the fresh wave of grief just that thought brought.

Rose curled and uncurled her fist as she fought against the air around her. She blinked rapidly, not knowing yet how to focus. Her big eyes looked up widely at Hannah's face.

"Rose, please," Hannah begged. "For me."

Rose responded by whimpering and hiccuping before beginning to wail again.

"Baby girl, what do you want? Tell me!"

Now Hannah was crying, too. Big, gulping sobs that stunned her.

She wasn't ready for this. She couldn't handle a baby. Hell, she couldn't handle herself. She'd been anticipating this baby because she'd known her mother would be there for her. Her mother would show her how it was done. Her mother would hand down that special magic that mothers had that made them endlessly patient, wonderfully wise, superhuman in strength. Her mother had promised her.

She'd promised her, damn it!

How dare Jim say it was okay to be mad at her? What did he know? He had a mother. He had a grandmother. Hannah had promised her baby. She'd promised Rose before she had a name, before she'd had toes or a beating heart, that she would have the best of grandmothers. She would have a grandmother who would weave her stories of old family legends, who would teach her to sing in a maddeningly off-key voice. Who would point out to her the great wonders in the world that could be really seen only from a child's height.

She'd promised. And now her mother was gone and Hannah was left alone, and she didn't know what to do.

Jim tried. He tried so hard. Hannah could still feel his arms around her, his soft, father's face alongside hers. He was grieving too. Hannah knew that she was breaking his heart by not sharing this with him, but how could he understand? How could he know the special weight of a child beneath your heart? How could he know just how quickly a woman tumbles for a faceless, nameless little being who makes her presence known through fluttering dances deep in the darkness of her body? Of her soul. How could he understand how that weight metamorphoses into responsibility, into commitment, into passion . . . into terror that you'll never be enough for the miraculous life you carry closer than you carry your dreams?

Her mother had known. Her mother had carried that weight nine times. She'd seen that weight survive into the light eight times and nurtured it to adulthood. She'd seen it spark in Hannah's eyes when she'd found out she would be a mother, when she'd seen her first ultrasound, when she'd felt the first skitter of a separate life in her. Her mother had held her own hand over Hannah's growing belly and promised as a mother, as a grandmother, that she'd be with Hannah and Hannah's baby to pass on the secrets that mothers were privileged to pass down to daughters for their daughters.

She'd promised.

And then she'd left.

And now Hannah held her daughter in her arms, terrified and awed and alone, the secrets never shared, the magic never given. She looked to this night and the next, and the month after that, and the year after that, and realized that irrevocably, she wasn't a daughter anymore. She was only a mother now, which meant she had to know. She had to be responsible before she felt she'd learned the lessons.

"What do I do?" she begged aloud for all those years she would have to guide this little girl to adulthood without her teacher to guide her.

"Basics," she could almost hear her mother say in her pragmatic voice. "Clean diapers. Food. Food is a key word with babies. And don't believe that crap about not needing a pacifier . . ."

The rest of the words were faint in the back of Hannah's mind.

"Pacifier," she said, clutching at straws. "I'll try the pacifier."

Hannah lurched to her feet, Rose still stiff and unhappy, and stumbled over to the sky-blue chest of drawers that her mom had painted to match the ceiling. Tucking Hannah under her arm like a squirming football, she dragged open the top drawer and pawed through it.

"Magazines, bottles, diapers, pacifier, papers . . ."

Hannah stared at the stack of papers she'd just

unearthed from the bottom of the drawer. They were yellowed and crisp, tied together with a purple ribbon. For a moment Hannah couldn't touch them. The hair on her neck stirred and she fought an urge to call Jim into the room.

Rose drew a breath, and Hannah plopped the pacifier she'd found into place. Rose gulped, hiccuped, whimpered. But she was quieter. Hannah felt a stab of hope.

She reached in and pulled out the papers. Then, with the baby safely in her arms, she took them to the rocker and unfolded them. Some of the handwriting was babyish, large crayoned letters. Some was bubbly, as if the words had spilled like ink across the page.

"Oh, my God . . ."

They were letters. Letters she and her mom had written back and forth to one another a long time ago. Her mom had always insisted on their writing letters to each other, saying she and her own mother had done it that way. Hannah always thought she wrote them just to make her practice penmanship.

She'd forgotten. All those years ago, and she'd forgotten it.

Dear Mom— Hannah stopped, the words blurring a second beyond tears, then took a steadying breath to go on. *I think I have it figured out. I want to be an astronaut. They get to fly up in the air and spin without weight. Don't you think that would be cool? Forget horseback riding. I want to be up in space. No one to bother me. What do you think? Love, Me.*

Hannah lowered the letter, trying to remember

when she'd written it. She looked down at Rose and smiled. Mouth working rhythmically around the blue plastic, the baby was finally asleep. Hannah sat back and continued reading.

Dear Hannah, I think you would make a lovely astronaut. Remember when you're up there to look for all of your pink houses. Since you do own all of those in the world. And don't forget about Dad's birthday coming up. Why don't you draw for him? He loves your pictures. Write back soon. I Love You, Mom.

Flipping through the letters, Hannah picked one up from her later years.

Mom, I know that I haven't written in a long time, but I've been so busy. I have exams next week and papers to write. I guess I'll bring you up to date on everyone. Sally likes Frank. Frank likes Jody. Sally refuses to be in the same room with Jody because Jody says she doesn't like boys. Why not? She's a girl, shouldn't she like boys? I asked my teacher, and she said to ask you. I'm in high school, I don't know why they just don't explain it. Well, Bobby is captain of next year's football team, so I told him not to think too much of himself. That's all I can think of now, I'll write soon. Love, Me.

Hannah, Sounds like a busy life to me. Remember, it's okay if you don't do so well. I know how hard you have been trying lately in school. Your dad appreciated the dinner you made for him on Father's Day. There are just so many of you, and he appreciated the time away from the kids to sit and have a nice dinner. We haven't had tea in a while. Tomorrow night let's make a big pot and talk. I Love You, Mom.

Hannah looked at her mother's handwriting for

a long time. She noticed the long loops on her *g*s and *j*s. She followed the pattern of the letters with hungry eyes.

Hannah pressed a hand to her chest. Her eyes flooded and spilled over. Her breath choked with the sudden rush of tears. She closed her eyes, trying to stop the hotness. She gulped in air and tasted loss.

"Why? Why, Mom? Why did you leave me? You promised me you'd stay. You told me I could trust you, and I believed you. God, I was so stupid to believe you." Hannah began to rock Rose, hoping to control herself. It didn't work. "Why did you have to die? Leave me empty and searching for someone. Someone to hold me and let me cry with a box of tissues ready, someone to listen and unfalteringly love me. Just a little longer. That's all I would have needed. Don't you get it?"

Hannah abruptly stood up and with shaking hands set the baby in the crib. Still clutching the letters, she paced the room, a technique her mom had taught her to calm down. She held her arms tightly around herself. She walked, finally, back to the chest her mother had made for Rose and opened the drawer to put the letters deep inside.

There was another piece of paper there. A fresh one with shaky handwriting. Carefully slipping the bundle of letters into a deep corner, Hannah pulled out the fresh paper and unfolded it.

Hannah, I love you. Always remember that. I know how you feel. I know you're lost and confused. I know the way you search your baby's eyes for answers when she cries. Don't you think I did that too? I was left with no mother. No support. No way to become a child again in someone's arms. You would cry during the night for no reason. You tore my heart apart. I wrote this letter for you because I know how angry you are at me. I know you're frustrated. I know you need me. This is the best I can do.

I will always look over you and your new family with a love only a mother can have. Don't worry, baby. You're ready. I know you better than you know yourself. I know you can handle it. But don't hold it in. Let it all out. Be mad at me. Kick my gravestone, curse, swear. But know I am here, whenever you need me. Remember that your father needs you too. Help each other. And know I love you with all of my heart. I love you and the rest of my children. You now understand the love of a mother. Understand my love is undying.

Hannah could hear her mother's voice in the words and found herself, unbelievably, smiling. Tears flowed freely down her cheeks, dripping from her chin. Refolding the letter, she curled into the rocker, her knees tucked beneath her chin. She looked up to the mobile above Rose's bed that her mom had made for her. It danced with butterflies, stars, and fish. Dreams and whimsy, her mother's rare gift.

For a long time she just sat in the silence of her daughter's room. She just sat in the darkness, where the night whispered secrets and magic could live. Where pink and orange giraffes reached a hand-painted sky.

Finally, as the birds began to wake in the trees, Hannah rose and walked into the den. Settling down at Jim's desk, she pulled out pen and paper. She sat for a second, then put a date on the top and began writing.

Dear Rose, It's four in the morning and you're sound asleep. I just put you down. I wish you could have met Grandma. She was a neat lady. I remember we would have talks over tea. That's where I learned everything I know. I'll teach you everything in due time, don't worry. Grandma adored all of her children. We used to write letters back and forth to each other. We were always so busy, that's how we communicated. I hope you and I can write letters to each other.

Today is the day I brought you home. To tell you the truth, I have no clue what to do with you. Hopefully we'll learn together. You'll understand when you're a mother what I am talking about. Just remember something Grandma always told me. "As long as you are happy and healthy, nothing else matters, except wearing clean underwear in case you are in an accident." I'm going to give this to you when you're ready. All I want you to know is that no matter what, I will always love you. Rose, remember me always. Tell stories about me to your children, and remember to write. I love you always. Mom.

Hannah folded the letter in thirds and held it for a minute. Then, the new sun gilding her movements, she got up and walked over to hide it away in a safe place.

She was just coming back to her bedroom when Jim walked out. "Hey, Mom," he greeted her, wrapping his arms around her. "How's our daughter?"

Hannah smiled and nestled her head against her husband's great heart. "She's beautiful. I think my mom would have loved her."

Jim laughed. "I think your mom would have spoiled her rotten."

Hannah felt the first flush of exhilaration. Of exultation. She felt the magic transform into the sun. And so she laughed.

"Yep. Pony in the backyard by the age of four."

Out of Time

Wendy Hornsby and Alyson Hornsby

Photo by Lee B. Phan

INTRODUCTION

This is the second short story that my daughter, Alyson, and I have written together, and we found the process to be both challenging and rewarding. The first obstacle was geography: Alyson is in college in Washington, D.C., and I am on the far side of the continent in Southern California. Most of the discussions about plot and character took place over the telephone until the semester was over and Alyson was home for the summer. Finally able to sit down in tandem in front of the computer, we worked in turns. Alyson sketched in plot, and I filled in detail. And then we switched places, editing each other as we went. It was fun. The story isn't about us; no one in the family died in Butte, Montana. But we both learned a few things.

"Mom, did Nana have a lover?" My twenty-one-year-old daughter, Lainey, sat cross-legged on the floor of my mother's attic, an ancient steamer trunk open in front of her, an old shoebox full of snapshots resting across her knees. "This guy, whoever he is, is really good-looking."

"Nana, a lover?" I said. "Never."

"He is definitely a prince, Mom. And he's all over Nana. Look at him."

"Not now. My hands are full." I pulled a broken lamp from a jumble of dusty castoffs in a far corner and sent it down the trash chute we had rigged from the attic window to a dumpster in the yard below.

Six months after my mother's funeral, we had finally managed to sell her old house, the house where I grew up. I had put off the task of attic and cellar cleaning, and all the memories stored there, until there was no more time to stall.

All weekend we'd had plenty of help. My brother and his wife and various old friends had all joined Lainey and me in a happy sort of campout, the accommodations becoming more and more spartan as the furniture and rugs were disposed of, one room at a time. By Sunday night most of the heavy work was finished, the general patching and repairing had been done, and there was new paint throughout.

Monday morning Lainey and I were alone in the house, and there was still more work to do than I thought it was possible to finish in the few days left to us. By the afternoon we were exhausted, overwhelmed, dirty, and short-tempered as we felt the press of time. Just the same, that Monday was a rare pleasure: We'd shared few full days alone together since Lainey had moved away to college three years earlier.

Trying not to sound like a shrew, I said, "Honey, if you stop to look at every old picture, we'll never get the house ready for the new owners by Thursday."

"I know, I know." With the shoebox in her arms, she uncoiled from the floor and came over to me. Holding the picture that had captivated her so that I could see it, she said, "Just look at him, Mom. Do you know who he is?"

Dust motes swirled around us, an effect like a gauze filter before my eyes, as I looked at the face.

Four days spent sorting heirlooms and keepsakes and just plain junk Mother hadn't gotten around to tossing out had left me emotionally purged. Old issues that were stirred up with the dust I dealt with in turn and put away. By day two, I could gather up Mom's forty-five-year accumulation of frilly Mother's Day cards and her collection of baby teeth and send them all down the trash chute without an instant's hesitation. By day three even her antique teacups stirred little interest. Suddenly, however, a face gazing out of a faded photograph opened a deep, dark emotional closet I had forgotten existed and left me short of breath and light-headed.

"That's my father," I said. "Your grandfather, Richard."

"Whoa. My grandfather?" Lainey grinned, happy at the discovery. "Go, Nana! I can't feature her in a big romance with a guy this gorgeous. Nana wasn't what you would call a beauty or a bundle of laughs."

"She was once."

Lainey grew thoughtful. She brushed her fingertips across her grandfather's face before she put the picture back into the box, which she cradled in the crook of her arm. "You never talk about your father. All that you've ever said is that he died."

"I was only six years old, honey. I don't remember very much about him."

She watched me until I felt uncomfortable. To get out from under her stare, I said, "Will you help me move the big table out of the corner?"

She sighed, and shrugged elaborately. Tucking a stray strand of hair under her bandanna, she walked with me through the maze of boxes marked for Goodwill or labeled with the names of various friends and relatives. Men from my mother's church were going to haul away the leftovers for us on Wednesday.

"Nice table." Lainey knelt to examine the heavily carved legs. "Can I have it?"

"Certainly, but where would you put it?"

"I'm thinking about getting an apartment for my senior year. I can use the table as a desk."

"This is the first I've heard about an apartment."

"What's to tell? I don't want to live in the dorm with freshman scrubs. Besides, an apartment is cheaper than the dorm."

"Will you have a roommate?" I asked.

"Yes. We found a great place one subway stop from campus. It's great. All I need now is a desk."

"So you're more than just *thinking* about an apartment."

"I was going to tell you." She gave me a wry grin. "I'm an adult. I don't need my mom to cosign the lease."

"Of course you don't." I patted her bare arm when what I wanted was to cradle her in my lap. "If you want the table, tag it or it'll end up at Goodwill."

With her shirttail, Lainey polished a corner of the tabletop until the old mahogany shone. Looking at her reflection, she said, "You have Nana's picture on the family room wall with everyone else. Why isn't your father there beside her?"

"I don't know." I felt uncomfortable, challenged. "I guess I thought it would make Nana feel sad to see him."

"Why would she be sad? Grandpa Joe's picture doesn't make Grandma sad. Hell, she even blows him a kiss when she walks by it. You didn't take down Daddy's picture when he moved out, and we all know that Daddy makes you more than a little unhappy."

"Even if I don't see him anymore, he's still your father, and Grandma's son." I grasped one end of the table. "Help me, please."

"So, what happened to your father?" She was persistent.

"I told you, he died. Will you grab an end here?"

Lainey set the shoebox atop the table carelessly enough so that it spilled, snapshots slid out, scuffing a path through the dust. Her voice sounded tight. "You're doing it again, Mom."

"Doing what?"

"Shutting me out. What is the big deal? I thought we had established that I'm an adult. I don't need to be protected from the truth. And I think I'm entitled."

I started to protest, to defend myself. Then I looked at her sweet face, a face so much like my father's around the handsome eyes, and remembered him saying to my mother, "If you're angry with me, I wish you would simply say so."

"I'm sorry." I put my arm around Lainey. "I don't mean to shut you out. After my father died, mentioning him in this house was the biggest taboo. I loved him, I missed him terribly. But there was no one that I could tell how I felt. It still makes me uncomfortable to talk about my father because it was a forbidden topic for so long."

"Why all the silence? I mean, people die all the time."

"Nana had standards, even for the way people were supposed to die."

"Nana isn't here, Mom." Lainey smiled. "It's okay. Let it out."

"I don't know very much about what happened."

"Tell me what you know."

I shrugged. "My father died in Butte, Montana, six hundred miles from here. He was a mining engineer, working on a project. Mother—Nana—got a call late one night. The next morning she went away on the train and came home a week or so later with my dad in a shiny black coffin. That's what I remember most clearly, that big shiny coffin."

"What did she tell you happened to him?"

"She didn't," I said. "The only person who said anything to me was Essie, the housekeeper. All she said was, 'Your father passed, you poor little thing. What will your mother do?' "

"That's cold."

"Nana was overwhelmed," I said, feeling defensive of my mother, so recently gone. "I'm sure that Nana planned to talk it over with me and your Uncle Dickie when she could be more composed. But she never did. Her pain was very private, and I'm sure she thought she was protecting us. After a while, the silence was just habit."

"I look at these pictures," Lainey said, "and I don't know who most of the people are. Are they your father's relatives? My relatives? Where are they now?" Lainey collected the spilled pictures, squaring the corners before putting them back into the box. She looked askance at me. "Nana owed you more."

"I was only a little girl," I said, wishing Lainey, for once, would let an issue drop. "Nana wanted to protect me and Uncle Dickie. I never got the whole story, so what I remember is just fragments, flashes from the past that are like watching those faded old snapshots spill."

"What do you remember?"

I thought for a moment before answering. "I remember Nana taking her good black dress out of the dry cleaner bag and changing the shiny buttons to plain ones. I remember holding Nana's overnight bag at the station, and how heavy it was. My teacher brought over my schoolwork so I could do it at home, but I wanted to go be with my friends. There was a heavy fog the whole time Nana was gone. And I had a pain so intense one night that Essie called the doctor in."

"What was wrong with you?"

"Heartache. Loneliness."

"You had Uncle Dickie."

"He was just a baby," I said. "What puzzled me most was that no one came calling. This town is so small and so boring, that the biggest things that ever happen are weddings, births, funerals, and fires in green hay. The whole town will show up for a broken leg. I kept expecting neighbors and friends, the ladies' guild from the church, to be here clucking over the terrible thing that had happened.

"I thought Mrs. Caldwell would make us the same big coconut cake she took to the Proski family when Walter fell under the wheels of his tractor. There should have been tuna noodle casserole with potato chip topping, and Jell-O. Nothing ever happened without some kind of Jell-O showing up. But not for us that time."

"That's precious. Poor Mom." Lainey hugged me. "Not even Jell-O?"

"Nothing and no one."

"That's mean. You were just little kids."

"It's the way Nana wanted things. The gossip would have been brutal, but she put a stop to it right away. There was no funeral even."

"What did Nana do, throw the coffin off the back of the train?"

"Almost. Essie dressed up Uncle Dickie and me to meet Nana at the station. We went from there directly to the cemetery. Dr. Wilby, the minister, came with us, and Mr. Harper from the mortuary—he took the coffin in his hearse—but nobody else. Not even the director of the Sunday school came, and she was without question the best crier in the whole town."

Lainey chuckled. "Seems so strange."

"It was. I asked Essie whether things were done differently when someone died out of town, if maybe all of the fuss and coconut cake happened wherever the person had died."

"What did Essie say to that?"

" 'Don't get your good shoes wet.' "

"But there was some kind of service, wasn't there?"

"Dr. Wilby said a prayer, and Dad went straight into the ground. When I started to protest—I couldn't remember my dad's face, I wanted the coffin opened the way my grandfather's had been, just to be sure Dad was in there—Essie said, 'You hush, girl. Don't upset your Momma.' "

"What did Nana say?"

"Not a word. I think she was doped up just so she could get through it. As soon as we got back home, she took Dad's portrait off the mantel, stowed his clothes and books, his rack of pipes and his golf clubs, and any other evidence that he had ever lived in our house into that trunk where you found the pictures. And he was never again spoken of."

"Not even to Uncle Dickie?"

"No."

"Do you and Uncle Dickie talk about it now?"

"Never."

"Don't you think you should? He has kids himself. Doesn't he deserve to know something about his father? I mean, you remember some stuff, but he was younger."

"You don't understand, Lainey. There are other factors involved that complicate things," I said, trying to make it clear that she shouldn't inquire further.

"I never will know if you don't tell me." Lainey took hold of one end of the table and lifted. "So, what did your father do that was so terrible? Suicide?"

"No," I said, lifting my end of the table. "He was shot by an irate husband."

"O-oh." Her eyes grew round, her mouth dropped for an instant as all the pieces seemed to fall into place. We set the table down near the top of the stairs. "So when Daddy . . ."

"Excuse me." I didn't want her to see me cry, so I turned and fled out of the attic and down the stairs. My head was flooded with dust, but also with thoughts that hadn't entered my mind in years because I had tried so hard to forget they were even there. Somehow, one of those tricks of the mind, the enforced silence around my father and the impenetrable secrets that enshrouded my almost ex-husband became all mixed up together, grief and anger doubled.

Marriage is a private world. My mother had owed me some explanation. She did not owe me the whole truth. How much more was Lainey entitled to know about her father and me?

I remembered my mother coming off the train looking tired and fragile: white-faced, dry-eyed, her good black dress so wrinkled she might have worn it the entire five days she was gone. She held us by the hand but allowed no one close enough to hold her. I was afraid that if I cried she would collapse, and it would be all my fault.

I could taste the saltiness of the stream of tears that ran down my cheeks. I took the stairs two at a time so Lainey wouldn't hear me cry. The door to my old bedroom flew open and I ran to the mattress that was the only remaining furniture in the room, curling myself into a little ball just as I had that day when I was six years old and I learned that my father was gone. I wept for him and I wept for my mother, and for all the promises unfulfilled.

"Mom, you okay?" Lainey's voice wakened me from an exhausted sleep.

I raised my head to see her sweet face looking at me with worry and a little fear. I glanced at my reflection in the window and saw why she would be concerned about me. She had probably never seen me with puffy red eyes and a swollen nose. All through the divorce, I did my best to hide the depth of my feelings from her. Just as my mother had done.

I looked pathetic, felt pathetic, and I didn't want to show my weakness to Lainey. My daughter was so strong, I was afraid that she would just pity me.

"You've been asleep for an hour," she said. "I thought you might want to get cleaned up."

"Cleaned up for what?" I said. "What time is it?"

The doorbell sounded.

Lainey glanced at her watch, seemed almost panicky. "Oh, my God."

"Honey," I said, "would you get the door?"

"Would you? I am a mess." She pulled off the bandanna she had wrapped around her hair. "I'll be right behind you, but I need a minute."

I tried to pull myself together as I went down to the front door. I heard Lainey's sandals on the bathroom floor upstairs, and the scratchy sound of a hairbrush, water running in the basin. Needing more than a quick brushing and a face wash myself, I merely combed my fingers through my hair and stood up straighter. There was no one in town I needed to impress, but I was my mother's daughter: There were standards.

The front door had been left open for fresh air, so there was only a screen separating my disheveled self from the tall young man on the porch.

His was a face I hadn't seen before, but he smiled as if we should be friends. Was he the grown son of one of my old neighborhood playmates? I stepped closer to the door.

"Hello," he said in a voice that sounded vaguely familiar. "Are you Mrs. Murphy, Lainey's mother?" As I opened the screen, he stepped forward with his hand extended, nervous yet excited. "I'm Paul. We spoke on the phone yesterday."

"Yes, I remember. Lainey's friend from college." I took the offered hand. He was handsome, dark hair and lots of teeth. He wore khaki shorts and a rugby shirt, a pair of very old Nikes, and a fair share of confidence. I was curious about him, and maybe a little wary. I said, "Nice of you to drop by. Do you live in the area?"

Before he had a chance to respond, Lainey was next to me, smiling, her hair brushed smooth, a glow on her cheeks. The worried face she had worn upstairs had vanished. When she turned to Paul, her happy expression was a revelation to me. "Good, you two have met."

"Come in, Paul." I stood aside. "Lemonade?" I asked. *Exactly what my mother would have said*, I thought, feeling suddenly old. Should I have offered him a beer?

Lainey put her arm through his as if by habit and led him inside and down the long hall to Nana's kitchen. I followed a few steps behind, watching them. Paul was telling Lainey about his train ride from school, and she was laughing as I had never seen her laugh. Her eyes were bright, and she gave his every word her rapt attention.

As she reached for glasses from the cupboard, she said, "Mom's giving us the most wonderful old table that's been in Nana's attic for who knows how many lifetimes. It'll be perfect for the computer."

I refrained from repeating, "Us." Instead, I excused myself, went upstairs, brushed my hair, washed my face, changed into a clean shirt. I'm not sure they noticed that I was gone.

I had not been expecting a visitor, especially one of this sort, and I wasn't sure what I was supposed to do. Lainey had dated in high school, so I was used to meeting boyfriends who came and went with the seasons. But this one seemed different. She had never even mentioned him to me, yet they seemed to be serious enough to want to live together. I couldn't imagine why she wouldn't want me to know about her relationship with Paul. I never thought she was the kind of person who kept secrets.

I walked back to the kitchen, feeling like a snoop. Lainey was standing alone cutting apples and arranging them on a plate with cheese and crackers.

"Paul is in the bathroom washing up. The train

ride up from school was long and uncomfortable—
you know how that can be," Lainey said nonchalantly as she placed an apple slice in the middle of
a pinwheel of cheese. "Travel makes you feel so
grungy. Must be the train air."

"You met Paul at school?" I said, grabbing an
apple and a knife to join her.

"Chemistry class. Too ordinary, I know. Chemistry. He was my lab partner. He's really smart.
He's pre-med."

"How old is Paul?"

"Twenty-one, like me."

"And he doesn't want to live with freshman
scrubs next year either?" I was obviously digging
for information, and she knew it.

Lainey turned to me and looked me straight in
the eye. She smiled an embarrassed smile, knowing that I had caught on. "Mom, Paul and I are
planning to live together next year."

"I got that message," I said. "Aren't you rushing
things?"

"I wanted to tell you about Paul a long time ago,
but I thought you would be overwhelmed with
Nana, and then Dad and everything. I knew that if
you met Paul you would see how great he is and
wouldn't think it was a big deal."

"You don't give me enough credit, Lainey. I
think I had a right to know," I said.

"Of course you do, Mom. I just thought that
it would make you uncomfortable. Since the divorce you've been kinda negative and withdrawn.
I didn't want to give you a chance to say no until
you'd met him. I promise, Mom, he's not like my

dad, or your dad. When you get to know him you'll see that he's really great."

"I'm sure he is. But moving in together is a big step. How long have you known him?"

"Long enough."

"Are you two talking about marriage?"

"I don't think I ever want to get married." She looked me directly in the eye. "We all know how that turns out."

"Oh, sweetheart." I felt stung as I put my arm around her. "I have to admit I'm relieved; I think it's way too early to be planning a wedding. But marriage can be wonderful. Your dad and I had many very happy years."

"Happiness doesn't last forever. I mean, it would be great if it did, but I don't want to go through the hell that you had to go through. I saw what breaking up did to you, and now I'm seeing what it did to Nana." She looked so serious and so matter-of-fact. "I love Paul, but I'm too sensible to think that it will always be like this between us."

"No, it won't be just like this forever. What if it gets better?" My heart ached, realizing the impact my experiences had on her. "Maybe Nana and I look like disasters to you. But knowing what I know, I wouldn't have done anything differently. And remember, you aren't us."

"I know all that. But why risk it? Paul is good and honest, but I'm sure you and Nana thought the same things in the beginning. And look what happened. I'm not going to set myself up for the fall."

"Oh, honey . . ." I didn't know what to tell her. My marriage had ended like a bad soap opera, and the word "tragedy" could certainly be applied to Nana's situation. Still, I knew that wasn't the only way. "I don't know which clichés to give you. But it all comes to the same thing: Be friends first. When things got bad, too often I did the same thing Nana did. I froze everyone out, including your dad. I thought all our problems would just go away if I pretended nothing was happening. I wasn't a very good friend to your dad when times got tough."

"Mom, are you blaming yourself for Daddy's affair?"

"No. That was his decision. If nothing else, the breakup could have been less traumatic if we had all been able to sit down together. We should have included you more. Like Nana, I assumed you knew all that you needed to know and were old enough to understand. You always seemed so strong. You were my little trooper."

"I stayed strong because of you. I was afraid that if I broke down, you would, too."

"I'm sorry I put that burden on you, Lainey. Trust me, I know how heavy that load can be."

Lainey was misty-eyed, and the apple slice in her hand shook slightly. I looked at her and realized that I couldn't read her face. In some ways, this young woman was a stranger to me as she grew into her independence.

I said, "I love you, Lainey. And I always loved your father."

She raised her head, but her eyes slid past me as Paul appeared at the doorway.

"Can she cook?" he said, pulling a stool up to the kitchen counter.

"No. But I can open a deli package." Lainey seemed to have recovered in his presence. She wore a smile I had never seen her wear, and one that I hoped she never lost. She pushed the beautifully arranged plate in front of him. "Eat up. I'll bet it's better than anything you could get in the club car. At least it's prettier."

"Thank you. It's nice to have a fully stocked kitchen instead of the dining hall, huh?" He stacked a piece of cheese and an apple slice together and took a bite. Looking straight into her eyes, he said, "It's beautiful. Thank you."

"Any time." Lainey shrugged. "I was just telling Mom about the apartment."

"Good." He swallowed a bit hard, but managed to keep the smile. "We found a really great place, Mrs. Murphy. It was a steal."

"Tell me about it."

He did, his smile growing: one bedroom, an okay bathroom, a tiny kitchen off the living room that would be their study. An easy walk to the campus. I couldn't see anything under that warm smile that would suggest heartache down the road. He looked so hopeful and good. And trustworthy. Had my efforts to shield Lainey from unpleasantness made it impossible for her to trust?

"I hope you'll come see us once we've gotten settled," he said. "If you don't mind sitting on the floor."

"Lainey," I said, "I've kept a pair of Nana's rockers and the dining room chairs. Would you like to have any of them?"

"I would." She hesitated. "But you want them."

"Better that things are used than to have them gathering dust in my garage."

She reached across the table and took Paul's hand. "Mom's giving us the best old table. You'll love it."

I decided that at the moment I was one person too many in the kitchen. I finished my lemonade and excused myself.

"I'm going to go back up to the attic," I said. "Any volunteer help will be appreciated. There's so much work to be done. We'll never get this place packed up by Thursday unless we skip sleeping for the next few nights."

"We'll be up to help you in a little while," Lainey called after me. "Don't worry. We'll get it finished in time."

The old wooden stairs creaked as I climbed back to the attic. Strangely, my head felt clearer in the cloudy attic than it had downstairs. I found an unexpected comfort in the jumble and mess. I reached for a trash bag, ready to attack a pile of old newspapers when I saw the old mahogany table standing alone.

I grabbed a tag, wrote, "Goes in U-Haul," and tied it to a leg. The table was old, had been old even when my mother bought it to put in the entry of the house just a few years after my father died. She had said that she would put flowers on it and pictures of her children so anyone who came to the house would see how beautiful we were. She said it made her happy to see our smiling faces when she came in the door. I don't know when the table moved up to the attic. Maybe she got tired of

dusting picture frames: first there were two weddings, then four babies—my one and Dickie's
three—christenings, graduations, too many mile-
stones for one table. Or, maybe, there were too
many reminders.

I found a clean rag and began to polish the table.
Some of the frames had left marks on the surface, and I thought about all those faces, my family,
past, present. Nana had paired one of my baby
pictures with one of Lainey's in a tandem silver
frame. How alike we were, she would say, and
how I loved to hear it. She always attributed our
best features to her side of the family, never mentioned Dad.

I have my mother's strong nose and high forehead, but I also have my father's full mouth, a
legacy that is even more apparent on Lainey's
face. She also has his eyes, and her own father's
long legs and peaches-and-cream skin.

By the time I heard Lainey's light footsteps and
Paul's heavy ones bounding up the stairs, the old
table shone like the treasure it had once been.

"Wow, Mom. It looks fantastic." Lainey's face
was bright with pleasure. "Paul, don't you think it
will be perfect?"

"It is perfect." Paul seemed to share her excitement as he ran his hand over the surface. "This is
real furniture. I was planning to make a table out
of a door and sawhorses."

"There are two extension leaves somewhere
around here," I said. "You can make it larger."

"Thanks, Mom." Lainey hugged me. Her happiness was contagious.

"Too bad you didn't mention the apartment before Uncle Dickie drove off with all the dressers," I said.

She leaned into Paul, wrapped her arm around him, and gave me a sheepish grin. "You know what I'd really like to have instead?"

"Just name it."

"My grandfather's steamer trunk. It'll make a perfect dresser."

I looked over at the big trunk standing open where Lainey had left it. I asked, "With or without the golf clubs?"

"Without the golf clubs, but with the box of pictures."

I picked up the box of photos from the floor and pulled out the one that had captured Lainey's interest earlier, my parents together, young and in love. I showed it to her. "May I keep this one?"

"They all belong to you, Mom."

"I only want this one. I think it's time to make space for Dad on the family room wall."

Lainey looked a little suspicious. "You planning a rogue-husband gallery?"

"Not at all. I think I'll take down the portrait of your dad and send it to you. Maybe you can save a little space on the side of the table for him. And maybe some room for a little picture of your mother, too?"

"Like chaperones," she said, chuckling. "What are you going to do with the rest of the stuff in the trunk?"

"Take it home with me." What I was thinking made me feel a little bit guilty, certainly disloyal to my mother's wishes, but also stronger. I took

out my father's pipe rack and sniffed it, found
some remnant of the scent that had been his. "It's
time for a few things to be brought back out into
the open where they belong."

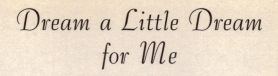

Dream a Little Dream for Me

Diana Gabaldon and Laura J. Watkins

Photo by Douglas Watkins

INTRODUCTION

All my early stories were collaborations. My sister and I shared a bedroom until I was fourteen or so, and we stayed up late almost every night, telling long, continuing, interactive stories, each with a cast of dozens, at least. Since I got my own bedroom, though, it's been a solo act.

Consequently, I wasn't quite sure how to go about this project of collaboration with my older daughter (Laura, age fifteen). I have collaborated on written projects with my husband, but those were all strictly nonfiction—computer manuals, software documentation, etc. I've never collaborated with anyone on writing fiction before. How do you go about writing a story together?

What we did was essentially the result of bad timing; owing to one thing and another—like book tours—we began work with two weeks to write the story, and for one of those weeks, I was due to be on yet another book tour, this time in the UK. Where to begin? How to go on?

The starting point was provided for us, courtesy of my younger daughter, Jennifer. On a spring trip to the Museum of Modern Art in New York City, Jenny showed an amazing facility at interpreting works of art that the rest of us (Philistines that we are) were merely inclined to squint dubiously at, muttering things like, "If that's art, I'm a baked potato." One particular piece featured a pillow and quilt, mounted on the wall as though part of a turned-down bed, lavishly splotched with paint.

"Those are the dreams of the people who've slept in that bed," Jenny explained, after her brother, Samuel, expressed a strong disinclination to sleep in a bed covered with miscellaneous unidentified substances (well, okay, "It looks like somebody's head exploded," is what he actually said. Sam's thirteen). "The dreams sink into the pillow, and then when someone new sleeps there, the dreams get into their head."

The notion of a pillow that came complete with built-in dreams struck me as a good one (people are always asking writers, "Where do you get your ideas?" The answer is "Everywhere." If you're lucky, you can steal them from your kids), and so when Laura and I began the story, that's what we started with.

We sat down together and brainstormed for half an hour. Who was this story about? What was her name? What happened in the beginning? What happened next? Laura thought there should be a cat in the story, and fortunately we had a model at hand—one Martin Van Tiltsnoot, Laura's personal feline.

With a rough idea of who and what, I sat down and sketched in the beginning of the story. Whenever I came to a bit of description, I left a pair of empty square brackets. I did a page or so, then quickly outlined the rest of the story, ran downstairs to throw my clothes in a bag, and charged off to the airport, leaving Laura with a handful of pages and the fax numbers of hotels from London to Edinburgh.

Laura filled in as much of the sketch as she could, and

upon my return, I typed in her contributions, we had a
final consultation on the shape of the denouement (that's
why there's a cat in it), and I spent the next day writing
in the last missing pieces. A final run-through by Laura,
for comment and emendations, and it was done.

I showed the final draft to Jenny (age eleven), who
read it solemnly, then handed it back. "That's pretty
good," she said. "It even made me smile in a couple of
places." What more could a storyteller ask?

It wasn't at all what she'd been expecting. Of
course, she wasn't sure what she *had* been expecting. "Inheritance" was one of those words
that made you think of heirloom jewelry and designer clothes and yacht cruises to the Caribbean.
Not *this*.

She wrinkled her nose, peering into the large
cardboard box. It was filled to overflowing with a
huge, puffy pillow. A pillow covered in soft black
velvet, with . . . things . . . embroidered all down
the sides and round the corners, in a riot of multi-
colored silk threads. What sort of things? Squint as
she might, she couldn't really tell. The embroidery
looked vaguely Russian, or maybe Celtic, with
lots of curlicues and loops feeding back on themselves, and millions of little sprouts that turned
into animals or flowers, or . . . just . . . well, just
things.

A faint scent of lavender drifted up from the pillow, mingled with peppermint, and something
sweetly musky—marjoram? It smelled like she
imagined dreams would—if dreams smelled.

She laughed at the thought of smelly dreams and looked again at the neat lawyer's letter that had accompanied the box. Yes, that was what it said, all right: This box contained her inheritance from her great-aunt, Natalia MacManaman Krenski. It was Mrs. Krenski's wish that her great-niece should derive great benefit from regular use of the bequest.

Rosalie sneezed three times. Great benefit. Great allergies, probably. No, she hadn't expected an inheritance at all, but if she had, it wouldn't have been a moth-eaten pillow, no matter how fancy.

Granted, Great-aunt Natalia hadn't been exactly wealthy. Rosalie had the dimmest of memories of the old lady, no more than a large, white-haired presence, spangled with antique jewelry, with a strong smell of stale tea and old-lady perfume. Her memories of Great-auntie's house were dimmer still; it hadn't been very big, though, because when she went into the kitchen to help Auntie make tea, she'd still been able to hear her parents hissing at each other in the living room.

Hissing. That brought it back. What she did remember was the cat.

He was enormous, with deep-green slanted eyes and thick black fur. He seemed to take on different shapes, sometimes a velvety chunk of charcoal, or a pool of black oil, or a shadow gliding along a wall. And always in the middle of whatever shape it was were those emerald eyes, watching things that only they could see.

She had followed him in and out of the tiny house, behind the furniture, under the sofa, trying for a closer look at those eyes, and finally, as though tiring of the game, he had sat down in the shadow of a blackberry bush in the front yard, and let her look straight into those glowing emeralds. She got up close, close enough to smell the heat and dust in his fur, the perfume of the small white flowers above their heads, and tried to look deep enough to see what the emerald eyes saw. She thought she saw the rise and fall of nations and empires. Faces appeared; no one she knew, but faces that seemed familiar nonetheless. Wars raged and discoveries were made. Great structures rose, lived, and crumbled away.

Through it all, she felt no fear, only serenity and an intangible feeling of power as she slid through green liquid, warm and embracing as a tropical sea. Then someone was shaking her, and her father was saying, "Rosie, sweetie, it's time to go."

She felt that she'd already been gone—and come back from an unimaginable distance, not knowing what she might have done. The cat was gone from his place in the shadows, but as she walked to the car, she felt the green eyes still watching her.

Great-aunt Natalia was one of her father's distant relations; they had found themselves near the small town in which she lived and stopped from some sense of duty. Rosalie was only seven at the time, but she had no trouble deducing from her mother's attitude that they weren't likely to find themselves passing that way again anytime soon.

"And that *disgusting* cad," her mother had said, sneezing and dabbing at her nose as they drove away. Her mother was terribly allergic to cats. "Lettig it sid on the table where people are *eadig*! It probably licks the spoods!"

Rosalie grinned. The black cat probably had; Phoebe did, unless she was careful to wash the spoons and put them away immediately.

Now she felt a presence at her elbow and reached back to rub the inquiring ears.

"Hi, Feeb," she said. "Practicing mental telepathy today, are we?"

The white cat rubbed up against her shoulder, blue eyes nearly shut, purring madly. She'd always wanted a cat—even before that visit to Great-aunt Natalia's? she wondered suddenly—but her mother's allergies had prevented it. "Please," Rosalie had begged. "It will live in my room and I'll feed it and its name will be Phoebe." But neither begging, coaxing, nor whining had had any result. "Kerchoo!" her mother said, and that was the end of that.

Rosalie smiled, remembering. When she had gotten her own apartment, she had gone to the pound to adopt a cat. As soon as she saw the white cat, she loved it. It was crouched on a box in the cat room, dirty, scruffy, and lord of all it surveyed. It was a male cat, but no matter; Phoebe was a nice name. Besides, she'd thought of her phantom cat as Phoebe for so long, she couldn't think of another name that pleased her.

Still purring, Phoebe leaped into the box, his paws sinking into the pillow's fluffy surface. He began kneading energetically, then turned around three times and curled up in a ball of somnolence.

Rosalie lifted a hand to shoo him off, but then thought better of it.

"Let sleeping Phoebes lie," she murmured. She glanced at her watch, realizing that she was already late, distracted by the arrival of her—ha!—inheritance. She snatched her coat from the rack, not bothering with anything else. She could comb her hair on the subway.

She was due to pick up a new job this afternoon, the manuscript of the latest book by Berenice LeGros. A freelance copy editor, Rosalie had never worked on a book by Ms. LeGros before, but she had heard that the famous author was given to larding her books with misspelled foreign phrases, gruesome medical procedures, and obscure historical details. Oh, well, she was getting paid by the page, and she could definitely use the money. Now, why Great-aunt Natalia couldn't have left her a few million dollars, instead of a ratty old pillow . . .

She glanced once more at the box that held her inheritance, shrugged, and left it on the table. Phoebe rumbled complacently, as if the pillow was stuffed with catnip. Maybe that was what accounted for the smell.

Her hair was a pale blond, the same silky texture as embroidery floss. Unfortunately, it was just as hard to handle, forming French knots all on its own. She tugged grimly at the tangles, swaying back and forth with the rocking of the train. Another tooth of the ancient comb gave up the struggle and popped out, the clatter of its fall lost in the whoosh as the train entered a tunnel. Rosalie gave up and dropped the ragged comb back in her purse. She'd meant to buy a new one, but it came down to a choice of a new comb or a bag of cat kibble for Phoebe—and that was no choice at all.

If not a million dollars, why couldn't Great-aunt Natalia have left her some of her jewelry? That must have been worth something!

"Why doesn't she sell some of that terrible baroque jewelry and move to one of those nice apartments for seniors?" her mother had demanded, coughing and sneezing into a handful of Kleenex. "Turd up there, dear; Highway Sixteed is the one you want."

Her father, squinting at road signs, had muttered something about Great-aunt Natalia probably not fitting in very well at your average rest home, then promptly taken the wrong turnoff. By the time they had disentangled themselves from the wilds of Weehunkus and got back on the proper road, Great-aunt Natalia and her foibles were long forgotten.

Now that she thought back, Rosalie did remember the jewelry, though she hadn't taken much notice at the time. It wasn't your usual old-lady-out-of-style-since-mastodons-walked-the-earth jewelry. It might not have appealed to her mother, but with the hindsight of college classes in art appreciation, Rosalie recognized it was a master's work—golden fountains still molten-looking, stones with odd but beautiful settings, and delicate silver scrolls embracing nests of pearls.

One piece in particular stuck in her memory. It was more a collar than a necklace, made of hinged plates, each with a different color of jewel set in the center. Not baroque, not that one. It belonged on a panther in an Egyptian pharaoh's court. Auntie hadn't worn it but had kept it in a golden box covered with inscrutable carvings—Rosalie had found it, snooping to and fro in boredom while the grown-ups talked. The black cat had sat on it, the Sphinx guarding ancient treasure. She wondered who Great-aunt Natalia had left *that* to; so far as she remembered her father saying, he—and she, of course—were the old lady's only living relatives.

And now only her. She sighed, thinking of her father. He hadn't left her much beyond his love of words and his complete lack of patience for people who couldn't spell. She was usually inclined to view these as priceless gifts—except when the rent was due, which it was this week.

Ribblemore, Knowlton, and Bent was one of the medium-sized publishing houses that hadn't yet been gobbled up by a multinational conglomerate. It occupied the top three floors of a shabby building off Times Square, sharing it with a newspaper office, a widget manufacturer, and twenty-three law offices. Normally, Rosalie enjoyed working for RKB; the managing editor was normally nice, if harried, and they paid decently. Since the last job, though, she'd been a lot more hesitant about entering the RKB building.

The reason for her reluctance was the new editorial director, Marjorie Wilton-Thomas. Marj DeFarge, the junior editors called her behind her back; those not directly in her power called her Marj the Large. Ms. Wilton-Thomas was tall, heavyset, designer-dressed, and positive that she was right, about everything. If anyone crossed her in this supposition—heads would roll.

Rosalie got off the elevator at Editorial, on the eleventh floor, and peered cautiously up and down the narrow lobby. She could see Marj DeFarge's door, just beyond the receptionist's area, but it was safely closed. With a sigh of relief, she pushed open the door and announced herself.

The manuscript was waiting, thank goodness. Gratifyingly fat, for someone getting paid by the page; it barely fit the confines of the manila envelope.

"Rosie?" said a voice behind her, high with surprise. She swung around, half expecting to find that Marj the Large had crept up on her after all, but instead was surprised to see Annabelle Preston—the next worst thing.

"Hi, Annabelle," she said with a weak smile. "Fancy meeting you here! I thought you were with Verbatron these days." Safely out of Rosalie's orbit, that was. Verbatron handled nothing but high-tech nonfiction—stuff requiring a technical copy editor, which Rosalie wasn't.

"Oh, I decided to come back to the world of Lit-ra-choor," Annabelle said gaily, waving a manicured hand in a graceful arc. "All that Internet stuff . . . BORinggggg! And what about you? Is this the magnum opus, at last?" She poked playfully at the envelope.

"No," Rosalie said, between clenched teeth. She'd been at college with Annabelle and had once made the mistake of confiding her dreams of being a writer.

"Oh? Well, do be sure to send me a synopsis—if you ever have one."

"A synopsis of what?"

A hot flush spread over Rosalie's cheeks as the new voice spoke behind her. Ms. Wilton-Thomas, picking the worst possible moment to emerge from her lair.

"Rosie's an aspiring novelist," Annabelle was explaining, with a trill of musical laughter that made "aspiring novelist" sound slightly less worthy than "aspiring sewage processor."

"Really?" Madame DeFarge frowned, what was left of her plucked brows drawing together in a circumflex of disapproval. "I thought Josie told me she was hiring you to do the copyedit on the new LeGros book."

"She is. I am. I mean—this is it." Rosalie clutched the envelope to her chest, as though it might serve as a shield. POSSESS ME, SWEET DEMON was written on it, in bold black letters.

"We *never* hire writers as copy editors," Marj said, lifting one brow at Annabelle, as though she were responsible for this breach of policy. "They always think they can write, and they go changing things in the manuscripts and annoying the authors."

"I'd never do that," Rosalie assured her, edging toward the door. "Never. I just . . . you know . . . the grammar . . . the punctuation . . ." If they took this project away from her, she'd have no income at all this month; she'd have to go back to waiting tables, coming home so tired she could barely write a few paragraphs before tumbling into bed. She edged toward the elevator, still babbling,

". . . house style . . . continuity . . . utmost respect for the author's words . . ."

"Hmmm," Marj said, looking dubious. But the gods smiled. The phone rang and the receptionist leaned over and murmured to Marj, who turned away, distracted.

"Byeeee!" trilled Annabelle, waving. "Good luck with the writing! Remember to send me a sample chapter if you ever finish anything!"

Feeling mangled, Rosalie stepped into the elevator, manuscript clutched to her chest. She stood fuming, wondering what sort of character defect it was that kept her from telling Annabelle Preston to go jump in the lake.

She closed her eyes and tried to do the yoga breathing that her best friend advised for stress. In to the count of four, out to the count of two, in for . . . she opened her eyes, wondering where the fragrance she had just smelled was coming from. It wasn't perfume, exactly. No, something quiet, musky and . . . er . . . very attractive. She swallowed, eyes fixed on the back of the man in front of her. It had to be coming from him; the only other people in the elevator were a couple of middle-aged ladies drenched, respectively, in Opium and Cinnabar. It was a wonder she could smell anything at all in the face of such competition, but she could.

He was wearing an old-but-good tweed coat with suede patches at the elbows, and his hair was just a little bit too long, curling dark and thick over his collar in the back. She would have liked to ask him what the name of his aftershave was, but she was much too shy to accost strange men in elevators.

She drew one last wistful lungful of his scent, and then the doors opened. He stepped out at once, to make room for the others, and she stood a moment, entranced by the way he moved—very graceful for such a tall man. Then a blast of Opium nearly knocked her down—physically—as the woman barged past her, knocking the manuscript out of her arms.

The flimsy envelope exploded on impact, and sheaves of Ms. LeGros's latest work of genius scattered all over the elevator floor.

"Oops!" said the Cinnabar-wearer, as she stepped delicately through the mess, leaving spike-heeled prints on several of the pages.

That pillow had been a bad omen, Rosalie reflected grimly, fighting her way up a crowded street hours later. First the rent, then her comb, then Annabelle. Then the ghastly women with no sense of smell in the elevator. And finally, the subway ride from hell: her train had suffered a power failure and they'd been trapped in a tunnel for more than two hours, giving a street performer dressed in a cowboy hat and sequined boxer shorts—and nothing else—ample opportunity to sing his entire repertoire, which consisted of "Home on the Range" and the first verse of "The Streets of Laredo," personally for every single person in the car. This had stretched everyone's nerves to the snapping point, and a fistfight had broken out between a Guardian Angel and a three-hundred-pound woman with a run in her queen-size pantyhose, who claimed he had been looking at her legs. The woman won the fight, sitting on her opponent and nearly crushing him to death, but was luckily persuaded to get off him before asphyxiation set in.

It was nearly nine o'clock by the time Rosalie reached home. The elevator, naturally, was out of order. Rosalie climbed—crawled, really—the twenty-two flights to her floor, thinking longingly of a cool shower, a light dinner, and bed. POSSESS ME, SWEET DEMON could wait until tomorrow.

The shower was cool, all right; the hot water was out again. Shivering, Rosalie wrapped herself in her terry-cloth dressing gown, wrapped her hair in a towel, and went into the tiny kitchen, where she discovered that dinner would be even lighter than she'd thought. Phoebe had pried open the tiny refrigerator and taken ruthless advantage of the slice of fish she'd been planning to broil.

"Bad cat," Rosalie muttered tiredly, getting out the peanut butter. After her meager meal, she dragged herself into the bedroom, wanting nothing but bed. Phoebe followed, full of fish and very pleased with himself.

"*Bad* cat!" Rosalie said, with a lot more vigor. Phoebe had done something unspeakable, right in the middle of her pillow. She swung around in accusation, to see Phoebe sitting in the doorway, a great big smirk of accomplishment on his face. A bad cat was bad enough; a smug cat was just too much!

"Dis*GUST*ing feline!" Rosalie yelled, heaving one of her teddy bears at him. Phoebe fled precipitately, and Rosalie followed. "Disciple of foulness!

You disgrace to the name of cat!" she cried, flinging her desecrated pillow after him. She chased him around the room as he bounded from sofa to coffee table like an incontinent mountain goat.

"Dismal creature," she panted, glomming him off the curtains up which he was trying to make his escape. "Disloyal fiend." Having thoroughly dissed her erstwhile companion, she exiled him to the bathroom and went back to survey the damage.

"Ick," she muttered, picking up her sodden pillow. She dropped it gingerly on the floor and stood rubbing her aching head. Sleeping without a pillow gave her a stiff neck. Well, perhaps Great-aunt Natalia's bequest would come in handy after all.

She plucked the velvet pillow out of the box and dusted it gingerly, checking for mites, bedbugs, or other hitchhikers. Nothing rose from it except another waft of an herbal fragrance. *Mm,* she thought, holding the pillow closer to her face. It smelled a little bit like that man on the elevator. Now, if she could just arrange to dream about *him.* . . .

A loud "MRRRRRROWWWW" echoed from the bathroom. Rosalie pounded the velvet pillow, wondering hopefully for a moment whether Great-aunt Natalia might have hidden her jewelry in it, but no promising lumps appeared. She pulled the covers up to her chin and sank back into the velvet pillow, letting its softness rise up over both ears.

"Horrible hairball," she muttered, and peacefully went to sleep.

She woke in the morning, refreshed in body but groggy in mind. She had dreamed all night, but not about Mr. Aftershave.

"Hi, Feeb," she said, letting him out of his prison. "You'll never *guess* what I dreamed last night!"

Phoebe, hungry after his incarceration, wasn't all that interested, but he kept his ears half-pricked while he gnawed his kibble, at least pretending to listen.

". . . so then all the bright-colored fish turned into M&Ms and started dropping down onto the sea bottom," Rosalie said, between bites of her Cocoa Puffs. One ear rose; Phoebe loved M&Ms.

"Only then the M&Ms turned into jewels, Feeb—all kinds of jewels!" The ear went down. If he couldn't eat it, Phoebe didn't want to hear about it. Rosalie slurped a spoonful of her cereal, only mildly disturbed to realize that it sounded just like the noise Phoebe was making with his kibble.

"Okay, okay. Well, anyway, the next thing I remember is another dream that was even better. I wasn't in this one, but it was great." She put down the spoon, licking milk from the corners of her mouth as she grinned at the memory. "Marj De-Farge and Annabelle the Ass-kisser were in an elevator with this man. He had a *huge* pile of ratty-looking pages in his arms and was begging them to publish his three-thousand-page fantasy epic. They were just giving him the cold shoulder, but then all of a sudden, he whipped an elevator key out of his pocket and turned off the power and told them he was holding them hostage until they promised to give him a contract." Rosalie laughed so hard at her memory of Annabelle's face that small Cocoa Puff crumbs flew across the table. "I even remember what it was called—'Revenge of the Cyber-Mammoths.' Heeheehee!" Phoebe looked bored.

Rosalie washed and put away the breakfast things, feeling cheerful, wide awake, and invincible—ready, in other words, to tackle POSSESS ME, SWEET DEMON.

She shoveled Feeb, who was busy doing his melted-marshmallow impression, out of the way, got the stack of manuscript, a packet of yellow sticky notes, and two red pens from her tote bag, then sat down to do her deep breathing and to recite her pre-work mantra: "Even if I can write a thousand times better than this, this is not my book. Even if I can write a thousand times better than this, this is not my book. Even if . . ."

The spirit of high-minded detachment induced by this exercise lasted for about the first thirty pages, to be succeeded by a tight-lipped grimness, which in turn faded into muttering and hair-pulling.

"Good grief, you idiot, if you don't know what *faute de mieux* means, don't use it! You nincompoop, who taught you to spell? Oh, for goodness' sake, I'm sure they didn't have land mines in 1752! Or did they?" She squinted dubiously at the page, then, with a deep sigh, inserted a sticky note and made a separate, non-sticky note to check the history of land mines at the library on tomorrow's research trip.

"How much do you figure they're paying her for this tripe?" Rosalie demanded, pausing in the midst of a sex scene she had been reading aloud for Phoebe's benefit. "Just listen to this! 'Slowly his virile member inched its throbbing way upward, the ruby-crowned head expanding'—no, forget it, you don't want to know what he did with it. You'd think it was a cobra being snake-charmed, not part of somebody's anatomy." She took a deep breath in through her nose. "EvenifIcanwriteathousand timesbetterthanthisthisisnotmybookEvenifIcanwrite athousandtimesbetterthanthis . . ."

In spite of the horrible prose, Rosalie found herself succumbing to fascination at what was happening in the story. At this stage she was mostly just reading, tagging only the most hideous errors. After she'd read the whole thing, she would go back and begin the tedious word- by-word corrections. The hero and heroine, after an initial showdown with the villain, were escaping down the Seine in a fishing boat filled with heaps of freshly caught squid (sticky note: "Are squid found in the Seine?"). The villain's boat filled with muscular thugs, was drawing closer, propelled by brawny oarsmen. The sails above the squid fluttered limply; the wind was dying. The hero was breathing enticingly down the heroine's cleavage.

Rosalie flipped the page, eager to find out what happened next. ". . . she stretched languorously on her couch of embroidered brocade and reached for another bonbon . . ."

"What?!" Rosalie exclaimed. "What about the squid? What about her titillating breasts?" She shuffled rapidly through the mass of pages, but it was true: Pages 143–189 were missing altogether.

Muttering under her breath, Rosalie phoned the publisher. She got Josie, the managing editor, who sounded much too cheerful for anyone with her job.

"Did you hear?" Josie scarcely waited for Rosalie's explanation before bursting into laughter. "Annabelle and Marj the Large got taken hostage in an elevator this morning!"

"No!" said Rosalie, clutching the phone tighter to her ear.

"Oh, yes!" Josie paused to slurp coffee. "Some crazed wannabe writer—said he wouldn't let them go until they promised to publish this huge manuscript he had. They were stuck in there for three hours! Security finally pried a panel off the roof and got somebody in to rescue them." Gurgling sounds came through the receiver, indicative of someone snorting coffee through the nose.

Rosalie felt a trifle light-headed.

"Don't tell me," she said. "The manuscript was called 'Revenge of the Cyber-Mammoths.' "

"How'd you know?" Josie asked, sounding mildly hurt. "Did you already hear this story?"

Rosalie asked for her missing pages, hung up as politely as she could, and returned to the table, feeling distinctly odd. It took some time before she was able to settle down to work again; she kept turning around to look at the pillow on her bed, as though the embroidered images might somehow have come to life behind her back.

Come bedtime, Rosalie was of two minds about whether to use the velvet pillow again. Still, it had given her the most comfortable—as well as the most entertaining—night's sleep she'd had in quite a while.

"Well, why not?" she said to Phoebe, pulling

her nightie over her head. "What harm can it do, after all?" Phoebe seemed to agree; in spite of her attempts to discourage him, he curled up next to her head, insisting on sharing the pillow and shedding vast quantities of white hair on the black velvet.

It was undoubtedly Phoebe's presence that made her dream about the white tiger, Rosalie thought, regarding herself in the mirror as she brushed her teeth the next morning. All that purring in her ear was bound to have some effect on her subconscious.

The tiger had escaped from somewhere; she'd seen the key, glinting as it turned in the lock of the cage door. The beautiful big cat had slipped free and, wearing a jeweled collar, strode through a great crowd of people, all of them screaming and shoving each other to get out of the way—though the tiger showed no interest in them, merely disappearing into the bushes like a scoop of ice cream melting.

It was the most beautiful thing Rosalie had ever seen. Half her mind was still on the dream when the phone rang. The other half was on her work, and between those twin preoccupations, she failed to recognize the danger in time and found herself weakly agreeing to meet Jasper Betancourt for a drink after work.

Jasper was what passed for her love life, if that was the appropriate term to use for a relationship in which the party of the first part could barely stand to talk to the party of the second part. However, the party of the second part was much too busy talking about himself to notice Rosalie's silence—or to take no for an answer when he called.

". . . so I told him it's tort law, we don't do torts, but he said he couldn't . . ."

"Uh-huh," said Rosalie, not listening. They were strolling up Fifth Avenue; at least she had the crowds and the windows to distract her from Jasper's endless rehashing of the day's events—or nonevents—in the law offices of Nibbs, Yodelberry, and Froodman. She'd bought them snow cones, in hopes that the ice would freeze his tongue, but no such luck.

". . . did a contract for *ten* million, but with a graduated payout, so . . ."

"Uh-huh," said Rosalie, still not listening, but for a different reason. She stopped suddenly, hardly able to breathe.

"What?" Jasper demanded, belatedly noticing that she wasn't walking. She couldn't speak; she only nodded toward the park. Jasper turned to see and dropped his red snow cone down the front of his pants.

It was just as she'd seen it in her dream; a huge, magnificent thing, all cream and snow and white velvet, gliding soundlessly through the concrete canyons of the city. All around her, people were screeching, shoving, cramming into the opulent storefronts to get away. Tossed by the crowd like a pebble in the surf, Rosalie made no effort to move. The tiger came nearer, and nearer still, and soon all she could see were the jeweled eyes, shining into hers.

It passed her, close enough that she felt the brush of soft fur against her hand, and then it was gone, a shimmer of white as it crossed the street and took the steps of a small plaza in a single bound. Rosalie began to laugh, with more than a touch of hysteria.

"What? What is it? Why are you laughing?" Jasper demanded. Having fought his way hero-ically back to her side, he was miffed to have her pay no attention to his feat.

"Look where it's gone," Rosalie gasped, point-ing. "They'll never find it in there!" The tiger had bounded into F.A.O. Schwartz, home of the most abundant, most expensive stuffed toys in the world—many of them life-size.

"Well, what do you think, Feeb?" Having—with some difficulty—persuaded Jasper that she really wasn't so traumatized by the afternoon's adventure that she needed company for the night, Rosalie turned back the covers of her chaste bed and regarded the velvet pillow with a mixture of trepidation and anticipation. "Shall we risk it again?" *As though there's a choice,* she thought. Cu-riosity alone would be enough, without Great-aunt Natalia's instructions—"Mrs. Krenski trusts that her great-niece will derive great benefit from regular use of her bequest."

"Great benefit," she told him. "Maybe I'll dream of money tonight—and find it in the street tomor-row!" She'd better find some somewhere; the rent was due tomorrow.

Phoebe didn't look up from his task of dismem-bering a large roach—his only socially useful ac-complishment. Still, when she lay down to sleep, the cat leaped onto the bed to join her, and she drifted off to sleep to the rhythmic sound of Phoebe sucking his soft pink toes.

She might have dreamed through the night. The only dream she remembered came just before dawn, frightening her out of sleep. She lay in bed, drenched in sweat, staring around at the objects in her apartment, rendered unfamiliar by the gray light, threatening in the shadow of the dream.

Unlike the others, which had been sharp and vivid, this dream had been shapeless—a drift of menacing darkness, shot through with flickers of red that sent tingles of dread down her spine. She had dreamed of money, but it hadn't been a good dream; she knew that much. She had felt something dangerous, along with a crushing sense of responsibility. She had to do something—but what?

She got up, staggered to the bathroom, and splashed cold water on her face. That made her feel a little better. It was only five in the morning, too early to get up. Perhaps she should try to go back to sleep. If she dreamed again, she might get a clue to what it was that was going to happen, what it was that she had to do.

The thought of the darkness she'd seen made her shiver, but Phoebe was there, sprawled comfortably across half the pillow, looking as though he'd never heard the word "nightmare." Reassured by his warm presence, she lay down and, after what seemed a long time, fell asleep again just as the sky began to lighten in the east.

The second dream seemed to have nothing at all to do with the first. She dreamed of the black cat—Great-aunt Natalia's cat, wearing the jeweled collar. He was playing with a small object, batting it to and fro on a black-and-white-tiled floor. A cockroach? No, it was shiny, and made a musical clinking noise when it struck a piece of furniture.

The cat came to rub against her ankles, and she bent to pick up the shiny object. It was a key, a small silver key. The cat looked up with its emerald eyes, and she felt a sense of peace come over her, as she breathed the scent of blackberries. She drifted into wakefulness, sunlight flooding the room and Phoebe's self-satisfied rumble in her ear.

She dressed slowly, wondering what to do. First things first, she supposed. It was rent day, she would have to go to the bank and withdraw some money from her dwindling savings account. Then a stop at RKB to pick up the missing pages of the LeGros manuscript—she did want to find out whether those two sex fiends really did it down in the hold with the squid—and then a stop for such essentials of life as Diet Coke and kitty litter. Then—

"What are you doing? Stop that! Bad cat!" She slapped at Phoebe, who had been gnawing the corner of the velvet pillow. Incensed, she snatched the pillow and brought it down on Feeb with a resounding *whap!* Phoebe flew across the room in one direction; something shot out of the pillow and flew in the other, landing on the floor with a metallic *ping*.

The hair prickled on Rosalie's neck as she bent to pick up the key. It was small and silver and bore the words, "First Metropolitan Bank—No. 310" across its head. The key to a safe-deposit box.

Rosalie swallowed, excitement dampening her hands. So there was more to Great-aunt Natalia's bequest than she'd thought! For the first time, she realized that there had been a key in all her dreams—this key. And jewels—all her dreams had been full of jewels; the fish who turned to candy, then to gems; the tiger with the jeweled collar; the black cat with his pharaoh's collar and his emerald eyes—yes, it had to be, it had to!

She slipped the key into her pocket, then quickly ran around the apartment, collecting everything for her run of errands. No sign of Phoebe; he must be hiding under the sofa, in a huff over being biffed with the pillow. She didn't take time to coax him out; let him get over it on his own. She picked up the heavy tote bag by the door, and slinging it over her shoulder, set out to find her fortune.

First Metropolitan was right next door to the building where RKB had its offices; that had to be a good sign, she thought. She hesitated on the corner, debating whether to pick up the manuscript first, prolonging the anticipation, or go directly into the bank. Her shoulder bag suddenly twitched, and she dropped it with a yelp. Phoebe, rudely startled, leaped out of the bag and took off down the street like a scalded cat.

"Phoebe! Phoebe, come back!" Jewelry, danger, and dreams forgotten, Rosalie ran after him, her heart in her throat. A flash of white and the screech of brakes as he ran across the street; another as he darted back, scared by the traffic.

"Phoebe! Phoebe! Stop!" Half-sobbing, Rosalie ran as fast as she could, pushing through the morning crowds on Forty-Second Street. She tripped over the sleeping bag of a homeless person sprawled on the sidewalk, stumbled, and half fell.

Looking up, she saw Phoebe racing like a streak of white lightning down the street. Then she glimpsed the glint of a revolving door and saw a man charging out of a building, his heavy foot landing directly on the fleeing cat. There was a heartrending yowl, a startled yell, and the sudden ringing of alarms.

As though in a dream, Phoebe saw the man turn, the gun in his hand, and she knew quite suddenly exactly what to do. She swung the heavy bag off her shoulder and with great calmness let it go. It seemed to travel through the air slowly, like a pebble dropped in molasses. She could follow every inch of its flight, just as she saw every movement of the man's body, arm drawn back, finger tightening on the trigger of the gun. Then the bag struck him full in the head, and he dropped to the pavement in a shower of books, red pens, and sticky notes.

"I expect the reward will keep your friend in tuna for quite a while." The young man smiled down at her, clicking his pen in and out. He wore the same old-but-good tweed jacket; journalists didn't have big wardrobes. He'd had his hair cut, though. The ends were feathered above his ears, thick and soft, black and shiny as a healthy cat's fur.

"I guess it will." She clutched Phoebe on her lap, preventing his efforts to escape and take advantage of the handfuls of M&Ms the bank people kept offering him.

"You live some way uptown," he said, consulting his notebook in case he'd missed anything. "What brought you downtown today?"

She took a deep breath, reminded of her purpose, and felt in her pocket. Yes, the key was still there.

"Well, that's quite a story," she said. "Do you have time to listen?"

"All the time in the world," he assured her, smiling. His eyes were green and faintly slanted. "Can I buy you a cup of coffee while you talk?"

"Sure," she said, smiling back. The key was warm in her fingers. "But first I need to check something. Why don't you come with me? If it's what I think it is, this may be a *really* interesting story!"

He brushed close against her as they walked toward the bank's safe-deposit vault, and she looked up at him.

"Er . . ." she said, suddenly shy, "that aftershave you wear . . . it's very nice. What kind is it?"

He glanced at her, surprised, then smiled. The sun from the high windows caught his eyes and made them glow.

"Not aftershave," he said. "It's handmade soap; my sister makes it." He lifted a hand and sniffed the back. "Yeah, I thought so. It's—"

"Blackberry," she said. "I thought so."

Charlie's Grave

Elizabeth Engstrom and
Nicole Engstrom Fourmyle

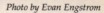

Photo by Evan Engstrom

INTRODUCTION

Thanksgiving dinner. I've retired from cooking it and Nicole is too busy. Her father was out of town and her brother in the army, so it was just the two of us with her two boys, aged three and five, at a nice restaurant with her father's credit card.

"The mother-daughter story," I started to say, and then Luke spilled his milk. The waiter came, and Joey wanted nothing but a grilled cheese sandwich, which this particular restaurant wasn't offering on Thanksgiving, and Joey wouldn't have anything else.

"Unconventional adoption?" Nicole offered when the chicken strips arrived for appetizers and the kids got quiet.

"Yeah, that kind of hits home, doesn't it?" I answered. I had adopted Nicole and her brother many years before. "What if—"

Joey spilled his hot chocolate and wanted his grilled cheese sandwich now. I gave him crayons and paper instead.

"Think there should be a ghost in it?" she asked.

"An unconventional ghost? We could try, although . . ."

The food came. The boys, full of chicken, began to fidget, then fight. Then they slid under the table, crawled

*out, and began staring at the other restaurant patrons.
We asked for doggie bags and hugged in the parking lot.
So much for Thanksgiving dinner on the town.*

*I'm so proud of her, you know, and my love for her is
so acute it sometimes hurts, but our lifestyles are aeons
apart. Sometimes there's no understanding, just an
aching. As there is between my mother and me.*

*But we keep trying. And occasionally we break
through. Sometimes understanding comes with a meal,
sometimes with a fly-by kiss, sometimes with a short
story collaboration.*

The note said simply, "Charlie died and your
dad had a stroke burying him. Come home."
Laura assumed that the Reverend Morganstern
had written the note and addressed the envelope,
per her mother's request. It wasn't her mother's
handwriting; her mother had no handwriting. And
her mother would insist that the reverend not em-
bellish the message at all, either. There were no
embellishments, not even a signature. There were
certainly no sentiments.

Laura canceled her appointments for the next
three days and had her secretary book a flight and
a rental car.

Finally, it was time to go home.

In a way, she was sad that she had waited so
long she wouldn't be seeing her dad, or so she assumed. But then, she had never expected to see either of her parents again. She had never wanted
to. And she didn't want to now, but she couldn't
ignore this summons.

She had never expected that her mother would need her.

She only hoped her mother didn't need her too much. Laura had a busy, full life, and while she wasn't proud of the thoughts she had about her illiterate, dirt-poor parents and their lifestyle, she wasn't about to compromise her hard-won financial independence and freedom.

Every Christmas, Laura tucked a couple of hundred-dollar bills into her Christmas card to them, and she assumed the money was received, though it was never acknowledged. They had had no other communication since Laura had moved away to go to college on a merit scholarship more than twenty years before. Her books were her life. She got straight As all the way through college, cementing her grants and loans and scholarships, studying summers and during term breaks. She worked part time in various medical laboratories, gaining important research experience as well as extra credit. She taught basic biology while getting her graduate degree and, once she was firmly ensconced as a research assistant at one of the larger pharmaceutical companies, wrote her dissertation and acquired her Ph.D.

Nice-looking, soft-spoken, hard-driven, and dedicated, she turned out to be Mymet Laboratory's biggest gun in soliciting research grants.

Her dirt farm heritage was a nasty little secret that she didn't want anyone to discover. She hated owning that attitude, but over the years it had become a habit.

At first she was too busy to go home. School and work kept her nose to the grindstone, and she couldn't get away, couldn't afford to get away to go back.

Then she was too proud. She had nice clothes. She could read and write. She studied the classics in literature classes. She mapped DNA genomes. She was a whiz at math and chemistry. She didn't know what she would talk about with her parents. She didn't want to see them through educated eyes.

Then she was too political. Her high-paid future at Mymet was predicated on her gracious, well-timed ability to extract big bucks from those government agencies with the grants. She also spoke at stockholder meetings, where she impressed not only the board of directors but those who held large blocks of preferred Mymet stock. Most of those people were old-money, conservative, squeaky-clean people, and they wanted those they associated with to have the same pristine background. Or at least the illusion of it. Laura worked hard to feel at home in those circles.

Then, as time and experience funneled wisdom into her head, almost against her will, she was too ashamed of herself to swallow her pride and come back home to the family she had deserted so many years ago.

And now Charlie was dead, her daddy was too, like as not, and her mama needed her. "Time to grow up, Laura," she told herself. "You'll turn forty this year. It's time to reconcile."

She had known her mama would die someday, and her daddy too, but Charlie? Charlie was never supposed to die.

On the plane, Laura made a fearless, realistic

appraisal of her life. She was professionally successful and personally a disaster. She had no mate; she rarely even dated. She owned a nice, professionally decorated apartment that had no soul. She had two good women friends, but distance was necessitated by her fictional history. They were professional colleagues before they were friends, and once she had told them the story of her middle-class upbringing, it had to add up on all fronts.

Laura kept a tight rein on her life. So tight it pinched. It choked her. Laura was afraid that if she eased up in any area—acquiring a boyfriend, getting intimate with girl talk, going on a wild spree of any kind, be it a rummy vacation in the Bahamas or a new hairdo or a trendy wardrobe or a whimsical redecoration of her bedroom—that she would lose the steel bands that held her carefully designed and constructed persona together.

If those bands ever loosened, backwoods dirtwater would leak out of her and pool on her thick-pile beige carpeting, and she would leave a barefoot, pigshit stench wherever she went.

She'd worked too hard to pull herself out of that sty. She refused to be sucked back into it.

But acknowledging her roots didn't mean having to move back into the dirt-floor shack, now, did it?

Her only pair of jeans—expensive designer jeans—were in the weekender valise in the overhead compartment. She had bought a pair of tennis shoes and a couple of light cotton tops that she could throw away when this trip was over. And she had packed a black dress, anticipating her daddy's funeral. She'd see to her mama, and then she'd go back to her high-rise apartment, and then she'd give it all some serious thought.

Who knew what she would actually find, once she got back to West Virginia? Older versions of the same kids she went to school with, she imagined. Working at the dime store and slinging hash at Tiddly's just like their parents did. They'd each have six sickly kids with ringworm and lice, and they'd live in old run-down trailers with rusted car carcasses in the front yards, leggy weeds growing up through their transmissions and out from under their bent-up hoods.

Laura felt sick to her stomach just thinking about it. She opened the in-flight magazine and looked at the upcoming year in fashion.

Enid Bridges heard from Donny Brooks that Enid's daughter had booked a room for three nights in Donny's little bed-and-breakfast in town. Enid couldn't quite imagine that Donny had the guts to rent out her son's old room, add a stack of flapjacks, and call it a bed-and-breakfast, although she guessed that's exactly what Donny offered. A bed. And breakfast. Donny's old house was right next to the post office, so it was in a central location, not way out Highway 38, like Enid and Whip's place.

But Donny wasted no time driving her old Ford on out to tell Enid that Laura was coming, and for that, Enid was grateful, if a bit shamed that the neighbors knew about it before she did. And they knew that Laura wouldn't stay in her own room in her own house. And now, on the morning of the day Laura was supposed to arrive, Enid looked around and didn't know what to do to prepare for her daughter's arrival.

The house was clean, Whip was bathed and fed and now slept peacefully on the sofa, the television giving him comfortable background noise. She'd changed the sheets on the bed Laura wasn't going to use, and put out fresh towels. A chicken stewed on the stove, and Enid had baked a cake the night before.

The chickens took care of their own selves nowadays, and after Charlie died, Enid went down to the police station and asked Mort if he would come take the two horses and four young beeves to auction for her. Mort and his son came by the following Saturday morning and left behind an empty barn and a simpler, emptier life for Enid.

The chores were done, the house was ready, there was nothing for her to do now but wait.

She paced the scrubbed kitchen floor one more time, then looked in on her husband. When he was sleeping, he looked like a normal man. It was only when he was awake and trying to talk, or laugh, or eat, or be normal that she could see the sag to the left side of his face. He tried to be Whip, he tried real hard, but a chunk of him was gone. He'd left a big part of himself up on the knoll, Enid figured.

There was nothing sadder than to see the mortality of one's mate. She'd always hoped she would die first, so as to never have to face life without Whip, but over the years she had grown strong, strong enough to help him through this, strong enough to see the end of their days, strong enough to hope that he died first.

She had become strong enough to endure being abandoned by their only child. Strong enough to insist that Laura come home. And Laura was coming. Today.

Whip needed to see Laura, if only for the last time before he died. And Laura needed to see her daddy. There wasn't anything Enid could do to change Laura's feelings about her family, though she would if she could. Laura had always been a high-spirited girl. And smarter by far than her parents by the time she was old enough for school. By the time she was in high school, she was spending all night, it seemed, at the little library, and she would bring big books home and try to talk about them at the dinner table.

Enid tried, God knows she tried, to talk to her girl, but the things Laura said confounded her and made as much sense as Chinese. Whip used to get mad and throw down his napkin, but Enid knew it wasn't Laura's fault—she was cursed with a big brain and a yearning for knowledge that came from somewhere outside their family traits. Enid was proud of her but afraid that all that book studying would come to no good when it came time to find a husband, raise a family, and cook the daily meat and potatoes. All that knowledge just puts restlessness in the soul. Or so she believed.

But she really didn't know. For all she knew, Laura had married well and had a passel of her own kids.

Except that Enid knew her daughter's heart well enough—or hoped she did—that if Laura had children, she'd want them to meet their grandparents, even if the only book those grandparents owned was the one that kept the bedroom door from slamming.

No, Enid was certain that Laura had never married, had never had a child. Enid felt it was in some way her fault that Laura was born so smart that she'd put her priorities in all the wrong order. It was as if Enid and Whip were supposed to have seven or eight kids, but when the time came, and they were only given the one, that one, that poor Laura, was cursed with the smarts of all seven or eight.

And that made her a misfit. The life of a misfit was never an easy one. Enid prayed every day that with all those smarts of Laura's, she would figure out a way to fit in. Well, they'd see, wouldn't they? Laura was coming home. Today. Enid fingered the worn lace on the edge of her fresh apron and tried not to worry.

Laura pulled into the driveway, scattering chickens. It was exactly the same. The driveway, the barn, the house, everything. Everything was exactly the same. She couldn't believe it.

Then a short, white-haired woman came out the kitchen door, and Laura barely recognized her mother. But the way Enid held on to the screen door so it wouldn't slam, and the way she took tentative steps down the shaky porch stairs, then held her hands clasped in front of her was as familiar and recognizable as the way out to this old farmhouse. Her fingers tugged on a threadbare apron that Laura remembered—an apron that should have become a dust rag twenty years ago.

She got out of the car, and the silence of the country stunned her for a moment. She had to consciously take a breath. The silence was familiar, as if it had been bred into her genes and she'd been fooling herself by living in the city all these years.

"Hi, Mama," she said simply and walked around the back of the car to hug her tiny mother. Enid even smelled the same. Ivory soap and baby powder.

"It's good to have you home," Enid said. "I know your father will be happy to see you."

"Daddy? I thought—"

"It won't be long now," Enid said. "Come see him while you still can."

Laura walked up those same split porch steps, through that same loose screen door, and into that same scrubbed kitchen. It was almost exactly the same—perhaps a little shabbier. The worn black spot in the middle of the kitchen sink had grown, the kitchen curtains were a little thinner from the sun and the regular washings, the wallpaper a little more faded. The linoleum had worn in a path right down to the black mastic. But the Blue Delphi plates were still on the walls and her high school graduation picture was still taped to the ancient refrigerator door.

"Whip?" Enid said and walked through the kitchen into the living room.

Laura heard her mother click off the television. She didn't want to go in there, but she had to, she knew she had to.

"Guess who's come to see you, honey? Can you sit up?"

Laura heard groaning and a couple of low syllables as she imagined her mother readied her father for company. "Come on in," Enid called.

Laura stepped around the corner into her childhood. The living room was exactly the same. Even the same old black-and-white television.

But her father wasn't. Thin and with few strands of white hair left, he sat propped up in the corner of the couch, surrounded by pillows. His pencil legs were covered by a crocheted afghan, and the scarred, workingman's fingers of one hand played the piano in midair.

"Hi, Daddy," Laura said, and his eyes brightened as he recognized her, but his mouth stayed still. She sat on the sofa next to him, and a tear dripped off his lower lid and skidded down his old cheek, lined from the sun and dotted with dark-brown spots.

"F-f-f-goddamn!" he said.

Enid laughed with fondness at him, while Laura looked at him in confusion. "He has a hard time talking," Enid said, "but he can still cuss."

Laura kissed his cheek, and though his father fragrance had turned to an old-man odor, she could still detect sunshine and fertilizer, hay and cow manure. Fresh farm smells. She took his restless hand in hers and kissed it, then held it still in her lap. There were no words for her emotion. There wasn't even any definition to her emotion. She was overwhelmed, and she didn't know what it was that overwhelmed her.

"Lemonade?" Enid asked.

"F-f-f-goddamn!" Whip said, another tear following the first down into a crease in his cheek, and he squeezed Laura's hand. She wished he'd squeeze it hard enough to squeeze a tear out of her eye. She felt full to bursting.

Enid brought three glasses of lemonade into the living room and opened the curtains to let in the late-afternoon sun. "So," she said. "Dandy new car."

"It's a rental," Laura said.

"I always liked a red car."

Laura watched as her mother helped her father sip some lemonade, more of it going down his chin than into his mouth. She laughed, teasing him with great affection as he groaned his frustration. She wiped his face, kissed his cheek, and then sat down again in a straight-backed chair on the other side of the coffee table.

The coffee table had the same empty nut dishes that had been there when Laura was a kid, each perched daintily on its own hand-crocheted doily.

"Married?" Enid asked.

"No, Mama," Laura said, indignation rising. "Don't you think I'd let you know if I got married or had any kids?"

"Don't know," Enid said. "I'd hope so, though. Too late now, don't you think?"

Laura looked across the table at the woman who had given birth to her but who was now a stranger, and Laura was amazed at her lack of propriety. That topic of discussion was way too personal. And yet. And yet, this was her mother.

She felt a familiar attitude coming on. She stepped into this house and she became a child again.

Well she wasn't a child, and she didn't have to put up with being made to feel like one.

Laura felt her blood pressure rise.

Relax, she told herself. Just relax.

"Suppose so," she said, telling herself that she could do this, she could endure this for a couple of days and then she could go home again, back to Minnesota, back to where she was comfortable, back to where she was a competent adult, back to where she knew who she was and what she was about. This would be but a very short period of time. She'd been uncomfortable before; she could put up with it.

Whip pulled his hand out of Laura's and began waving it around and making sounds with a mouth that didn't work and a tongue that lay flat.

"He wants to know how long you're staying," Enid translated.

"I'm going home Thursday," Laura said. "I have to leave here about noon."

Whip looked at Enid.

"Today's Tuesday," she said to him.

He nodded, put his hand back into his daughter's, then said something else that sounded like wailing to Laura.

"No, honey," Enid said. "She's staying down at Donny's."

A pang of guilt grabbed Laura. "I could stay here," she said. "I just didn't want to be any trouble."

"No trouble," Enid said. "Wherever you're comfortable."

Whip pulled his hand away from Laura's again,

and with a finger stabbed the sofa between them. She didn't need any translation.

"Okay, Daddy," she said. "I'll stay here."

He nodded again, then looked at Enid.

"He's ready for dinner, Laura," she said. "Will you help me in the kitchen?"

The television provided background noise, the stew pot bubbled with delicious smells, as Laura set places for two at the kitchen table and for one on the coffee table, per her mother's instructions. Enid mixed up dumplings, and they worked around each other in silence. If Laura closed her eyes, she could be a child again, her father due home from the fields for dinner, Charlie in the living room watching cartoons, Laura reluctantly setting the table when she'd rather be upstairs immersing herself in either her schoolwork or a novel that transported her far, far away from West Virginia.

She still wanted to be transported far, far away.

The air here smelled the same. It had that same poor, illiterate stink to it that she had always hated. That hadn't changed. That would never change.

"Here," Enid said, handing Laura a bowl of chicken and dumplings. "Go help your daddy, while I ice this here cake."

Laura didn't like being ordered around, but she was glad for something to do, and it wouldn't be a bad thing to help her father eat.

It was a terribly frustrating process.

By the time she realized that the kitchen towel

her mother handed her along with the bowl of soup was to put around his neck, she had dribbled chicken broth all down the front of his shirt. His swallowing was impaired, and she had to cut the chicken up into pieces so small it was almost as if she were chewing it for him, and every other mouthful he'd choke and cough and she would begin to panic.

"I'm sorry, Daddy," she said, close to tears. "I'm not very good at this."

"Me, neither," he said as clearly as if his language apparatus worked perfectly. What he did was make an incomprehensible sound, but Laura understood. She smiled, the tears overflowing her lower lids this time, and gave him a hug.

"F-f-f-goddamn!" he said, and they both laughed, or as close to it as they could come.

By the time he gave up, she had fed him maybe half a bowl of soup and spilled another third of it down the front of him. She kissed his temple and took everything back into the kitchen.

"He eat?" Enid was dishing up their bowls.

"About half."

"That's good. His appetite has been waning."

"I kind of made a mess."

"It takes practice. I'll clean him up."

Laura put ice water in their two glasses, then carried the steaming bowls to the table. Maybe it was a good thing she'd never married, she thought. She would never be able to take care of somebody like this. Never. Her mother fed him three, maybe four times a day, helped him bathe, shave, go to the bathroom, dress, sleep—oh, God, no way. No way.

"We thank you for the money you send every Christmas," Enid said.

Laura smiled.

"You must be doing good up there in Minnesota."

"It's a good job. It's a challenge, and a lot of fun. Next month I go to Washington to testify before Congress."

"No." Enid stopped doing what she was doing, turned and looked at her daughter with admiration all over her face. "Congress? The real Congress? In Washington, D.C.?"

"Yeah. It's about, you know, drugs. We want our new drugs approved by the FDA, because we could help people who need them, but the government makes us jump through too many hoops."

"What kind of drugs?"

"Well, we've developed a pill that can cure a yeast infection with only one dose. We think it should be available over the counter."

"You got anything that could help your daddy?"

Laura looked down at her plate. "No, Mama. Has he seen a doctor? Did you take him to the hospital? He should be on some blood thinners or something."

"No, no hospital. They'll just try to make him live longer, and he don't want to, not like this."

"Stroke victims sometimes recover lots of their former faculties. If he had some therapy . . ."

Enid just shook her head.

"Nobody thought Charlie'd ever speak either. Or dress himself. But he did," Laura said.

"Charlie was a little boy. God made children like little rubber balls. Your daddy, his bounce is gone." Enid smiled. "He spent it right, and he used it all up."

She was right, Laura knew. It was so odd to hear her mother talking of her husband's impending death without putting up a fight, though. She accepted it as if . . . as if . . . as if death were a part of life. Which it was, and Laura ought to know that by now.

Her old bedroom looked like a guest room, and Laura even had conflicting feelings about that. On one hand, she hoped they had preserved her childhood self in there, and on the other hand, she hoped they hadn't clung to her like that. And now that she saw they hadn't, she kind of wished they had. The furniture was the same, but the walls were newly white and the quilt and curtains were fresh. Everything of her childhood was gone, and the room was cool and as sterile as a room with handsewn quilts could be. They'd moved on. Did she think she had so much power over them that they would pine for her year after year for twenty years?

Laura snuggled down between the cool sheets with the warm quilt over her and listened for Charlie in the next room. But this wasn't her room anymore, she wasn't in high school anymore, and Charlie didn't sleep next door anymore.

"One day down," she said to herself, punched the pillow, took a deep breath of the familiar scent of her old room, and reached for sleep.

Enid got her husband cleaned up, into his pajamas, and settled down on the sofa for the night.

He lived on the sofa now—and would for the rest of his days.

She turned off the television and sat with him for a while, holding his hand, running her thumb back and forth across his forehead.

Laura will want to go see Charlie's grave tomorrow, she thought. *Maybe she'll drive that fancy red car into town and see some of her old friends too.*

"She's a beautiful girl," she said softly to Whip. "Smart and successful." A certain sadness mixed with the pride she felt. She was so happy to have raised an independent girl, an educated girl, who escaped the beatings of a drunken husband and the life of raising a dozen shoeless kids—the life so many of her classmates had fallen into.

But there seemed to be a certain soullessness to Laura's life instead. No husband to beat her, but yet no husband to love her either. Enid looked with fondness at Whip, who began to twitch in the early stages of falling asleep. What would her life have been about if it hadn't been about Whip? And no children for Laura, either. What would Enid have to be proud about if it wasn't for Laura? And Charlie, too, she supposed. Though he wasn't hers by birth, he might as well have been. And though he grew to be a man and they treated him like a man, he was always and forever a child.

Oh, God, she missed Charlie more than she thought possible. She didn't think she'd even miss Whip as much when he passed on.

Charlie had come to them so young, maybe six or seven, nobody really knew. He'd been dropped off or left behind or something at Tiddly's. Told the waitress his name was Charlie, but that's pretty much all he said before the accident over at the Sinclair station. He'd been sleeping in the pile of old catalogs in the back, begging for food with those blue eyes of his and that quick smile. The men took to feeding him like any stray, and he hung around, watching the men wrench on those engines. One afternoon Charlie was sitting on a stack of tires, watching the men, when an air hose busted loose from the compressor, snicked around, and the brass end of it crushed a hole in the boy's skull.

Whip was there filling up the gas cans for his tractor when it happened, and he grabbed the boy and brought him home.

Enid boiled up some darning needles, some sharps and a spool of thread, and with Charlie's head in her lap and his blood soaking through towels, she pulled up the pieces of bone by their edges until they pretty closely matched the curvature of his head. Then she sewed up the tear in his scalp with her sewing kit, wrapped the boy's head, and put him to bed in the spare room next to Laura's.

The next day he woke, and he could eat, but his eyes were vacant. It was a good month before life returned to those eyes. It was two years before language came to the boy, and maturity never did come. But he grew big and strong and loyal and hardworking. He helped Whip with all the chores, and acted like a little brother to Laura, and never failed to kiss Enid's cheek when he left for chores after breakfast or when he came home for dinner. Never missed. Never forgot.

Oh, she missed those kisses.

Laura was just a baby when Charlie came to them, and she mentally passed him up before she was three. But she seemed to understand that he was damaged, and while she never doted on him, she was never mean to him either. She just accepted him as being who he was, an older brother, kind of, who was always younger.

In the dark hours of the night, when sleep eluded her, Enid wondered if Laura had forsaken the family because she had spent too much of her time with Charlie. He was needier, so he got more attention. Would Laura be softer and have a bigger heart and a more normal life today if she had been raised with normal brothers and sisters? Or if she had been an only child?

What if Laura knew that Charlie cried for six months after she left? What if Enid told her that every Christmas when a beautiful card full of money came from the postman, Charlie would grab the card and have Enid tell him stories about Laura and the angels, for surely she lived with angels in Minnesota, or she wouldn't send pictures of them every year. Then the card would disappear into his room.

If Laura only knew how much Charlie had missed her. Would that make a difference to her?

Or would telling her just make her feel bad? What good would it do now?

"I did the best I could with what I had and what I knew at the time," she said softly to Whip, whose eyes fluttered open for a moment, then closed again. "I always tried to do right," she said, feeling the softness of Charlie's lips on her cheek, the freshness of his shave in the mornings, the buzz of his heavy reddish beard stubble in the afternoons. She thought of her beautiful daughter, asleep upstairs, and wondered when she last got a kiss on the cheek from Laura.

So different, Enid thought.

I did the best I could at the time, she thought. *And I'll do the best I can tomorrow, too.*

She kissed her husband's forehead, tucked the afghan up around his neck, turned off the light, and went into her bedroom, leaving the door open in case he needed her in the night.

Tiddly's was exactly the same, except the Naugahyde booths were now black instead of red. Laura wasn't really hungry, not after that enormous breakfast her mother had made, but she wanted to cruise through town, and Tiddly's was the center of the social whirl.

First she settled up with Donny Brooks—she hadn't canceled her reservation, so she paid anyway, despite Donny's protests. Donny fussed over her like a visiting diplomat, which made Laura uneasy, but she exited Donny's foyer as quickly and as gracefully as good manners would allow. Donny walked her out to the car, admired the rented Taurus, then said, "Sorry about your daddy, Laura." Then before Laura could respond, Donny added, "And Charlie, of course."

There. Somebody had finally said his name. Tears bloomed in Laura's eyes, and she accepted Donny's hug, squeaked out a "Thank you," got in her car, and blew her nose.

Enid hadn't said anything about Charlie. Laura began to wonder how he died. Why he died. He was only, what, forty-six? He was supposed to be there to take care of the folks, to be their son, their grandson, their great-grandson, to see them through the rest of their lives.

He was supposed to be there, absent Laura. He was to be the one to assuage her guilt.

What happened?

She repaired her makeup and drove the two blocks to the cafe. When she walked in, she remembered a few good times, when she felt a part of a crowd, and she remembered the bad times, when she felt ostracized by everybody.

Most specifically, she remember giving Randall Cosgrove his ring back in that corner booth. She'd cried as she slowly unwound the angora yarn from it, making him as uncomfortable as she could, for as long as she could, and the next day that same ring was on a chain around Cynthia Newcomb's neck.

Laura sat at the counter and ordered coffee, and it wasn't until it was served that she recognized the waitress. Lisa Mae Wolff.

Lisa Mae recognized her at the same instant, squealed and ran around the counter for a hug, then called into the back that she was taking a break. A younger, high-school-age girl came out to take her place. The cafe wasn't busy, so she set herself to refilling sugar dispensers.

Laura and Lisa Mae slid into a booth, where Lisa Mae lit up a cigarette and moaned about her feet, then they settled right down to gossiping. Lisa Mae still wore her hair bleached yellow and ratted high up on her head. Her lipstick and nail polish were as pink as the apron she wore over a white blouse and jeans. They had never been very good friends in high school, but all that class distinction seemed to melt away in the perspective of their approaching forties. They talked and laughed about all their old classmates, most of whom lived an unenviable life.

"But look at you!" Lisa Mae said with admiration in her eyes. "We always knew you were too smart to stick around here. You escaped this place, and it was a good thing you did. You're the only one who did. Some got as far as Wheeling, but that's not far enough. Most settled right here, or down yonder."

Laura knew that "down yonder" meant the hollow with the tin shacks and old run-down travel trailers. Alcoholism, disease, incest, and murder weren't uncommon down there. Living down yonder was a horrible life sentence, and Laura didn't know how people ended up there, knowing about it the way everybody did, but there were never many vacancies there.

"How many kids you got?" Lisa Mae asked.

"No kids," Laura said. "I never married."

"You never married?" Lisa Mae's eyes, rimmed with all that black makeup, grew large. "You queer?"

"No. Busy."

"Never married, and no kids. Wow, I can't hardly imagine that. I'm on my second husband now, and Jimbo is a good guy. I've got three kids and he's got three, so together we've got us a houseful." She fished around in the pocket of her apron and came up with a pack of cigarettes and a plastic case full of photographs.

Laura was amazed that Lisa Mae would carry photographs of her kids in her pocket at work. But she did, and she unfolded them, and showed Laura the pride of her life, and seemed to delight in every one of Jimbo's kids as much as her own. "I tell them, 'You learn to read, and you learn to cook, and you don't never end up down yonder.' Good advice, don't you think?"

Laura nodded. "If they can read, they can do anything."

"Yep. Wouldn't give 'em up for the world." Lisa Mae repocketed the photographs. "Sorry about your pa," she said. "And Charlie."

"Thanks."

"Charlie used to come in here for a cup of coffee with a tiny scoop of ice cream in it almost every day."

"He did?"

"A real gentleman, that Charlie." Lisa Mae's eyes turned sad. "Then he started having those fits. Your ma, sometimes she had to handle him all by herself, and that Charlie, he was a big guy."

"Fits? You mean seizures?"

"You know, cracked head and all."

Laura nodded, trying to imagine her tiny mother handling Charlie during a grand mal seizure.

"But you got kids, you do whatever it takes, that's for sure." Lisa Mae checked her watch. "I got to get back to work or I'll get my skinny ass fired. Let me bring you a piece of pie. Mo makes it fresh every morning, and it's good as it gets. My treat."

A moment later, a hot piece of apple pie with a

scoop of ice cream landed on the table in front of Laura, along with a dispenser napkin and a fork, but Laura was still lost in the echoes of Lisa Mae's statement: "You got kids, you do whatever it takes."

Lisa Mae stayed in this town, married twice, raised her children, was personable and friendly to everybody, even those who had treated her badly in high school. Laura had never treated her badly, but Laura never liked her much either. And Lisa Mae dealt with it. She didn't run away, abandon her heritage, she just lived with it. And here she was, friendly and giving and loving, to someone who had run away from home, someone who had denounced this jerkwater town, and Lisa Mae with barely a high school education.

And Laura, with all her fancy education, had left her tiny mother to deal with Charlie's seizures. And her brain-damaged father.

You got kids, you do whatever it takes.

You accept their brain damage, and you accept their abandonment.

Laura put a bite of pie into her dry mouth, swallowed it with the last of her coffee, left a ten-dollar bill on the table, waved to Lisa Mae, who waved back, and stumbled to the door. She couldn't wait to get back to her mama. Laura had never learned to do whatever it takes. Her life was one selfish act after another.

Her mother's life had been one charitable act after another.

Guilt surged like bile. Maybe it wasn't too late to make restitution. Maybe it wasn't too late to figure it out. She drove fast back to the farm, but she drove carefully. She couldn't afford to be killed—or worse yet, injured enough so her mother would have someone else to care for—before she made amends. If she ever could make amends for the last twenty years.

She pulled into the drive amid a scattering of chickens, got out, and ran to the front door. "Mama?" she called, but the house was quiet. The breakfast dishes had been done.

She put her purse on the kitchen table and went into the living room.

Whip was sleeping on the sofa, a game show playing softly on the television.

Laura walked into her mother's bedroom, but the bed was made and the room tidy.

"Mama?" she called upstairs, but there was no answer, so she walked up softly.

Her bed was neatly made. She walked into Charlie's room and found it to be in perfect order as well. *Sweet boy*, she thought, her heart squeezing. She looked at all the toys on his dresser, race cars, mostly, lined up by their mother on a lace doily. *That has to be a new addition,* Laura thought. She couldn't imagine Charlie living with doilies in his room.

The house was so clean. Neat and clean. And now that Laura thought of it, it had always been this way. Why did she always think of down yonder when she thought of home, instead of thinking of how fresh and scrubbed everything was inside her parents' house?

There was a stack of comic books on Charlie's

nightstand. Laura sat for a moment on his bed, fingered the familiar bedspread, then picked up the comics.

Underneath them was a stack of Christmas cards.

Laura recognized them instantly, and a pang of grief threatened to double her over. She put the comics back down on top of the cards, went down the stairs and out the kitchen door, holding it back so it wouldn't slam and wake up her daddy.

The chickens ran over to see if she had any leftovers for them, but she just stood there, needing her mother, overwhelmed with emotion that she didn't know how to identify or how to handle.

Then she saw a worn path through the weeds behind the house. She followed the path with her eyes and saw a small figure, cotton dress flapping transparently around the legs, standing on top of the ridge.

Laura started running.

Enid stood looking down on the mound of dirt that had begun to grow a good cover of weeds already. By the end of the season, nobody would ever know that Charlie was buried here, and that was probably just as well. He'd been a good man, but he came in mystery and he left in mystery and he lived a good, helpful, simple, loving life. It was fitting that he didn't leave much behind except those ripples of goodness. Enid thanked God that the town had no doctor, and the sheriff had actually come to help her finish putting Charlie in the ground when Whip couldn't. No paperwork. Charlie had never had any paperwork to begin with, he sure didn't need any to end with.

"You just keep on making those angels laugh, Charlie boy," she whispered to him as she saw Laura come up the hill.

Laura was young and strong, stood straight and looked you right in the eyes. Enid could not be more proud, although she would rest a little easier if Laura were married and had someone to take care of her. Women weren't meant to live alone and fend entirely for themselves. Life was to be shared, and while that wasn't always easy, it was really the only worthwhile thing.

Laura put an arm around Enid's shoulders and they stood looking down at Charlie's grave for a long, silent moment.

"No marker?" Laura asked.

"Only in our hearts," Enid said.

Laura nodded, and Enid saw a drop darken a spot of dirt at her feet. Enid was cried out, but she was glad Laura had a chance to loosen up and expel a little of her grief.

"I have to get back," Enid said. "Rufe Hoskins will be dropping by soon."

"Rufe Hoskins? What for?"

"The neighbors take turns coming by every day," Enid said.

"I don't even know my neighbors," Laura said with a catch in her voice.

"You could," Enid said, her arm tightening around Laura's waist.

Laura shook her head, her emotional glacier splitting and cracking right before Enid's eyes. "I don't know how."

"Well, then," Enid said, realizing that missing

her daughter's university graduation was nothing, now that she had an opportunity to see her daughter finish her real education, "come along and see Rufe. We'll show you."

Laura turned and wrapped her arms around Enid, and Enid felt those soft lips on her cheek, softer even than Charlie's. She held her little girl as long as she could, absorbing as much of that pain that she could, and then it was time to let the grief lapse for now and go back to the real world.

" 'Bye, Charlie," she said. "See you tomorrow, honey."

" 'Bye, Charlie," Laura said.

"Can you bake a pie?" Enid asked her. "Your daddy loves a cherry pie."

"Teach me," Laura said, and took her mother's hand.

Bound by Hoof and Nail

Anne McCaffrey and Georgeanne Kennedy

Photo by Orla Callaghan

INTRODUCTION

I learned how to ride at the South Orange, New Jersey, Arsenal, where the cavalry kept a troop of army remounts during the thirties. I learned about horses when I moved to Ireland and, at age forty-five, bought my first horse, Mr. Ed, who was an eleven-year-old dapple gray heavyweight hunter. He also had a great "pop" in him, as they say here in Ireland, and was dressage trained—if you put a double bridle on him.

Georgeanne started riding in Ireland at ten, and at eighteen she took her Irish Certificate of Equitation Sciences and the British Horse Society Assistant Instructor's Certificate.

But we decided it would be more fun to write from a dyed-in-the-wool sheep farmer's viewpoint—which Gigi's husband certainly has.

Did you honestly think that we'd let you in on all those secrets we've learned while handling horses for a sum total of ninety years?

The summer of 1994 was one of the best Ireland had enjoyed in close to a decade. No one could say for sure when spring ended and summer began—only a gradual warming in daily temperatures marked the change from one season to the next. Each morning dawned bright and clear, and by mid-June the entire country was enjoying unbroken sunshine from first light until close to ten o'clock at night. Why, even people returning from holidays in the Mediterranean weren't half as brown as those who'd stayed home and sunbathed in their own back gardens! Needless to say, as a farmer, I was able to tackle many jobs much earlier than in previous years. My fields were fertilized, hedgerows trimmed, and waterways cleared by the first week in May, and when the long-term weather forecast was for more of the same, I took out my clippers and sheared my flock of sheep by mid-May. Chores that would not normally have been started until the end of June were now completed, and I found myself with more free time than I'd ever had before in my life.

Now, a person can sit and watch the grass grow and the lambs fatten for only so long before tedium sets in. By the first week of June I was like a schoolkid let out on vacation, with too much time on my hands, the whole summer stretching before me, and nothing to do. My wife of just six months, Jean, took pity on me and asked if I'd like to accompany her and her mother, Andrea, to Kilkenny for a two-day horse show they were attending that coming weekend. I was at first reluctant, but Jean had a way about her that I found hard to resist.

"John, why don't you come with us?" she said, her green eyes twinkling at me as she spoke. "You'll have a blast, and anyway you've never really seen us work together before. We're quite a team, even if I do say so myself."

"I'll feel like a square peg just *watching* you two. You know I have to *do* something or I'll go out of my shiggin' mind with boredom," I said, not unaware of the faint note of petulance in my voice.

"Listen," Jean said, standing in front of me and holding both my hands as she made, and held, eye contact with me. "There's plenty of things you can do to help us when we're not working in the show ring. All those years riding with the pony club must have taught you something, even if you did stop riding when the call of the sheep grew too loud," she said, chuckling. "You know how to tack up a horse—I've seen you do it, you know—and you're well able to help us water and feed the horses as well as muck out the box each morning. And if you're really intent on being useful, you can share in the driving. And when we *are* in the ring and there's nothing for you to do, I know for a fact that part of the show grounds is devoted to agricultural machinery and other farm-type stuff." Jean stood her small frame on tiptoes and kissed me on the lips. She was a smart gal, she'd saved the hook for last; she knew I couldn't resist farm machinery or any other mechanical gadgets.

It took a couple of seconds for me to work out the details in my head, such as asking my neighbor to check my sheep each day, before I agreed to Jean's suggestion. Andrea, when apprised of this latest news, was absolutely over the moon.

"Fabulous news!" she said, hollering loudly. It was unintentional, but occasionally my mother-in-law could sound like a stiff-upper-lip type when, really, she'd been born and bred—and lived her entire life—in the gentle county of Wicklow.

"Sorry, I didn't mean to roar at you, dear." Andrea smiled, running her hands up and down the sides of her thighs in what I had come to recognize as her "calming" mode. She was a slender, wiry woman, with thick brown hair and green eyes, and even in her middle years she was still prone to freckle in sunny weather. I noticed a new splash of freckles across the bridge of her nose now.

"It's just that you've never really seen us work together before and we're quite good . . . at the exhibition stuff, I mean." I had to smile at her. Andrea had the most charming way of putting things; if she was unsure of your understanding of what she meant, she'd throw in an explanation as an afterthought, almost as if she were reassuring *herself* of what she really meant. I'd noticed that she had a knack of making people feel exceptionally comfortable; she never belittled or condescended, and managed, without really trying, to dispel self-doubt in anyone who came in contact with her. I suppose she was a bit of a Florence Nightingale to the soul—without the medicine, of course.

I had seen Jean and Andrea work together a few times, but never in front of a crowd. They had a small business that Andrea had taken over from her father, the Colonel, when he passed away, and between mother and daughter they managed to break and bring on young horses—and sometimes ponies—to a very high standard. Andrea and Jean didn't specialize in making any one type of riding animal; they simply let the horse show *them* what he or she could do best. Over the years, Andrea's unique ability to get the best out of any horse she worked with turned her into a bit of a celebrity among the horsy crowd. Some horse show organizer, familiar with Andrea's ability, had asked her to show off the skills of one of her horses at a show, sort of as a gimmick to help pull in the crowds. Andrea's "act" had been a huge success, and since then she had graced many a show with her talent, including Jean on her outings as she grew older.

To the ordinary observer it may have appeared that Jean was learning her mother's secrets by osmosis, but I noticed that the two spent an increasing amount of time perfecting the techniques that Jean had learned from her mother. Perhaps Andrea was ensuring, as best she could, that the lifelong endeavors of her father and then herself would not be lost to the next generation that would take over the Hartshorn legacy.

Never without prospective buyers or lucrative deals in the offing, Andrea nevertheless kept the family business small, having no more than seven horses stabled and in work at one time. Of course they had other animals, resting or growing in the many paddocks surrounding the yard, but to have any more than seven horses in work at one time was, Andrea felt, too much. Anyway, seven was her lucky number, she said. Between Andrea and Jean, they had a thriving business and managed to "make" animals that were not only used to entertain at equestrian events but were also sold on as show jumpers, dressage horses, three-day-eventers, hunters, and good old family hacks. They had made quite a few marvelous little ponies too, but anything under fourteen hands high was too small to carry Jean's weight. My wife was small but not minute!

Andrea's and Jean's talents were well known throughout the echelon of equestrians in Ireland and England, and they had a steady stream of prospective buyers for their stock. In April they had sold a young horse to a German buyer for what seemed to me crazy money. The horse, Zulu, was only five, and even to my novice eye he was a magnificent animal. He was quiet and controlled when ridden, and Jean said that he was naturally very athletic. But when he was put to a show jumping fence, Zulu turned himself inside out to fly over that obstacle with total abandon, and feet to spare! I had to laugh when I thought back to that evening in April and how Zulu had performed for the German buyer.

The German, Otto, and his Irish contact, Kevin Callan, arrived later in the day than expected, and subsequently they were in a bit of a rush to see the horse.

Andrea rode Zulu first, showing off his gaits through collected walk to a medium paced canter, with a few dressage movements thrown in for good measure. When Zulu's mouth was frothing with saliva, Andrea reined him in and dismounted. She'd once explained to me that a horse exhibited a flexible and adaptable nature to prospective buyers if worked by more than one rider. So I wasn't surprised to see Andrea hand Zulu's reins over to Jean when she dismounted; it had become common practice for Jean to ride all the jumping horses over fences after Andrea had warmed them up. What I hadn't expected to see

was Andrea and Jean make the briefest of contact
with the palms of their right hands, almost as
if one were passing some secret to the other. It
happened so quickly and lasted so briefly that I
thought perhaps their hands had brushed together
by accident.

I thought nothing more of their quirky little
exchange as Jean vaulted onto Zulu's back and
proceeded to deftly put him through his paces in a
workmanlike fashion. When they'd trotted, cantered, and loosened up a bit more, Jean put Zulu
over some of the fences set up specially for the occasion. She sat very, very quietly in the saddle, and
I noticed Andrea nodding her head slightly in approval. When Jean had shown the horse to his best
advantage, she dismounted and offered Zulu to
Otto to ride, then came over to stand outside the
arena with Kevin, Andrea, and me.

The German rider quickly repeated what Jean
had done in dressage movements and then indicated to Jean and Andrea that he would try a few
small fences before attempting the larger ones.
Cantering Zulu down the long end of the school,
he popped him over a small spread fence without
mishap. But Otto was used to "setting his horses
up," to use a phrase of Jean's, for each fence; he sat
deeply in the saddle and rode Zulu to take mea-
sured strides so that he would meet each fence at
the correct takeoff point. After the horse jumped a
few more, increasingly larger fences, it became obvious, even to me, that Zulu wasn't used to being
told when to take off for a fence, and he started to
fret at the bit. I suppose the horse had had enough
and wanted to prove just what he could do. So

when Otto tried to set him up for a combination of two fences, one to be popped right after the other with no stride in between, the horse gave one mighty leap and jumped both fences together, nearly throwing his rider out of the pad and into the blue skies above.

"My Gott! He jumps dis vay alvays?" Otto sputtered at Jean as he hurriedly corrected his position on Zulu, pulling the horse up to stand in front of us. "Dis is fantastick! He jumped over fifteen feet vide and four feet high!"

"It looked more like four and a half feet high to me," Kevin said, to no one in particular.

"Ya, he cleared it well?" Otto asked Kevin.

"With inches to spare," Kevin said. "I don't think we need look any further, Otto. You've found your next rising star. But if you'll permit me, I don't think you need 'ride' this horse to his fences as you're used to doing. Just let the chap at them—he knows what he has to do," Kevin said, grinning. "He has a clean vet certificate, doesn't he?" he asked, turning to Jean and Andrea.

"It's in the house. I can get it now, if you want," Andrea said.

"I have no doubt he's clean—sure, he's one of your horses. Let's go inside and take a quick look at his papers and such. Then let's talk money," Kevin said, rubbing the palms of his hands together and ushering Andrea out of the arena toward the house.

Andrea and Jean had made an excellent deal with Kevin, and Zulu was shipped off to Germany the following week, aptly renamed "Zulu Star" by Otto. With the proceeds of the sale, Andrea and

Jean later bought two new animals and had a great chunk of change to spare.

The morning we were set to travel to Kilkenny I rose early to check my sheep, leaving Jean curled up in bed with her dreams. Later, I drove the short distance to Andrea's house and her adjoining stable yard. I found Jean in the tack room, stuffing a trunk with equipment and muttering to herself not to forget an extra set of bandages, "just in case."

"Hi, Jean," I said, "anything I can do?"

"Oh, yes. I'm almost finished, but be a pet and throw three bales of hay and four of straw on top of the horse box, please. There's a cover you can lash over them when you're finished. Don't want a trail of hay and straw to follow us to Kilkenny."

I left my wife packing and muttering and hauled the heavy bales of hay and the not-so-heavy bales of straw onto the top of the horse box, then lashed them securely in place with the cover Jean had mentioned. When the job was done, I pulled errant strands of hay off my clothes and noticed Andrea lunging a giant gray horse in the outdoor arena. I had the perfect vantage point for watching her from the top of the horse box, so I sat myself down cross-legged and chewed on a piece of hay while I watched her at work.

Andrea talked to the horse constantly, telling him to increase his pace, or to turn a circle, or to halt and step back a few paces. The horse obeyed his mistress at every command. I was amazed at the talent this woman had and glad, too, that she shared it so freely. Andrea's ability to make people comfortable around her was magnified tenfold when she was with horses. They just *knew* that she wouldn't harm them or ask them to do anything they didn't want to do. Of course, this always worked in her favor, because all her horses wanted nothing more than to please her. I suppose they were just like children, so earnestly eager to please.

Andrea finished lunging the horse and reined him in to her.

"Jean," she said, calling out loud enough that she'd be heard. "We're ready for you now."

Jean came out of the tack room, pulling her long brown hair back from her face into a quick knot, which she secured at the base of her neck with a hair clip.

"We'll start with the usual warm-up routine and then see if old Bixby can throw in a few new tricks for us, okay?" Andrea said, winking at Jean as she approached the giant horse. Jean nodded in agreement, gathering herself to mount the horse. But just before she vaulted to Bixby's back, she passed her right hand over Andrea's outstretched palm. They were doing their little secret hand-shake routine again, and I wondered if perhaps more was happening in front of my eyes than I could imagine, or even begin to fathom. I shook my head at the thought and abruptly brought my attention back to Jean as she settled herself comfortably on the horse's back, sitting just behind the vaulting roller they used instead of a saddle. Andrea unclipped the lunge line from the cavesson and then removed that piece of gear from the horse's head. She gently pulled at his left ear and muttered some endearment that I couldn't hear.

Anne McCaffrey

With only the vaulting roller on his back and no bridle or halter on his head, Bixby stood quietly, flicking his ears to and fro, waiting for his mistress to command. Andrea moved away from Bixby, to the center of the arena. Jean folded her arms in front of her and waited patiently with Bixby. Andrea clicked her tongue and said to Bixby, "Away, Bixby." The horse pulled up his head fractionally, arching his neck and tucking his nose down so that it was perfectly vertical to the ground. He walked away from Andrea and moved to the edge of the arena, turning to the left when he reached the short end. He walked on while Jean sat on his back, her legs resting loosely at his sides. Even from the distance of my vantage point I could see that Jean wasn't giving the horse any commands with her legs, and her arms remained folded and idle in front of her.

"Walk long, Bixby," Andrea said. The horse lowered his head slightly and lengthened his stride into a walk that looked loose and relaxed. Andrea allowed Bixby to walk on a long stride for about ten paces and then called out, "Halt." Bixby stopped in his tracks. Now, I suppose this horse, or any horse for that matter, would get used to a certain routine to the point of being able to anticipate the next command, but Jean had once told me that Andrea liked to vary each workout, to keep her animals from growing bored.

"Five paces back, Bixby." He shortened his neck and carefully stepped back five paces, then stood, absolutely square and still. Jean raised an eyebrow and smiled at her mother.

"That's a new one, Mum," she said, and Andrea

smiled back at her daughter, acknowledging the compliment.

"Canter slow, Bixby," Andrea said. Bixby tensed his haunches under him in one movement and pushed with all the strength of his back legs from a full standstill into a rocking, evenly paced canter. Jean barely moved an inch on his back as he cantered around the arena; she was glued to his back, a human extension of Bixby's body, completely in unison with his movement.

"Circle small, Bixby," Andrea said, stepping back a few paces to allow the horse a clear passage around her. "Go large, Bixby," she said, as the horse completed his circle. Bixby continued to canter on the outside track of the ring. He was nearing the top end of the ring where he had first started to work.

"Down the center. Canter odd, Bixby," Andrea said. The horse turned lengthwise down the center of the arena and continued to canter, but I noticed that after every three strides he would change his leading leg, giving the appearance that he was hopping. I smiled to myself as I watched this giant horse playing hopscotch up the center line of the arena.

"Change rein, Bixby," Andrea called, and he smoothly continued cantering, turning to the right at the top of the arena, keeping to the outside track. When the horse was nearly abreast of Andrea, she called out to him, "Walk, Bixby." The horse walked, flowing effortlessly from one pace to another.

"Come to me, Bixby." The horse walked over to his mistress and gently reached out his head to her. "What a marvelous horse you are," Andrea said, caressing his muzzle with gentle hands. Bixby snorted, blowing into her hand. Jean vaulted off Bixby's back and gave him a huge hug and a pat on the neck.

"You're a grand fellow, aren't you, old Bix?" Bixby lowered his head, so that Jean could scratch an itchy spot just behind his left ear.

From my seat on top of the horse box I felt slightly let down when Bixby's schooling session was over. It was uplifting to watch such an enormous animal work without the use of lunge line or whip, and I wanted to see more.

"John?" Andrea said loudly, not realizing that I had been a silent witness to the training session. I waved to her from my perch.

"Over here, Andrea," I said and clambered down the ladder that was fixed to the side of the horse box.

"John, I'm wondering if you'll give us a hand for a few minutes? We want to try something with Bixby that we think will please the crowd down in Kilkenny." I walked the short distance from where the horse box was parked and joined Jean and Andrea in the arena, absently giving Bixby a pat on the neck.

"What can I do you for?" I said, smiling as I used a favorite bass-ackwards phrase of mine.

"Just stand at Bixby's withers," Jean said, smiling, "and bend your left knee." I complied, only just realizing, as she grabbed my leg below the knee, what she had in mind.

"Oh, no, you don't!" I said hastily, raising my hands in protest as I planted my left foot firmly on the ground and stepped away from Jean and Andrea. Bixby turned his head to look at me.

"You're not getting me up on that mammoth to make an ass of myself!" I protested.

"John, you'll be perfectly safe, really," Jean said. "He's completely bombproof—as you've witnessed—and really comfortable. Listen, if you want you can hold on to the vaulting bar, there, on the roller." She pointed to the substantial-looking piece of leather-covered metal that protruded from the top of the roller that encircled Bixby's belly. I passed a critical eye over the horse and then looked at my wife and mother-in-law from under a raised eyebrow. They stood close to one another, mother and daughter, and I sensed that these two women were bound by some indefinable connection that went beyond genes and maternal-filial bonds. They had reached an agreement that I knew nothing about, and I sensed that every moment they spent together resulted in a huge exchange of knowledge between the two, although not always passed verbally. An understanding rested comfortably over these women, and I guessed that Jean was in the final stages of taking over the business her grandfather and then her mother had built up so carefully. Andrea undoubtedly had many more active years to live, yet I couldn't help but wonder whether her unerring sense of what was right, of what should be, had compelled her now to pass on the essence of skills honed over two lifetimes. I suppose their work with horses wasn't work to them at all; it was a way of life, and Andrea was only ensuring that it would carry on.

"You'll do just fine, dear, I promise," Andrea said.

I looked from daughter to mother again and shook my head. They had me hooked, and they knew it. I would look like a simpering ninny if I didn't at least give it a try.

"You two are some pair, you know," I said, as I collected myself in front of Bixby's withers and proffered my leg to Jean. On the count of three, I jumped and Jean hoisted my not inconsiderable frame onto Bixby's back. I tried to arrange my body in what I remembered to be a decorous fashion.

"Just sit as relaxed as you possibly can and hold on to the roller bar, okay?" Jean said. I nodded and watched silently as my wife and mother-in-law walked away from me to the center of the ring, wondering what antics they were going to get up to. Andrea gave Bixby the command to walk on, and the horse took to the outside track at a comfortable walk.

"Trot, Bixby," Jean said. I was startled and turned to look at my wife, as I didn't know that she too worked with Bixby from the ground. I thought it was solely Andrea's special skill that could make Bixby perform so freely. Jean must have guessed what I was thinking, because she smiled at me and tapped her index finger lightly on the bridge of her nose. This had been her secret.

"Walk, Bixby," Andrea said this time. He walked. "Halt, Bixby."

"Five paces back, Bixby," Jean said.

"Oh, no," I said, as Bixby carefully paced backward five steps. "You're not going to have him canter straight from halt with me on board! I'll go right out the back door and end up on my ear in the dirt." I guess I must have sputtered a bit, because Jean and Andrea spontaneously burst into laughter at my protest. When Jean stopped chuckling, she said, "Don't worry, we'll do this nice and slowly."

"Walk, Bixby." He walked.

"Trot short, Bixby," Jean said, and the horse flowed into a lovely springy trot, the likes of which I'd never felt before. It was as if the horse's feet were bouncing off the ground, and with each stride forward for a split second he must have been floating.

"This is nice," I said. "I could get used to this."

"That's the plan," said Andrea. Bixby was nearing a short end of the arena and Jean said, "Cut across, Bixby." Bixby cut across the length of the arena diagonally, and I could see that we were taking a perfectly straight path that would bring us to the opposite short corner of the ring.

"Trot long, Bixby," Jean said, nudging her mother gently as they exchanged grins. Bixby lengthened his stride in trot; his neck lowered and he threw his forelegs out in front of him, propelling himself forward with the immense power of his back legs. Well, if I'd thought the horse was floating before, this long trot was ten times better. With each stride, Bixby seemed to hang for ages, all four feet in the air at once, and then he'd rise up again, powerfully, to hang in the air once more. Surprisingly, I wasn't thrown about at all; the balance and tempo of his stride glued me to his back more than it would have if he'd been walking.

"Hey, this feels great!" I said, smiling at Jean

and Andrea. Bixby reached the short end of the school and slowed his pace to allow for the approaching corner.

"Canter slow, Bixby," Andrea said, and with the smoothest of transitions Bixby flowed from trot into rocking-horse canter. It was the loveliest feeling to have such a giant of a horse gently bouncing underneath me. When Bixby started down the long side of the ring, I felt completely relaxed and capable of riding the horse at this pace forever.

"Snake around, Bixby," Jean said, and Bixby cut across the arena, heading straight for the opposite side. When he reached the other long side of the school, he turned a tight half circle in the other direction, changed his leading leg, and continued to canter straight across the middle of the ring to the long side whence he'd started "snaking." He continued looping back and forward across the arena in the shape of a snake, and I suddenly remembered this movement from my days as a pony club rider; it was a limbering exercise that our instructors had called "a serpentine." Bixby reached the short end of the ring, and Andrea called to him, "Go large, Bixby." Bixby complied, cantering fluidly around the arena with me grinning like a gormless idiot on his back.

"Trot, Bixby," Jean said. "Walk, Bixby." Bixby moved from canter to trot to walk in a seamless flow. This horse was sheer magic to ride.

"Come to me, Bixby." We turned off the track and headed to the center of the ring. Bixby halted a pace away from Jean and Andrea, and I let out a contented sigh, more from the sheer enjoyment of riding Bixby than from my previous anxiety of falling off.

"I have one last thing to show you, John, before we finish," Andrea said, stepping forward to pat her horse.

"Take a bow, Bixby." Without any warning I felt Bixby lower his forehand under me, stretching one leg out in front of him while sort of curtsying with the other.

"Hey, what's this!" I said, afraid I'd fall off from a standstill. If it hadn't been for the roller bar I might have ended up on the ground at Bixby's feet. I grabbed onto the bar to steady myself. Bixby slowly completed his bow and then stood up normally on his front legs. I laughed out loud and patted my mount soundly on the neck.

"Thank you, ladies, and Bixby," I said, "for giving me the ride of my life. He really is a fantastic horse, a definite master at his job." I patted Bixby on the neck again, unable to stop smiling.

When I'd dismounted, sort of slithering off his back, the three of us walked Bixby to his stable. I helped untack and rub him down before we gave him a drink of water and then a scoop of oats mixed with sweet feed. When Bixby was settled and crunching on his lunch, we made our way to Andrea's house to get something to eat before we loaded the horses into the box and headed off to Kilkenny.

It was after three o'clock when we finally left for Kilkenny with Bixby, a young show jumper named Freeser, which Jean was going to enter in competition for the first time, and Melodia, a mare that Andrea rode in working hunter classes. The horse box was designed to transport six horses, seven at a pinch, but because this was a two-day show and we were bringing only three horses, Jean and Andrea planned to use the horse box as a stable at night. It was a very cozy piece of machinery, and before they loaded the horses, I had a good look inside it. There were partitions that could be secured during transportation and then easily moved to make comfortable "stalls" for the horses at night. On either side of the box were four windows, which Jean told me would be opened at night so the horses could look out. Ceiling vents also lined the roof to lend additional air circulation. Neat little metal hoops on hinges could be pushed flush with the wall while the horse box was moving; at night the hoops could be pulled up perpendicularly and securely latched in place to hold feed and water buckets. Numerous metal rings hung from the walls just below the roof, and these, I was told, were used for tying up the horses and their hay nets. All in all, the horses would be very comfortable because enough room was provided, when each stall was sectioned off, to allow them to lie down if they chose to.

When the horses were safely loaded, Jean and Andrea stowed their riding gear in the back of the cab, where two sleeping sections were neatly tucked away over the body of the horse box proper. At night we would be able to hear if any of the horses were having difficulties, yet remain secluded from them by the solid wall that separated cab from box. With a final look around the yard, Andrea climbed into the driver's seat and I followed Jean up into the passenger side with our overnight bags in hand.

"Who'll look after the yard while we're gone?" I asked as I stowed our bags in the sleeping compartments.

"Oh, Rick Evans will come in while we're at the show," Jean said. "He's just at the end of a six-week leave from racing, after a bad fall. He messed up his collarbone and smacked his head pretty badly at Punchestown racetrack, and the Turf Club automatically forbids jockeys to race until the club doctor deems them to be over their injuries. Four weeks is about the norm for a collarbone, but Rick's whack on the head added another fortnight to his mandatory recovery period. Poor sod. But he says he loves to get a break from the racers and ride our animals for a change. Personally, I think he loves a quiet ride out after all those years of riding hot-blooded racehorses. And being able to run the stables without all the usual hustle and bustle he's used to in a racing yard must be a pleasant change."

Andrea handled the horse box easily as we turned off the small side road from the stables onto the major roadway that would lead us toward Dublin and out onto the road to Kilkenny. The journey would normally take about two hours by car, but the horse box wasn't designed for speed, so we took our time, planning on about three hours of travel before we reached the show grounds. We weren't in any hurry to get there, as the show didn't start until the following morning, so we stopped along the way to have a break and a cup of tea. When we were ready to go, Andrea asked if I'd like to drive the remaining miles, and I gladly sat in behind the steering wheel, only too happy to have a chance to try this Rolls-Royce of a horse box.

"Mother, you'll never get him out from behind the wheel now. I told you he's a fiend for machinery and all gadgets mechanical," Jean said, smiling at me. Andrea chuckled and crossed her arms, snuggling down to doze for the rest of the journey. We passed the remainder of the trip in amicable silence, and when we were about six miles outside of Kilkenny town, I roused Jean from a nap to give me directions to the show grounds. We were nearing the end of a two-lane highway and Jean told me to take the next turn left, when a filthy-dirty horse box came up on our right side and passed us out. The driver then pulled in front of me and indicated that he was going to turn left too.

"Someone's in a hurry," Jean said.

"Look," I said and pointed to the back of the horse box, where someone had written "also in white" on the back door of the dirty vehicle with a finger, exposing white paint underneath. "Now, that's a hoot," I said. We turned off the motorway and followed "also in white" the few remaining miles to the show grounds.

We were in the heart of county Kilkenny, one of the most beautiful parts of Ireland I'd ever seen . . . next to Wicklow, of course. The land was verdant and fertile and boasted some of the best pastureland in the country. Farmers took great pride in their land around these parts, every field we passed was securely fenced and the hedges were neatly trimmed. Not a scrap of sheep's wool was caught on the wire fencing, and the grass was lush and emerald green—prime grazing land.

A series of sharp bends loomed ahead of us, and Jean told me to watch for a small break in the hedging after the last bend. That would be the entrance to the show grounds, a twenty-acre field donated to the show committee by a local farmer for the two days of events. As we pulled off the road, a small man in tweeds and a cloth cap waved to Andrea.

"Hello, there, Missus," he said, a grin splitting his face. "Glad to see you here again this year."

"I wouldn't miss it for the world, Joe. It's good to see you looking so well. It's a grand old summer we're having, isn't it?"

"To be sure, to be sure, Missus. And long may it last. Now if only we'd get a wee drop of rain at night and sunshine all day long, then the farmers would be happy too." He laughed and pulled his cap off his bald pate, slapping it against his thigh.

"And sure, aren't you a farmer, yourself?" said Andrea, smiling at Joe.

"I passed that job on to my son this winter, and glad I am to have done so. I'm too old to be running all over the countryside chasing after sheep and cattle. And sure, isn't it time for the son to be minding the father? Nowadays I just take my time and do whatever pleases me," Joe said, pulling his cap squarely back onto his head.

"Well done, Joe. We can't take the fruits of this life with us, so we might as well pass them on or share them around." Andrea smiled and waved at him as I pulled the horse box further into the field and parked where Jean indicated. The field was almost dead flat and neatly laid out in twenty show rings of varying sizes, roped off with short wooden posts and white tape. Some of the rings were smaller than others, and Jean told me that these were for show classes and other events that wouldn't have very large entry numbers. I parked the horse box nose end into a large hedge, and the three of us clambered out of the cab to unload the horses.

Once we got Bixby out, Jean handed his lead rope to me and I moved him a safe distance away from the box so that he could examine his new surroundings. Poor old Bixby must have been holding on to gallons of water, because he immediately relieved himself, groaning in the process. Andrea had hold of Melodia, who was more intent on sampling the succulent grass in Kilkenny than anything else. Freeser, with Jean in tow, whinnied his head off, calling to any and all horses within earshot. A horse or pony—I couldn't tell the difference—answered from a nearby horse box, which, when I was able to locate the source of the whinnying, turned out to be the dirty white box that had passed us on the road.

We allowed our cargo a good quarter of an hour to just stand and gaze about or walk off stiff, travel-weary legs, before we watered them and then tied them to metal rings that lined the outside walls of the horse box. Jean pulled off their light travel rugs, leg and tail bandages, and we gave them a quick brush-over before we set about the task of converting the horse box into three stalls. I noticed that Andrea was having a bit of difficulty manhandling a section of partition, so I politely shooed her out of the way.

"Go off and scout out the show grounds, Andrea. We can manage all right," I said, and Jean nodded in approval at my suggestion.

"He's right, Mum. These partitions aren't as light as they used to be," Jean said, smiling warmly at her mother. "Why not go find some buddies of yours and see what news they have. We'll catch up with you when the horses are all settled and fed. Then we can think about having some supper. I'm starving." Andrea laughed at her daughter and touched her arm in appreciation.

"Thanks, you two. My back isn't able to lift as much as it used to, and I guess I'm more tired from the journey than I ought to be. I'll see you in a while," she said and wandered off toward a large group of white tents.

Jean and I applied ourselves to the task of preparing the stalls for the horses once we had the partitions securely in place. We added a full bale of straw to each stall unit, putting big banks of it along the walls to protect the horses from getting friction sores. As well as lending additional comfort, Jean told me, the straw banks helped stop the horses from getting cast at night if they chose to lie down, and, in winter, the banked straw kept the stable warmer. We finished bedding down the units and then slid open the partitions to allow the horses to be reloaded into their separate stalls.

The partitions themselves were another piece of ingenious engineering that I marveled at. Each partition was actually made up of two sections, but once fitted into slider grooves sunk flush with the floor of the box, they could be fixed into place or partially opened to provide access for the horses and for people. Once a horse was settled in his stall, the smaller section could then be pushed into place and latched down via a bolt that slotted into the slider unit on the floor. The partition panels stood only a little under five feet tall, so the horses could see each other and, more important, we could see into the stalls without having to unlatch each section. Of course, there was access to the stalls via a small companionway that ran down the entire length of one side of the horse box. There wasn't much room to maneuver in the companionway, but at least we could put food and water into the stalls without having to unhook each section. Another nifty little feature was a small "groom's" door, which was located just behind the cab of the horse box and opened onto the companionway. If we needed to get in to a horse in a hurry, we could just crawl in through the groom's door.

Jean decided to load Melodia first, because she didn't care where she was as long as she had food. Bixby was next, and then we loaded Freeser last, so that he could have a perfect view of the comings and goings around him. The back ramp of the horse box was left down so the horses would have loads of fresh air, and also be able to see what was going on around them. With the horses safely settled in their stalls, we pulled buckets and feed from a storage compartment situated below the groom's door. Jean handed me three hay nets and I filled each one with three sheaves of sweet-smelling hay. While Jean was mixing up the horses' feeds, I filled their water buckets from a large container we'd brought along with us. I nestled each bucket into the rings mounted to the walls and started to hang up the hay nets. Jean came up the companionway with a bucket of feed for Melodia and chuckled at my bungled attempt at hanging a hay net.

"You have to secure the net very high on the wall. Otherwise a horse may just paw at it and get his leg all caught up. Horses are rather silly at times, and if they feel that they're trapped or caught in any way, they'll sometimes panic. Although old Melodia here would just keep on chomping no matter *what* she was hanging out of!" She smiled at me and adjusted the hay net so that it hung neatly, without any rope dangling in harm's way. Then she gave Melodia a pat on the neck, and we moved on to Bixby's stall, where I successfully tied his hay net to Jean's satisfaction. I had finished watering the other two horses and tied up Freeser's hay net by the time Jean came back with two more feed buckets. I settled Bixby's bucket in place, giving him a pat on the neck, while Jean fed Freeser.

"Now we can feed ourselves," Jean said, licking her lips, and without further ado she linked her arm in mine and marched us down the ramp and toward the show tents.

We passed the dirty white horse box while a man and a girl who looked to be about thirteen years old were unloading a pretty white pony. The man stood at the foot of the ramp and seemed to be in a hurry, waving his arms about and calling to the girl to get a move on. As the pony was slowly backing out of the box, the man waved his arms again and the pony threw its head up high, bringing its front legs off the top of the ramp in a half rear. The girl let go of the lead rope and the pony smashed its head off the top of the box. We could hear the thud from where we were and watched as the pony hurriedly backed itself off the ramp and stood on solid ground, dazed and shaking its head.

"Oh, Daddy, now look what's happened!" the girl said to her father, close to tears as she ran down the ramp to grab the pony's lead rope.

"He'll be all right. Just let him have a graze for a bit while I get his stall ready. Sure, 'twas only a bump on his head. He'll be grand in no time." The girl slowly walked the pony away from the horse box toward us, cooing and encouraging him every step of the way. The pony gave one final shake of his head and stood looking about.

"That was a nasty bang on the head," Jean whispered to me as we passed the girl and her pony.

I thought nothing more about the girl and her pony as we crossed the field toward the show tents, where we could see Andrea talking with a group of people outside. As we approached the group, Andrea caught sight of us and waved.

"Ha, here they are. Jean, you remember the Langans, and Joe and Dot Giltspur?" The group all smiled at Jean and asked after her health.

"I'd like to present my son-in-law to you all: John Flanagan, this is Helen and Frank Langan—they're running the show—and Joe and Dot Giltspur—they've been in this business for ages, which is more years than I care to remember," Andrea said and laughed heartily with the Giltspurs. "Helen and Frank have kindly asked us to join them for supper, and with Helen's cooking I know we're in for a treat."

"Mm, I can't wait," said Jean. "John, you'll be in heaven with this woman's food. Helen is renowned the length and breadth of Ireland for putting up a grand old spread. When can we eat?" Jean said impishly, and we all laughed at her frankness.

Helen and Frank Langan had set up a small table to the rear of one of the larger tents, which we learned was to be used as the refreshments tent over the next two days. The catering company had left tables and chairs and most of the heavier equipment already set up in the tent, so it was easy enough simply to move a few chairs and a table outside. Helen had the table set with a fresh linen cloth and cloth napkins and—I could hardly believe my eyes—crystal wineglasses.

"Whoa!" I said to Helen. "You certainly know how to get through these horse shows in style. I don't think I've sat down to such elegance since my wedding day."

"Hey!" Jean said, giving my arm a tender thump.

"No offense, Jean, but we're always in too much of a rush to get the food into us to pay attention to the niceties of it all," I replied, laughing. She laughed too, for we were both remiss in this area.

"I've always maintained that if I'm going to make a good meal I might as well make a good table, and I suppose years of the same practice just become routine after a while," Helen said. "Don't worry yourself over such things, dear," she added, patting Jean's arm. "You have other things to occupy your time." And she winked at us both.

"So, Jean Hartshorn—or should I say Flanagan now?" Frank said, and Jean nodded her head in assent. "Are you going to show us all up tomorrow with that marvelous jumper of yours I've been hearing so much about?"

"I'll give it my best shot, Frank," she said, sitting down in the chair Frank offered her. The rest of us were shown to our seats and settled down while Helen brought out a tray, laden with dishes, from the refreshments tent.

"I hear that you have no lack of talent, young woman," Joe said, adding to Frank's compliment, "and are bound to follow in your mother's footsteps." Jean said nothing, merely smiling at Joe.

"Now, my dears," said Helen, uncovering four dishes to reveal her delicious offerings. "We have a cold chicken salad with fennel, roasted and chopped hazelnuts, and fresh tarragon; a salad of green beans, red peppers, more fennel—I love the stuff—and artichoke hearts smothered in a light olive oil dressing. There's a quiche with onions, ham and goat's cheese topped with asparagus spears, and to finish, good old strawberries and cream. Frank, be a dear and pour the wine."

With a flourish Frank put one arm behind his back and took the stance of a sommelier, inclining his body slightly as he poured each of us a glass of wine.

"Ladies and gentlemen, for your dining pleasure this evening, I have selected a precocious little Bordeaux that will caress the palate and cleanse

the soul. Bon appetit!" Dot clapped her hands together with pleasure at Frank's routine, letting
loose an infectious chuckle that made us all laugh
with her.

We spent two and a half very pleasant hours
eating and talking the evening away, and when I
looked at my watch it was after nine-thirty. Jean
let out a huge yawn, which immediately brought
on a yawn from me. We hastily but politely thanked
Helen and Frank for a lovely evening, and Dot
and Joe for their company, then excused ourselves.
Andrea seemed set to make a night of it and said
she'd see us in the morning. Arm in arm, Jean and
I wandered back to the horse box as the night sky
began to settle over Ireland.

We passed the dirty white horse box, and Jean
stopped in her tracks.

"That's funny," she said. "I could have sworn
they were going to stable the pony in their horse
box tonight, but the partition is still wide open
and I can't see anything inside." We tried to peer
inside the box, but in the fading light it was hard
to see. Jean shrugged her shoulders and linked her
arm in mine again. But as we passed the horse box,
we saw the little girl sitting on the grass near the
cab, holding the pony's lead rope. The pony's head
was hanging down, and as we stepped closer we
could hear the girl quietly sobbing.

"Are you all right?" I said to the girl. "Where's
your dad?" She looked up at us, startled, and I
could see that her face was smeared with dirt and
clear tracks where her tears had run. I stepped
closer to her, Jean's arm still linked in mine.

"What's wrong, dear?" Jean said, releasing my

arm and stepping forward quietly to crouch down
next to the girl.

"Fairex won't go back in the box, and every time
I try to get him in he stops at the top of the ramp
and throws his head up. Then he charges back down
the ramp again. He must have dragged me down
that ramp a dozen times already," she said, sobbing
bitterly. "And I don't know where Daddy is. He
tried to help, but Fairex just got worse and worse,
so Dad went off about twenty minutes ago to get a
friend of his to help."

"Would you like us to try and help you?" Jean
said gently.

"Oh, would you, please?" The girl looked up at
Jean and me, and I thought I felt my belly flop at
the sight of her anguished face. Jean must have
had the same feeling because she stood the girl on
her feet and hugged her briefly.

"Here, now, let me look at you first, and we'll
wipe away those tears and dirt marks," Jean said
and brought a clean handkerchief out of her
pocket.

"What's your name?" Jean said to the girl.

"Rosaleen."

"Well, my name is Jean, and this is my husband,
John. Has Fairex had anything to eat since you un-
loaded him this evening?"

"No," said Rosaleen, shaking her head.

"Well, I know it'll sound strange to you, but
why don't you go get a small scoop of feed for
him, put it in a bucket, and bring it back here to
me? I'll hold him while you're gone. Okay?" Rosaleen nodded her head and scurried off to get the
bucket of feed.

Jean held the pony's lead rope in her hand and gently rubbed his back just behind his withers. "You poor little man," she said. "You've had quite an old day of it, haven't you?" The pony raised his head slightly, and Jean tentatively slid her hand up his neck and gently felt between his ears. The pony didn't move.

"Well, that's a good sign. From the sound of that smack we heard earlier this evening, I thought he might have bashed his poll rather badly. I guess he's all hangdog because he's hungry and fed up and afraid to go back into the box again for fear of another wallop on the bean. Well, we'll soon sort that out. I think a sensible old trick Mum taught me is the best solution to this problem." And she smiled at me.

Rosaleen came back with the bucket, and Jean turned the pony around and led him a few paces from the bottom of the ramp. Then she turned to Rosaleen.

"Rose—may I call you Rose?" Rosaleen nodded her head and smiled.

"Do you know that there are three things about horses that are very important to remember? Of course they love to be fed, but above all else they're creatures of habit, so they like to follow a routine that they're used to. They also like to be happy, so that means that they need to be looked after well, and ridden regularly, and cared for properly. But mostly they need to know that they won't be harmed, and old Fairex here thinks he's going to get hurt again if he goes up that ramp and into the horse box. So, here's what *you'll* do." Jean gently calmed Rose's mounting fear with a reassuring touch to the cheek.

"Give him a handful of nuts and tell him how wonderful he is." Rose took a handful of nuts from the bucket, and Fairex immediately perked up his ears, chomping noisily on the tidbit.

"John, would you please get half a bale of straw from our horse box and shake it out so that it looks lovely and inviting? Oh, and while you're in there, please open up the groom's door so that Fairex can see some light at the end of the tunnel." She smiled at me and added to Rose, "Fairex isn't stupid, you know. He'll see that we're making a cozy and inviting bed for him."

With Jean, Rose, and Fairex all patiently watching me, I shook out the straw, pushing some of it into banks against the walls. Then I opened the groom's door and, as an afterthought, pushed all the roof vents open as I left the box.

"Now, Rose, walk him forward to the edge of the ramp. I'll be right by your side the whole time. Then give him another few nuts, telling him that he's the best pony in the world." Jean's voice was gentle and encouraging.

"Now, this is where it may get a bit tricky, but we'll just take it very slowly, okay?" Rose nodded her head, her eyes wide and trusting.

"Lift his right foreleg and put it on the ramp and place a few nuts just in front of his foot." Rose did as she was told, and Fairex gobbled up the nuts quickly.

"Now I'm going to make a trail of nuts that will go all the way up the ramp and into the horse box, and when I come back down I want you to take the bucket from me and go and stand inside the horse box, but not so far in that Fairex can't see you. Okay?" Again the nod of the head.

Jean patted Fairex on the neck and gently rubbed around his eyes, telling him he was a wonderful, brave pony. She ran her hand over his head and down to his muzzle, caressing the soft skin. She bent her head and slowly blew into the pony's nose. Fairex let out a gentle snort as if clearing his nose.

"That's a good sign," said Jean. "It means he's relaxing." Slowly Jean continued to rub the pony up and down his neck until his head dropped down low, then she gently clicked her tongue and encouraged Fairex to take a step forward. The pony put his left foot on the ramp and, sniffing the nuts at his feet, gobbled them up hurriedly. Jean clicked at him again, and the pony walked forward another pace so that a hind leg was now on the ramp. He gobbled up the reward that lay at his feet. Very slowly, and with more patience than I've ever seen in any person before, my wife led Fairex up the ramp, praising and patting him every step of the way. When they were near the top of the ramp, Jean said to Rose, "Gently rattle the bucket, Rose, and call out some encouragement to Fairex. He knows your voice."

"Come on, Fairex, you can do it. Good boy," Rose said, rattling the bucket of nuts. With his head still down, Fairex finished up the last nut on the ramp and calmly walked the last few steps into the horse box without batting an eye.

"What a great fellow you are!" Rose said, delighted with her pony and sounding relieved that her ordeal was over. She patted him on the neck and then hugged him. Good old Fairex stuffed his head into the bucket and contentedly chomped down his long overdue dinner.

"I can't believe it," said Rose. "I thought I'd never get him to set foot in the horse box again, the way he was carrying on earlier. Thank you so much, Jean. Thank you so very much."

"It's all right, Rose. I'm glad I could help you. Just remember that you'll have to load and unload Fairex a bit slowly for a while. How about if I give you a hand tomorrow morning, first thing? We'll unload him before he has his breakfast and then we'll load him again, just the way we did tonight." Rose's face blossomed into a huge smile, and she gave Jean an awkward hug.

"I'd like that a lot, Jean. Thank you. Good night." In the fading light I spotted a shape approaching the horse box and from the size, I reckoned it could be none other than Rose's father. Jean saw him too and turned to link arms with me.

"See you tomorrow, then. Sweet dreams," Jean called out to Rose, and we left her chattering excitedly to her father about Fairex and the bucket of nuts.

"You were pretty fantastic back there, Mrs. Flanagan. I'm very proud of you," I said softly, kissing her head and hugging her close to me as we walked. "I know that you're an accomplished horsewoman, but I had no idea that you were a horse charmer as well. Has your mother passed on any other hidden skills I should know about?" I said, a light teasing note to my voice. Jean stopped in her tracks and turned to me.

"It's funny, John. It's always been a forgone conclusion that I'd take over from Mum, but we never knew when. I suppose that now I'm married to you, Mum's decided she can turn things over to me and gradually ease herself out of the business," Jean said and then paused, struggling with what she wanted to say. "I get the strangest feeling every time we work together; it's as if Mum is willing me to absorb her knowledge and experience. Sometimes when I'm riding a difficult horse, I suddenly know what to do without knowing how I know it!" She gave a nervous little chuckle and looked up at me, a brief hint of uncertainty flickering in her eyes, and I tipped her chin up with my hand, caressing her pretty face and gently rubbing away her uneasiness.

"It's all right, love. I've noticed those secret handshakes of yours. It looks like the passing of a baton in a relay race. Don't fret, though. Your mother is simply ensuring that the family talent lives on in her daughter. And jeez, what a talent it is! You *have* the knack bounding around inside you, right down to your toes—or should I say hooves." I smiled at my wife, glad that she was mine.

Jean stood in close to me, hugging me around the waist, and then she reached up with both her hands and pulled my head down to hers. She kissed me long and deeply and I thought I was in heaven. We stood holding each other for a long time and with Jean tucked in tight against my body, I sighed deeply, wondering what adventures would find us tomorrow.

The Glass Case

Kristin Hannah

Photo courtesy of Hannah Family

*A rare family photograph of author Kristin Hannah with
her mother, Sharon, and her younger brother, Kent.*

INTRODUCTION

Memories of my mother are precious commodities. She was always there for me, picking me up when I fell down, carefully placing Band-Aids on the mortal wounds of a tomboy's childhood. Later, she was the one I went to for advice. We talked endlessly about boys and friendships and life. By word and example, she gently guided me into the fast lane of young womanhood.

That's what I miss most of all, just talking to my mother. Now, as I warily approach the fourth decade of my life, I remember what she used to say when she put those silly Band-Aids on my wounds, and I say the same thing to my own son. This will sting a bit . . . but a kiss will make it all better.

What better description of life and motherhood is there?

I wrote this short story as a tribute to my mother. Like the heroine in the piece, I often find that I house my fragile memories of Sharon on a shelf too high to reach, in a glass case that I leave closed. It is nice—and necessary, I think—to take them down and dust them off every now and again and remember. . . .

So, Mom, this story is for you. I know that—somewhere—you're reading it and telling all your friends that your eldest daughter is a big star . . . and

*why not? I tell my son that his grandma lives in the big
star that hangs above our pond in the backyard. The one
that even in the blackest night showers our family with
light.*

Like many young mothers, I am overworked,
underpaid, and in serious need of a makeup
intervention. Every time I look in the cracked mirror above my bathroom sink—which I try to do
about as often as I make pie dough from scratch—
I hear my mother's voice: *Oh, April, you could be so
pretty if you'd just take a little time with yourself.*

It's sad that this is the only time I hear my
mom's voice, and unfair as well. Right up to the
end, even as she lay in a narrow hospital bed that
smelled of starch and hopelessness, she loved me.
I remember how tightly she held my hand, her
knuckles bony and blue-veined and sadly translu-
cent for a forty-two-year-old woman. She'd looked
at my swollen, pregnant stomach and started to
cry. "I just wanted to hold your baby's hand,"
she'd whispered brokenly. "Is that so much to
wish for?"

There was nothing I could do but pick up a
scrap of white tissue and dry her cheeks. We both
knew she would die in a sterile white room tucked
into the southeast corner of a concrete high-rise
that was miles away from our hometown. That
she would never hold my baby in her arms.

I was seventeen. Young and naive. I didn't know
how much I would come to miss her. Like the horrible night when my milk first came in . . . or
during midnight feedings . . . birthday parties . . .

tooth fairy visits. I didn't know then that every happy milestone in my life would carry with it a shadowy lining of loss. But she knew.

Probably it's just as well that I remember her scolding me. Although it's been years since her death, the other memories are still tender to the touch.

Besides, I *am* pretty, in an I-got-pregnant-too-early-and-never-fulfilled-my-potential sort of way.

It was because of the town I grew up in, really. That's the realization I've come to. If I had grown up in Bridgeport, Connecticut, or New York City, the only daughter of two Nobel Prize–winning scientists, I am certain my life would now be different. I would look beautiful and polished and self-possessed at twenty-seven, instead of more than a little tired and old before my time. These are the things my mother wanted for me. The road I turned away from.

I grew up in Mocipsee, Washington. It was—is—a town not unlike a million others in America. Population 4,320. Mostly dairy farmers. Every spring the river floods the valley, and the nightly news flashes pathetic, heart-wrenching pictures of toothless men saving stranded animals. Packing sandbags is a normal after-school activity during the soggy months of the year.

High school football is king in Mocipsee. In 1986 we almost won the state championship, and though we lost, the town went crazy, closing down the shops and streets to party in celebration of how close we'd come.

That was the night I first met Ryan. I knew who

he was, of course. In a town that idolizes football, the team quarterback is God. But guys like Ryan didn't talk to girls like me.

We were out in the Kupacheks' cow pasture—the standard party place in town. A hundred drunken teenagers crowded around a handful of silver kegs. Someone had brought a battery-operated radio. Tinny, scratchy songs hacked through the night, one after another.

I couldn't believe it when Ryan came up to me. "Hi," he said. "You're April Palmer, right?"

I knew even before I opened my mouth that I was going to say something incredibly stupid. What I said—precisely—was, "Uh-huh."

That was all I could come up with. I winced, waiting for him to laugh at me and walk away, but he just stood there, one hip cocked out, his hand curled around an empty plastic glass, his blue eyes fixed on my face. I offered to get him a refill—anything that would prolong the moment.

"I don't drink," he answered. "If I'm going to make the pros, I have to stay in top shape."

I remember staring at him in shock. A goal. A goal for the *future*. No one in Mocipsee thought about life after high school. No one went to college. A job at the makeup counter at Nordstrom's was the best we could imagine. Most of the men around town wore their letterman's jackets well into their fifth decade, and in the taverns there was always a discussion going on about some football game that had taken place fifteen years before.

Naturally, I fell in love with Ryan right then. That, in and of itself, was hardly noteworthy. The amazing thing was that he fell in love with me back. From that second on, we were as tight as shoelaces. It was only a matter of time (it could be tallied in nanoseconds) before we were having sex in the backseat of his old Ford Fairlane.

I was seventeen when I got pregnant. The first semester of my senior year. It wasn't all that unusual, a girl my age getting pregnant. None of my girlfriends thought much about it. We laughed and giggled and designed imaginary nurseries, drawings and all. In home ec, we looked up layette patterns and asked what babies ate. We pictured a tiny, pink-faced girl with my black hair and Ryan's blue eyes.

Now, of course, I see the sadness in all of it, the tarnished truth that we were girls who'd grown up in the rainshadow of the women's movement and still thought Mrs. Cleaver was the ideal woman. We asked so little of ourselves—and most of us got exactly what we asked for. Funny how that works.

The boys weren't any better. The football team rallied around Ryan, slapping the "stud" on the back. As if knocking up a teenaged girl was tantamount to throwing a touchdown pass.

The first time I really thought about what it meant to be pregnant was when I told my mother. I remember so clearly how I felt that night, all filled with pride and fear. When I squeezed Ryan's hand, I could feel his slick nervousness, too.

"Mrs. Palmer?" Ryan said softly, after the dinner dishes were cleared. He stood alongside the fireplace, his hands jammed in his jeans pockets. He shifted from foot to foot, rocking on the linoleum floor like a tiny wooden boat in a rough sea.

My mom came out of the kitchen and looked at us. I wonder now, all these years later, if she missed my father in that moment, if she'd wanted a hand to reach for, but it had been years since my dad had visited any of us.

I went to stand beside Ryan. "We have something to tell you." I didn't realize that my hand had moved to my stomach, that I was gently caressing the worn flannel of my shirt.

But Mom noticed. It hurt me, those silent silver tears streaking down her cheeks. "Oh, April . . ." She sighed, staring down at her work-stained hands. "I wanted so much for you."

They were words I'd heard many times. My mother was always talking about what she wanted for me. She always told me I could be anything— an astronaut, a cardiac surgeon, a ballet dancer.

I always wondered where my mother collected her big dreams. She had grown up in Mocipsee, the third daughter of five children. She'd gotten pregnant at sixteen, dropped out of school, and gotten married. By twenty, she was a divorced woman raising two small children on a cleaning woman's wages. We used to drive by Grandpa Joe's sometimes when I was a kid, and Mom would always point to the tiny white clapboard house and say, "That's why you go to college, April, so you don't end up renting a place like that for thirty years and then die without a penny to show for it."

Now that I'm a parent, I understand. Sometimes

in the middle of the night, I wake up in a cold sweat. In the quiet moments before I reach Ryan's hand beneath the covers, I wonder if I've planted dreams in my children's hearts and souls. I wonder if they believe they can be anything.

"I'll provide for her, Mrs. Palmer," Ryan had said with a thick catch in his voice, and I knew that my mother's tears were scaring him too.

My mother looked away for a long, long time, then at last, when my anxiety was a living, breathing presence that skittered up and down my skin, she stopped crying. "Well," she said, valiantly attempting to smile, "I guess we've got plenty to do. Let's get started."

We didn't know then that the wedding she was already planning would never come to pass, that I wouldn't have eight girlfriends beside me in pink taffeta dresses and a church full of flowers. We didn't know then that my mother had less than two months to live.

After the diagnosis, the wedding didn't matter. Ryan and I got married in the small Episcopal church on Front Street, a hurried affair with only the immediate family in attendance. Already my mother was getting weaker. Already my brother and I were donning the somber black look of orphaned children.

We learned quickly that life was different than we'd thought. The best quarterback in Mocipsee history was a long way from good enough for the big leagues. There was no professional sports contract—had we ever *really* been that naive?— but there was an offer of college tuition from a small, nearby community college. Ryan got a degree in business and is now the district appliance manager for Wal-Mart. We have built a good life, Ryan and I. Not perhaps what we expected, but what can grow in the shallow ground of so many disappointments?

I see it in his eyes sometimes, the regret over lost boyhood dreams. He shows it quietly, in flashes of reflection on a Sunday afternoon, with the Seahawks playing on television. But I see. I know. And I ache for him.

Oh, he loves me and I love him, but still, on rare occasions, we allow ourselves to peek into the dark rooms of what might have been. We try to look away, but it can't be done quickly enough. Ryan sees himself in Joe Montana, and he wonders secretly if he should have tried harder.

And me . . . well, when I peer into those unlit rooms, I see the shadow of a woman who never existed. The woman my mother wanted me to be. As I approach my third decade of life, I feel vaguely unformed, a work in progress.

I had three babies in five years. The first and second were accidents, and after that, I figured *What the hell?* My boobs already looked like air-to-ground missiles, and I'd forgotten what it felt like not to be nursing. We moved into a nice manufactured home on a wooded lot near the school, and in a fit of immaturity gave all the children "B" names. Bonnie, Billy, and Brad.

I stopped at three—afraid that the next would be Beethoven.

Looking back, of course, I wish I had thought it through better. Our last name is Bannerman, after all. But we were young . . .

Our oldest, Bonnie, is ten, and already she is beginning to frighten me. Any day she's going to ask me about periods and dating and things that I want to remain irrelevant for another ten years. Billy is eight, a little athlete beginning to form the same dreams that fueled his daddy, and Brad, my baby, started kindergarten just three weeks ago.

Time goes too quickly.

This is the advice my mother should have given me from her hospital bed. Instead of vague, unknowable quips like "Be careful what you wish for," she should have told me that time slides away on a hillside of loose shale and takes everything in its path—dreams, opportunities, hopes. And youth. It takes that fastest of all.

I do not feel young anymore. Sometimes when I pass the picture of my mother that hangs on the playroom wall, I stop. I stare at her face, wondering what she would look like now, all these years later. Would she still be coloring her hair to the sandy shade of her youth or would she have yielded to gray at last? Would she still wear those funny pink tennis shoes with the hearts and flowers on the white laces?

Her blue eyes stare back at me, holding the memories of my life. I remember when she used to wear her layered hair in a thin ponytail, tied up with a strand of fuzzy purple yarn; I remember the purple ceramic heart necklace she always wore, the one I made for her in the fourth grade. A big, lopsided heart with a thumbprint in the center. She wore it for years and years, and then lost it gardening one summer afternoon. She missed that necklace for the longest time. At the time, I thought it was silly, missing an ugly necklace, but now I understand. Time goes too quickly.

"Your thumb was so tiny," she once said, reaching out of habit for the absent bit of ceramic. "How will I remember now how little you used to be?"

"Hey, Mom," I say softly, touching the cool glass of the picture. I no longer wait to hear her ghostly voice—those innocent, hoping days are gone. Instead, I turn away from the picture and get on with my day. I load the dishwasher and pick up a pile of toys, I pull wet clothes from the washer and cram them into the dryer, thumping the On button. In less than an hour, I am expected at the bus stop to meet Brad, and there are a million things to do between now and then.

The bus is late.

I glance at my watch again. It has stopped—nothing unusual about that, not for the $13.95 drugstore special with the plastic band—but the casual reminder that money is tight irritates me. A quick fingernail thump on the glass gets the tiny hands moving again. Not that it matters particularly. My internal "mommy clock" is more accurate than any man-made bit of wire and metal. The bus is late.

Beside me, our white German shepherd puppy, Rex, moans despairingly, a sound like the slow leak of air from a punctured tire, then he curls around my feet and closes his eyes to wait for the little boy who loves him. For the past three weeks, this has been our routine, mine and this puppy who requires more supervision than a hyperactive toddler (at least children wear diapers) and who has insinuated himself into the consciousness of our family. Already we are beginning to wonder how we survived suburbia dogless. At least, Ryan and the kids are wondering. Me, I remember well, thank you very much. I remember when I didn't have to keep an FBI security-level count of every shoe in the house; I remember when no one and nothing peed on the carpet. But then Rex bounds across the yard at me, tripping over his own too-big paws, his pink tongue dangling from his mouth, and when he starts to lick my face and curls around my feet like a pair of familiar slippers, I am as lost as the rest of my family.

Every day at precisely 12:15, we leave the house together and head for the bus stop on the corner of Peabody and Cross Streets. The puppy drags me from tree to tree, so hard that already I wonder how it will be when he weighs one hundred pounds. Of course, by then I may weigh two hundred pounds and I may drag him from ice cream shop to beauty parlor.

In the distance I hear the bus, rattling and wheezing over the pockmarked pavement of the street. Rex jumps to his feet and starts wagging his tail, winding the nylon leash around my legs.

"Rex, stop it," I say with the tired resignation of a woman who has said this same thing to this dog before. Without waiting for Rex to stop, I gingerly extract myself from the makeshift cocoon and bend down to pet him. "Sit." I try to sound like Ms. Woodhouse, authoritative and certain. I come off more as Pee-Wee Herman, and Rex ignores me.

The bus pulls up to the curb. I hear the shudder of the brakes and the *whoosh-clank* of the doors opening. Immediately, five- and six-year-olds stream down the steps and onto the sidewalk in a laughing, jostling, centipede of blue jeans and T-shirts.

As usual, Brad isn't with them. He is always the last off the bus, my little talker.

Smiling, I head for the open door. "Hey, Claudine," I say, peeking my head inside, "where's—"

Claudine looks concerned. Her gloved fingers coil nervously around the big black steering wheel. "Brad wasn't on the bus today. Was he supposed to be?"

"What? *What?*" The leash falls from my fingers and lands with a soft thump across my feet.

"Don't panic, April," Claudine says, although I can see that she is having to work to keep her voice even. I know that she is thinking of Calvin and Suki, her own kids. "He's probably in the school office right now, trying to call you. That's what happens most of the time."

Most of the time.

I push those words away and focus on the others, *trying to call you.* They are a lifeline. While I've been standing here, waiting, doing nothing, my boy has been trying to call to say he missed the bus.

I mean to mumble a thanks, maybe manufacture a smile, but it doesn't happen. Instead, I turn and run. In some distant part of my brain I can hear Rex loping beside me, his leash snapping and clanging on the cement; at any other time I would worry that the puppy might trip over the strap and hurt his throat. Right now, I can't even think straight. All I know is that my precious six-year-old is out there somewhere, my baby who doesn't understand yet about crossing the street and isn't afraid of strangers.

I hit the house at full stride, crashing through the screen door. There is no message light blinking on the answering machine.

"Stay!" I bark at Rex, knowing this word has no meaning for him. I take a precious second to unsnap his leash and snag my purse, and I am gone again.

It takes several tries to get the car key in the ignition. "I'm coming, Bradley," I whisper over and over again as the engine sparks to life and I jam the gearshift into reverse.

It is thirteen blocks from our house to the elementary school. I make it in four minutes—four minutes that feel like a lifetime. Fishtailing into the parking lot, I wrench the old car into park and get out. In two strides, I am running.

He is all right. He's in the principal's office—just like the time Bonnie missed the bus in first grade.

I refuse to remember that they called that time, long before I left for the bus stop.

Then I see it.

"Oh, my God . . ."

Suddenly I am not running anymore. I can't. I feel as if I am walking under water. The air resists me, draws the oxygen away until I can't draw a breath.

Slowly, so slowly, I move toward the small blue container that lies fallen on the grassy hillside in front of Mr. Robbin's third-grade classroom.

A Power Rangers lunch box.

The fear I have been fighting explodes inside

me. I sink to my knees in the grass; my fingers are trembling so badly that it is difficult to pick up the box. I fumble with the plastic latch for a second— *lots of kids have Power Rangers lunch boxes, this isn't Brad's*—then the latch works and the front gapes open. Out tumbles half a peanut-butter-and-honey sandwich on wheat bread and an empty vanilla pudding container. Through the plastic baggie, I can see that the sandwich is soaked with honey— just the way he likes it. A metal spoon clangs against the side. He has remembered this time to bring it home.

"Mrs. Bannerman? April, is that you?"

It is the principal, Mr. Johnston, and the casual tone of his voice severs the thin strand of my hope. He obviously did not expect me; he has no idea why I am here, kneeling in the grass, pawing through the remains of my child's lunch. For a second—a heartbeat that brushes into eternity—I cannot look at him. When at last I do find the courage to turn, to lift my chin, my eyes are burning and coated with tears. "Bradley . . ." I whisper his name, hearing the hopelessness echoing in my voice. "Is he here?"

"Bradley? Didn't he come home? I saw him standing in line for the bus."

Through my tears I stare down at the leftover lunch. I clutch the half-eaten sandwich, bringing the baggie to my nose. The peanut butter smell is strong, even through the plastic. It is the smell of little boys everywhere. I allow myself a memory— peanut butter smeared in his hair, on his cheeks, on the scratched metal tray of his high chair. I remember laughing at the mess as I swept him into my arms and carried him to the bathtub. It was four years ago, that day, when he was just learning that food was for eating, not for playing with.

Four years ago . . . yesterday.

I think for a second that I can't take the pain, that this heart of mine will simply stop beating—for how can it beat when my son is missing?

"Come on, April," the principal says quietly. "We should call the police. The longer we wait . . ." Thankfully, his words trail off.

Like mothers have done for centuries, I get up, I go on. I do what I have to do. "Yes," I answer, and though my voice is a frayed remnant of itself, it is a triumph. For already, before this tragedy has truly begun, I can imagine the end. I am an old, old lady. My eyes are wild and I live in a box under the freeway. I haven't spoken in fifty years. Not from this moment on.

The last word I ever spoke was to the police when Mr. Johnston handed me the phone.

"My son, Bradley, is missing," I said. "He is six years old."

I am sitting on the front porch when Ryan gets home. Already the house is swarming with well-meaning police officers. They are poking through my son's room, picking up toys and opening drawers. I cannot watch. They act as if the secret to his disappearance is *here*, in the one place on earth where he was safe. In my arms is Teddy, the tiny patchwork bear Bradley sleeps with.

Ryan stops in front of me. It takes forever, but I manage to lift my head and look at him. His beautiful blue eyes are filled with tears, and I realize that I have never seen him cry before. I ache to join him, to feel the relief of tears, but I am dried up inside, the tears a hard knot in my chest. It is all too real now; my husband is here and I have to tell him everything that has happened, and when the words leave my mouth, I know I will fall apart.

Behind Ryan, a roving red police light throbs from its static place on the top of the patrol car, slicing through my yard in surreal bursts.

I force the enormity of my fear into tiny compartments. Details. These I can handle. "I called Susan. She'll pick up Bonnie and Billy after school. We'll have to tell them, of course. But I thought . . . not yet."

Ryan kneels before me, his big hand caresses my face, then curls protectively around my chin. He is crying openly now, my strong, silent, honorable husband, and his pain breaks what little bit of my heart remains.

"We'll find him," he says to me in a voice I barely recognize.

In that instant, I love him so much it is a dull pain in my chest. "Yes."

He moves around and sits beside me on the porch, pulling me close. Together we stare out at the yard—at the lawn that always needs mowing and the flower beds that always need weeding. I think of how often I have bitched about the lawn. How could I have missed the obvious?

This backyard of ours needs only one thing. Children. Children playing and laughing and drinking water from the green garden hose on a hot summer's day. I close my eyes in shame, wondering when I let things get so tangled. Was it only a few hours ago when I thought my life was unfinished and unformed? It feels like forever; the idle thoughts of a selfish child.

I lean against my husband, gathering strength and courage from him. Time falls away from us; I have no idea how long it has been when a police car pulls up in front of the house. A uniformed man gets out and slams his door, walking purposefully toward us.

Ryan's arm tightens around me, and I know he is feeling it too, this sudden, numbing rush of terror. I stare at the policeman's emotionless face, thinking the same thing over and over again. *Don't say you're sorry.*

A tiny sound, a moan, escapes me. I can't hold it all in.

The policeman stops and gives us a gentle smile. The gentleness of it is almost more than I can bear. "Mr. and Mrs. Bannerman?"

"Yes," Ryan answers.

"We need a photograph of Bradley . . . to put out over the wires."

I deflate, relieved momentarily. *A photograph.*

I think of Bradley's T-ball picture, tacked to the wall in the kitchen, the one where he is wearing a black batting glove and a toothless smile. I think of all the times he missed the ball and all the times I said, "Don't worry, pal, you'll be as good as Billy one day."

"Mrs. Bannerman?" the policeman says.

Wordlessly, Ryan gets to his feet. I know I should go with him, find the photograph for my husband, who can't find the carton of milk in our refrigerator, but I can't move. I stare helplessly at the policeman, trying awkwardly to smile. In seconds, Ryan is back with the baseball picture. The policeman nods stiffly, tucks the small picture in a manila envelope, and leaves us alone again.

Ryan sits beside me, and the tiny patch of concrete between us seems to span continents. All I can think about is this morning, my last moment with my son. I zipped up his backpack and sent him off to school. Had I told him how much I loved him then? Or had I been my normal frazzled self, thinking of the hundreds of chores to be done after he left? I can't remember.

"I don't know if I can make it through this." At the admission, control rips away like a damp tissue, and I am crying. Ryan takes my hands in his, cold flesh against cold flesh.

"We'll get him back," he says.

I can't answer. Suddenly I am missing both my son and my mother. Of all the people who have passed through my life, she is the one I need now. I want to curl into her arms and be held. I want to smell her Pert shampoo and Estée Lauder perfume. I want her to tell me that Bradley is okay, that we'll find him. She is the only one I will believe.

It is almost nightfall—four hours since Bradley disappeared. A light rain has begun to fall. Is he warm enough, my baby who is out in the night all alone? Did I remember to put a coat in his backpack?

I am standing at the picket fence, staring out onto the street that yesterday was as familiar as the back of my hand and now looks as foreign and frightening as the lunar surface.

Two hundred forty minutes since we were plunged into the nightmare. I am broken now, utterly lost. Ryan is in the house, talking to the police. He feels better if he is doing something, trying to help. Me . . . there is nothing that will make me feel better, and trying only reminds me that my child is gone.

A breeze rushes along the street, slanting the rain across my face. It smells oddly of apple pie and carries with it a picture of my mother rolling out dough, then wiping her hands on her apron and coming toward me. Then crying, in that soft, unassuming way of hers, almost as if she had no right to weep at all. *Oh, April . . . I wanted so much for you.*

The words have a resonance tonight, a sad wistfulness I never noticed before; perhaps I wasn't ready to see until now, this very moment. The disappointment was about my mother's life, not mine, an expression of her dissatisfaction with her own life.

"I still love him, Mom," I say quietly, tasting the salty moisture of my own tears. And it is true. After all these years—because of them and in spite of them—I still love my husband. Not in the starry-eyed teenaged way of long ago, but fully, deeply, and with all my tired housewife's heart.

My mother could never have said that about her husband. That's why she wanted me to be an astronaut, or a surgeon. My father ran out on us early, and so my mom lived her whole life in Mocipsee, in a rented white house on a shaggy lot at the edge of town. She wanted more for me because she wanted more for herself.

I stare out at the sparkly street. Something glimmers at me, a knowledge that I've been seeking for most of my life, and I know all at once what it is. For years I have kept my mother's memories in a glass case, thinking that they were too fragile to touch. But now I have to examine them, dissect them, and understand what part she played in who I am and how I feel about my life.

She led me wrong; I see that now. My loving, much-loved mother made me believe that happiness couldn't happen in Mocipsee, that I was wrong to want Ryan and my children and my home.

It saddens me to realize how much her hopes and dreams hurt both of us. For most of my life, I have been caught up in missing what I didn't have, and so I didn't see what was right in front of me. "I *love* the life I have, Mom. I'm happy. I'm sorry—so sorry—if it wasn't enough for you, but it's enough for me. As long as I've got Ryan and . . ." I can't get the words out, I am crying too hard. *And my babies, Mom. All I need are Ryan and my babies.*

I stand there, sobbing, until the rain begins to slow. In the sudden quiet I hear the uneven rhythm of my heartbeat. *Help him get home, Mom. Please . . .*

The wind moans softly, and in the sound I hear footsteps. I know it is my husband, come to rescue me with a kiss. As usual, he knows when I am most vulnerable, and he is there. My handsome quarterback husband who now coaches Little League and sells toaster ovens.

His arms curl around me. I lean back against him, comforted by his embrace. Though I have an ocean of tears left inside, I put them aside, leaving them for another time. I turn and look up at my husband through moist, stinging eyes. "I love you."

"I love you, too."

I start to say something else, to reveal all that I have learned about my life in the last few moments, when I see a shadow across the street, small and insignificant, huddled at the dark post of a streetlight. Before I know why, I am moving, then running.

The light flickers in the rain, and I see him.

It is our Bradley, standing all alone, shivering with cold, clutching the slick canvas of his backpack. His rosy cheeks are streaked with dirt and dried tears.

I scoop him into my arms, holding him tightly, crying into the damp tangle of his little-boy hair. Ryan wraps his arms around both of us. The rain begins anew.

Brad hooks his legs around my waist and leans back in my arms, looking worriedly at us. "I missed the bus."

I set him down on the ground and kneel in front of him. Sniffing hard, I swipe at my tears with my sleeve and draw a deep breath, trying to look grown-up. But the terror has left its mark deep, deep inside. I can't seem to stop shaking. "I went to the school. I found—" It wells up again in my throat. All I can see is that lunch box, abandoned in the grass. I know it will be with me always, that horrible memory. With a supreme effort, I force myself to finish. "I found your lunch box."

"I musta dwopped it. I was following a cwow. He was eatin' my lunch. When I looked up, the buses were gone. I knew I was in big twouble."

Ryan is staring at him, unsmiling. "You should have gone into the office and told Mrs. Freemont."

Brad's eyes fill slowly, heartbreakingly, with tears. "I know."

"How did you get home?" I ask quietly.

"I don't wanna tell you."

Ryan touches Brad's shoulder. "Come on, son." It is his best dad's voice, infused with gentle steel.

Tears streak down my son's apple cheeks, and each one seems to scald me. "Billy and Bonnie walk home from school every day."

He walked home alone, my baby who has never been allowed out of the yard by himself. I squeeze my eyes shut, but this darkness is worse. All I can think is, *What if?*

Beside me, Ryan kneels. His knees pop at the movement, then thump onto the sidewalk. "All this time, while your mom and I have been . . ." His voice breaks, and for a second, he is only mine, not a grown-up father talking to his son about something important, but my husband, my lover, who has just tasted his first helping of fear. Like me, he will never be the same again. Then he recovers. "You made it home all by yourself?"

I think: *Bless him.* Bless this man who has exchanged his boyhood dreams for a Wal-Mart register and full medical benefits. Bless him for finding his voice when mine is tangled somewhere so deep inside of me that I can't even find the hoarse, ragged start of it.

It takes me a second to realize that Bradley hasn't answered. I glance at Ryan and know instantly that he has noticed the silence.

"Bradley?" Ryan says. "You have to tell us what happened."

Brad flinches, blinks back another bulbous tear. "Mommy—" He reaches for me.

I draw back from his tiny hands. As much as I want to hold and comfort him, this is a time for answers. "Bradley, how did you get home?"

His voice is tiny, a reversion to the baby talk he abandoned years ago. "She said she knew you."

A stranger. He is talking about a stranger.

"Who said that?" It is Ryan's voice, not mine. Mine is lost again.

"Alice," Bradley says.

"Alice?"

"Like Alice in Wonderland. She found me. I walked for a long time . . . then I got scared. It started to rain and it got dark out. I din't know where I was. I sat down on the curb all by myself, and then she was there, sittin' beside me."

"What did Alice do?" Ryan asks in a thin voice.

"She said, 'I been waitin' a long time to meet you, Bradley.' I *told* her I wasn't allowed to talk to strangers, but she laughed and said she most certainly wasn't a stranger. She said she knew my mommy and daddy."

"Then what?"

Bradley sniffles and blinks away his tears. "She brung me home. I tried to get her to come into the house, but she said she couldn't go no further. I told her my mommy would want to talk to her."

"What did she say to that?" I ask.

He shrugs. "I think it made her sad, 'cause she started to cry. Then she said to give this to Mom." He reaches into his pocket and pulls something out.

I stare down at the object in my son's hand, and feel suddenly as if I am falling. Behind me, I hear cars rolling down the street, the tires squealing on the slick pavement. But it seems light-years away as I stare at the tiny, misshapen pottery heart in my son's tiny palm. I can see the thumbprint, still as clear as day, made so many years ago in art class.

Remember? a voice whispers inside me. *Remember how little your thumb was?* And suddenly I can smell it, a whiff of Pert shampoo and Estée Lauder perfume. In the leaves overhead, I hear a rustle of sound, and it sounds achingly like my mother's laugh.

"What in the—"

I cut Ryan off. "Did she say anything else?"

Bradley gives me a shrug. "No—oh, yeah. She said to tell you that she got to hold my hand."

"April?" Ryan asks, touching my shoulder.

I stand up and look around, down the rain-slicked streets, searching the shadows for one that is familiar. *Mom?* When I see nothing, I close my eyes and draw up images, the ones I've kept inside glass for so long. Surprisingly, they don't shatter and break and cut me with their sharp edges. The one that is clearest is of my thirteenth birthday party, when she carried a pink cake into the dining room. The other, darker images of her last days feel as far away as another continent.

I love you, Mom.

The leaves answer me, a whisper-soft sound that will stay with me for the rest of my life. In their sandpapery dry echo, I hear her voice, the voice I've longed to hear for years. *I only wanted you to be happy.*

I know.

"April?" Ryan says my name softly, but I can't answer, not now when I am laughing and crying at the same time. I hold on to their hands, my husband's and my son's, and in the warm press of their flesh, I feel connected and complete. I am a twenty-seven-year-old housewife with no formal education, living in a house that was put together in a factory somewhere, and yet I know now that it is more than enough. It is everything.

About the Authors

Eileen Dreyer

With twenty-four books under her own name and her romance pseudonym, bestselling, award-winning author Eileen Dreyer has garnered credits in suspense, romance and romantic suspense. Her novel *Bad Medicine* was nominated for the prestigious Anthony Award. She lives in St. Louis, Missouri, with her family which includes daughter and coauthor **Kate Dreyer**, who, at sixteen has already been published in poetry and is secure in her position as Queen of the World.

Elizabeth Engstrom

Elizabeth Engstrom is the author of five books, including the historical suspense thriller *Lizzie Borden* and the internationally acclaimed *Lizard Wine*. She has had dozens of short stories, articles, and essays published in a variety of publications and spends her non-writing time either in the woods with her dog, or teaching fiction at seminars and conferences around the world. **Nicole Engstrom Fourmyle** was born and raised in Hawaii and now lives in Oregon, where she breeds Persian cats, works as a manager in a supermarket, and raises her two sons.

Joy Fielding

Joy Fielding is the author of twelve novels, including *See Jane Run* and *Missing Pieces*. Her first major success was *Kiss Mommy Good-bye*, which Signet published in 1981, followed by other Signet paperbacks *The Other Woman*, *Life Penalty*, *The Deep End*, and *Good Intentions*. She and her lawyer husband have been married for twenty-three years and have two daughters. They divide their time between homes in Toronto and Palm Beach. **Shannon Seyffert** is an aspiring singer-songwriter, as well as an actress and model.

Diana Gabaldon

Diana Gabaldon holds a master's degree in marine biology and a Ph.D in ecology, and spent a dozen years as a university professor before turning to write fiction full time. Her books include award-winning novels *Outlander*, *Dragonfly in Amber*, *Voyager*, and *Drums of Autumn*. She lives in Scottsdale, Arizona, with her husband and three children.

Eileen Goudge

Eileen Goudge is a distant relative of novelist Elizabeth Goudge, and draws on her own rags-to-riches life story in creating romantic novels she describes as "dysfunctional family dramas." Starting with the bestselling *Garden of Lies*, all four of Eileen's titles were published by Signet. Her other titles include *Such Devoted Sisters*, *Blessings in Dis-*

guise, and *Trail of Secrets*, all of which have sold millions around the world. She lives in New York, and is married to talk-show host Sandy Kenyon, whom she met over the phone while being interviewed on the radio. In addition to speaking fluent French, daughter **Mary Bailey** is also conversant in the language of mother-daughter communication—the most difficult of all!

Kristin Hannah

Kristin Hannah received an undergraduate degree from the University of Washington, and a law degree from the University of Puget Sound. Following the birth of her son, she exchanged dusty law books for dirty diapers and settled down to be a full-time mom. It was during the first magical—sleepless—nights of motherhood that she began writing fiction. Her award-winning books have appeared on many national bestseller lists, and her latest, *Home Again*, recently won the National Reader's Choice award and was named by *Publishers Weekly* magazine as one of the five best love stories of the year.

Wendy Hornsby

Wendy Hornsby is the author of seven mysteries, including five Maggie MacGowen novels, *A Hard Light*, *77th Street Requiem*, *Bad Intent*, *Midnight Baby*, and *Telling Lies*. She has won an Edgar award for her story "Nine Sons," which appeared in *Sisters in Crime IV*. She lives in Long Beach, California, where she is a professor of history at Long Beach City College. Her first book for Signet was *Telling Lies*. **Alyson Hornsby** is a student at the

American University. This is her second published story.

J. A. Jance

J. A. Jance worked as an insurance salesman, a high school English teacher, and a school librarian on an Arizona Native American reservation before turning to fiction writing. Her J. P. Beaumont series set in Seattle spans over a dozen novels, and has garnered her two American Mystery awards. Recently, she's begun a new series featuring Arizona sleuth Joanna Bradley. She lives in Bellevue, Washington.

Faye Kellerman

Faye Kellerman's novels combine gritty police procedurals with an in-depth look into the world of Orthodox Judaism. Her series protagonists are Peter Decker, a Los Angeles police officer, and Rina Lazarus, a widow with young sons who assists him on his cases. The first novel in the series, *The Ritual Bath*, won the Macavity award for best novel. She lives in Beverly Hills with her four children and her husband, novelist Jonathan Kellerman.

Anne McCaffrey

Anne McCaffrey is regarded as one of the bestselling science-fiction writers in the world. Her Doona, Pern, and Rowan series have all won worldwide acclaim. A winner of both the Hugo and Nebula awards, her recent novels include *Freedom's Choice, Masterharper of Pern*, and *Acorna: The Unicorn Girl*, coauthored with Margaret Ball. She lives in Ireland. **Georgeanne Kennedy**, née

Johnson, trained and qualified as a riding instructor and horse trainer soon after she left school. Chronic illness forced her to quit her chosen career in the early 1980s, but she continues to enjoy wonderful dreams of noble, dancing steeds.

Debbie Macomber

Debbie Macomber is an internationally published author. Her novels have appeared on several bestseller lists, including the *New York Times* extended list, receiving awards and acclaim. Debbie's role of wife, mother, and author has expanded to include motivational speaking, and she gladly shares her secrets for success with enthusiasm, encouragement and inspiration.

Joan Lowery Nixon

Joan Lowery Nixon is the author of over one hundred novels and has won many awards for her books for young people, including four Edgar Allan Poe Awards for Juvenile Mysteries, and the International Reading Association Paul Witty short story award, and serves as president of Mystery Writers of America. She lives in Houston with her husband. **Eileen Nixon McGowan** has coauthored and produced many mystery weekends, cruises, and charity fund-raisers.

PENGUIN PUTNAM

online

Your Internet gateway to a virtual environment with hundreds of entertaining and enlightening books from Penguin Putnam Inc.

While you're there, get the latest buzz on the best authors and books around—

Tom Clancy, Patricia Cornwell, W.E.B. Griffin, Nora Roberts, William Gibson, Robin Cook, Brian Jacques, Catherine Coulter, Stephen King, Jacquelyn Mitchard, and many more!

Penguin Putnam Online is located at
http://www.penguinputnam.com

PENGUIN PUTNAM NEWS

Every month you'll get an inside look at our upcoming books and new features on our site. This is an ongoing effort to provide you with the most interesting and up-to-date information about our books and authors.

Subscribe to Penguin Putnam News at
http://www.penguinputnam.com/ClubPPI